thinking man's Rx

"Have you ever heard of telepause?" the doctor asked.

Cheney wrinkled his brow. "I don't think so."

"It seems to be a stage in the mental development of telepaths. The psi abilities become incredibly acute and somewhat unstable. The headaches are symptomatic of the inability to shut out any mental processes that impinge on your mind. And there is a strong increase in sexual desire."

"Is there anything that can be done for it?"

"Oh, yes." The doctor lied with what he hoped was the proper veneer of breezy confidence. "The Agency has seen this happen before—it usually only happens to the best telepaths, by the way—and they tell me they have a very effective program for treating it."

"That's a relief," Cheney said.

But Cheney did not know that the Agency's "effective program" was assassination. I⬛⬛⬛⬛⬛⬛⬛⬛⬛⬛⬛⬛⬛d every tim⬛⬛⬛⬛⬛⬛⬛⬛⬛r treatmen⬛

was the perfect cure, worked
—and he was next in line for

mindflight

by
stephen goldin

a fawcett gold medal book • *new york*

MINDFLIGHT

© 1978 Stephen Goldin

Published by Fawcett Gold Medal Books, a unit of CBS Publications, the Consumer Publishing Division of CBS Inc.

ISBN 0-449-13980-8

Printed in the United States of America

10   9   8   7   6   5   4   3   2   1

dedicated to the Trimbles
John & Bjo
Katwen & Lora
for being originals
in a world of imitations

acknowledgment

I'd like to thank my wife, Kathleen, for giving me the use of her idea—and for her usual superb job of constructive criticism.

—Stephen Goldin

part i:

earth

chapter 1

Alain Cheney sat quietly in the spaceliner's passenger lounge, face buried in his hands. He caressed his forehead delicately with his fingers, as though by massaging the skin outside his skull he could ease the pulsing pain that was growing within it. His eyes were closed against the bright light of the room, and he had intentionally slowed his breathing down to a steady, rhythmic pattern to help him cope with the pain.

There was a presence approaching him. With a minimum of mental exertion, Alain could read that it was a ship's steward who had noticed this one passenger left sitting in the lounge. As the man came nearer, a picture of conflicting emotions grew sharper in Alain's mind. The steward was concerned because the passenger was not looking well; he was also annoyed because he'd hoped to leave the ship early, and this complication could conceivably delay his departure.

As he came within what he considered acceptable limits, the steward spoke aloud. "Are you all right, sir?"

Alain lifted his head and opened his eyes. He looked straight into the man's face and tried to project both confidence and normality. "Yes, fine, thank you."

"Almost everyone else has disembarked, sir." Assured now that the passenger was not ill, the steward's mood shifted subtly over to impatience. As an afterthought he added, "Were you needing any further services?"

"No, I . . . I just wanted a few last moments here in the lounge before leaving. It was such a nice trip that I wanted to store up my memories of it by sitting here awhile longer. I hope I'm not inconveniencing you."

"Oh no, sir, not at all," the steward said, while all his thoughts contradicted his words. This *was* an inconvenience, and the sooner the passenger left, the better the steward would like it.

"I was just about finished anyway," Alain said, standing up. The calm of the room had been shattered for him; the steward would now be hovering over him constantly with subtle hints that he should be on his way. The mental oppressiveness would only make his condition worse. He might as well leave and face the inevitable crush outside.

Alain took one last look around the lounge. He had spent a great deal of time here on the journey from Leone to Earth. Even though the ship had carried nearly a hundred people, comparatively few of them were ever in the lounge at any given moment, which meant that the number of minds pressing onto his own would be minimal. He had spent most of the voyage staring into the infinite blackness of space, letting all sensations go numb and reveling in the oblivion the enormous viewscreens provided.

Now those same viewscreens merely exhibited the hell that was waiting for him outside the ship's hull: Vandenberg Spaceport, Earth—a seething mass of humanity in perpetual Brownian movement down the scrubbed tile corridors. It was hard for him to think of Earth as "home" anymore—he had spent so little of his adult life here that he felt almost a stranger to its ways.

The steward's relief was almost tangible as Alain left the lounge and began walking down the halls to the main hatch. There would normally have been a smartly dressed attendant standing at the doorway to wish him good-bye, but the ship had been aground so long that the attendant had left the post; maintenance crews were now swarming over the ship, checking out its condition after its trip through interstellar space and preparing it for its next voyage in a couple of days. The mechanics paid scant attention as Alain walked out the hatchway and started down the ramp toward the customs building.

Leaving the ship was like a physical blow; every step down the ramp was a hammer pounding at his skull. Ahead of him and through those ominous double doors were people—hundreds, if not thousands, of them—each

9

thinking individual thoughts and broadcasting them randomly into the air. To Alain Cheney, a trained telepath, it was a raucous shouting that could not be stopped simply by plugging his ears.

Most telepaths used drugs to dull their powers and drown out background "noises." Knowing that he was landing on Earth, an overcrowded world, Alain had downed two extra trimethaline capsules earlier that morning, but his precautions seemed inadequate now. Even trimethaline did not help much these days.

By the time he reached the foot of the ramp, the telepathic din was a surf pounding at his skull. He paused, bracing himself for the ordeal to follow, then pushed open the doors and entered. The audible clamor only added to the psychic Babel beating on his brain. Mobs of people pushed through the large open chamber before him, shoving and shouting in impersonal confusion. Loudspeakers blared incoherently from the low ceiling, and no one paid them the slightest attention. Vidicams in the upper corners scanned the scene coldly, noting any and all possible transgressions. Guards armed with variable-speed Horgan z-beam repeaters were stationed every few meters throughout the throng to correct any situations the vidicams spotted.

There were more vidicams and guards than he'd ever seen here before, he noted as he pushed his way through the riot of colors and the stench of all the mingled bodies. Nearly twice as many. *Things must be tight,* he thought. *Maybe I should be glad I don't live here.*

His luggage had already been offloaded and was sitting on a counter. Alain waited in line, suffering through the tensions of the people around him until his turn came. He gave the customs officer his claim check number, and his suitcase was pulled from the rack and placed on the inspection table.

"Travel card," the officer said routinely. Her thoughts revealed she was bored with her job. It was near the end of her shift and she was anxious to get home.

She inserted the card in the comp slot and looked to her screen for a readout. Her eyebrows arched slightly as she scanned the information; although her face did not register much emotion, her thoughts were abundantly clear to the telepath. She looked at the special orders and checked Alain's appearance extra carefully in comparison with the photo on the readout. She stared back at Alain, and one hand reached surreptitiously under the table to press the special "attention" button. "Your papers seem to be in order, sir," she said evenly, "but there is a question about the baggage. You'll have to speak to my supervisor. Come this way." And she opened the gate to let Alain through.

"If you insist." Alain was trying desperately to keep his face free of the pain he felt at the overflow of thoughts and emotions bombarding his mind. He'd never suffered from ochlophobia this severely before, but he braced himself against it and followed the officer into a small, brightly painted office where a man was waiting for him.

This dark-haired man was thin and weaselly and looked much too young to be in this line of work. He was wearing civilian clothes: a silk pullover shirt with wide blue and red diagonal stripes, dark blue trousers that fitted tightly at the thighs and then bagged ridiculously the rest of the way. The pants legs were tucked into blue suede boots that reached to mid-calf. The young man's eyes were steadfastly serious.

The man stood up as Alain entered. Dismissing the customs officer with a curt wave of his hand, he faced Alain and said, "These interstellar voyages are quite wearing, aren't they?"

Alain had been expecting his contact to be somewhat older and dressed with considerably more conservatism. But there could be no mistake; this somber young man had delivered the proper recognition signal. "I've made the run often enough before," Alain said, giving the appropriate countersign.

He could tell from the other's mind that the preconditions of the rendezvous had been completed, but the contact was still showing signs of irritation. "Where have you been? Your ship docked two hours ago."

"I had personal duties to attend to."

"I've got more important things to do than sit around

here all day waiting for you." Visions came to Alain of a busy office, piles of correspondence, hectic routine. They vanished quickly, though; this young man knew how to keep his mind in order when dealing with a telepath, and very few extraneous details escaped to the surface.

The contact walked over and belatedly offered his hand. "I'm Morgan Dekker. I've been instructed to see that you're well settled in while you're here." His handshake was firm, his tone cool and efficient. "Your bag is already on its way to the hotel room we've arranged. Come with me."

The two men left by a back entrance and began walking down a long, dim corridor. "I must commend old Tölling on his efficiency," Alain said as they walked. "This is the best-handled arrangement I've been through yet."

Dekker stiffened. A blur of conflicting images raced through his mind before he brutally closed the door on them again. "Gunnar Tölling was terminated seven months ago," he said brusquely.

The other man's tone sent a chill down Alain's spine. Gunnar Tölling had been in charge of Operations ever since Alain had joined the Agency. That he could be "terminated" so abruptly spoke volumes about what was happening here on Earth these days. Alain wondered whether "terminated" meant what he thought it did.

Dekker's manner indicated that questions would not be welcomed, but Alain could not let the subject drop with so ungraceful a thud. "Who's in charge of Operations, then?" He tried to make the question sound nonchalant.

This time Dekker's voice was a little warmer. "Joby Karns."

That news was both surprising and welcome. Alain had gone through the Academy with Joby Karns; she was a very beautiful and resourceful woman. The two of them had even been lovers for a brief—very brief!—period; it hadn't worked out, but he'd always had warm feelings for her since then. He hadn't heard anything about her for the last ten years—and now here she was, suddenly, his boss.

"That's very good news," he said aloud. "She and I go back a long way together. I hope I'll have a chance to see her while I'm here."

"I doubt it. She's at headquarters in New York, and very busy."

They reached the end of the corridor and stepped out onto a pirt platform. Dekker stepped up to the signal box and rapidly punched out a series of numbers, then inserted his plastic ID card into the slot. Within minutes, one of the personal, independent rapid transit cars came gliding quietly up to them and stopped.

The pirt car was little more than a large box on wheels, with seats inside for as many as four passengers and small windows for viewing the passing scenery. There were no guidance controls, merely a control panel into which the destination's coordinates could be entered. The machine drew its power and instructions from the computer lines buried beneath the streets.

This particular car was painted red and white on the outside, with a neutral gray interior. The inside walls had been painted and scratched on with standard graffiti comments. The two men got in and Dekker punched their destination into the car's circuits. The doors clicked shut and the vehicle rolled off along the street.

Neither man spoke during the journey. Dekker was busy keeping up his mental shields; he obviously had been informed that Alain was a telepath and was determined not to allow very much of himself or his thoughts to slip out. Alain, while curious about this strange young man, was too busy fighting off the throbbing pain in his mind to bother with more than a superficial glance into the other's thoughts. Instead, Alain leaned back in his seat and closed his eyes, trying as best he could to let tranquility wash over him. It wasn't easy.

Occasionally Alain would glance out the window as the pirt car made its way to his hotel. He was vaguely disturbed by what he saw. Was it only his imagination, or were things looking dirtier, less cared for than during his last visit here? The people who clogged the streets were all dressed in brightly colored clothing, but the mood was anything but cheerful. Pedestrians stared fixedly ahead, scarcely bothering to look at the world on either side of them. There were neither smiles nor frowns in evidence, and the overwhelming feeling that bombarded his mind was apathy. People just did not care.

There's always been a listless portion of the population in any human society, Alain rationalized. *It's probably just the route Dekker programmed that's taking us through a less affluent neighborhood, that's all.*

But the depression that began on the trip from Leone to Earth remained with him even after Dekker dropped Alain off at the hotel where his reservations had been made. The telepath flopped down wearily on the bed and tried in vain to blot from his mind the impinging impressions from people in adjoining rooms.

I'm glad I'll be seeing the doctor tomorrow, he thought. *Maybe he can suggest something for this condition.*

Dr. Javier daPaz looked suspiciously at the file projection on his computer screen. It was a profile of the telepath he was scheduled to examine tomorrow, Alain Cheney. He had seen the man on three previous occasions, once every two years when he was called in from the field for the required mental and physical tests.

There were two lines scrawled at the bottom of the notes on the last examination. Translated from daPaz's personal shorthand, they read, "Signs of incipient psi instability noted. Telepause likely within two to three years."

Not much to hang a death sentence on, is it? he thought bitterly. He dreaded the examination tomorrow and what he feared he'd find in Cheney's mind. He dreaded even worse the consequences of his findings, for there would be no way to hide them; the Agency would be monitoring all his instruments and would know the results as soon as he himself did.

He had joined the Agency many years ago as a dedicated young doctor, full of zeal at the thought of doing his own small part to help Earth's defense against the outsiders. But as the years wore on, the sheen of his enthusiasm was eroded by the rust of cynicism. He began

14

noting the recurrence of certain patterns—the most disturbing of which was the one that occurred in the strongest, ablest telepaths once they reached the stage of development labeled "telepause." Once that was diagnosed, they never returned for subsequent examinations.

He was not sure when he realized the telepaths were being deliberately eliminated by their own side. At first, his assumption was that they were simply being reassigned to less strenuous duties in view of their delicate condition—but gradually that opinion was turned around. There was no single cause; merely a word here, a significant glance there from the Operations people— little clues that weighed on his mind and made him uneasy with his task.

Then, just after the last case he'd diagnosed, he happened to spot a small item in the evening newsfax about an unidentified body being washed up on the beach near San Luis Obispo. The woman had had red hair and only four fingers on her right hand . . . which sounded suspiciously like the woman he'd recently diagnosed as telepausal. Try as he would, he could find no other information on the dead woman—and a call to the coroner in the area brought him a sharp reminder to mind his own business.

He'd taken a week's vacation time and gone on a binge of drinking and drugging to try to wipe the guilt out of his mind, but the death was not so easily forgotten. He thought then of leaving the Agency, trying to decide whether it would be an act of bravery or cowardice. He had reached no resolution and, from sheer force of habit, slipped right back into the Agency routine once his vacation was finished.

Now the problem was facing him again, in a way he could not avoid. Tomorrow, Alain Cheney would walk into this office with a probable case of telepause. And then . . .

DaPaz rose from his desk, went into the adjoining bathroom and looked at his prematurely lined face in the mirror. *And then what, doctor?* he asked himself. *What will you do then?*

15

chapter 2

Despite the fact that she was more than five minutes late for the briefing, Joby Karns entered the conference room the very embodiment of poise and elegance. Her lean, supple body was clad in a simple black and red dashiki. She didn't need to dress up to make herself beautiful; she knew that her copper red hair and her unlined face made her look a good ten years younger than she really was. Her beauty could only be enhanced by the power that accompanied her position. A thorough knowledge of her assets and her influence gave her all the confidence she needed.

Her blue eyes scanned the room, noting that everyone else was here: Marina Shekova of Budget; Ho Li Wan, "Public Relations" (in essence, propaganda); Colonel Adaman Haiphez, Military Liaison; Karl Junger of Counterintelligence; Cohila Buturu of Technical Services; James Tennon of Cryptography; Romney Glazer of Internal Security; Phyllis Rokowsky, liaison to the director; and standing at the front of the room ready to conduct the meeting, Hakim Rajman, in charge of Assimilation and Correlation.

A council of equals, Joby thought wryly. *But some of us are more equal than others.*

She could tell they'd been waiting specifically for her to arrive before starting. She gave them a curt nod as she sat down.

"How good of you to come, Joby," Romney Glazer commented acidly, as only he could.

"It's nice to know I'm missed," she replied. She saw no need to apologize to them, or even to explain that she'd been waiting for the long-overdue call from Dekker about the arrival of Alain Cheney. It still hadn't come, and she was beginning to worry that something might have gone wrong. But she owed no explanations to anyone here—least of all to a putzer like Glazer.

"Joby already knows most of what we're going to discuss," Hakim Rajman said from the front of the room, cutting off the bitter exchange. "It was her agents who discovered the problem. Perhaps I should let her explain the initial stages."

All heads turned once again to her. Joby remained in her seat as she said, "Three days ago, the Leonean Defense Ministry staged a complete shutdown of all our operations there. I mean 100 percent. All our sources either evaporated, closed their mouths, or 'disappeared.' All our monitoring devices were either ferreted out and destroyed, or neutralized in some other way. The logical inference is that something is happening inside there, something so monumental that they're willing to tip their hand that they knew our sources, rather than let us get the faintest whiff of what it is."

"There are other reasons for housecleaning," Karl Junger said. "A change in administration sometimes wants to get off to a good start by making sure all the spies are out of its closets. Or some overeager junior assistant may want to please his boss—or he may be trying a power play to replace him by showing him up as inefficient."

"Or perhaps," Romney Glazer spoke up again, "perhaps Joby's people were so clumsy that they were finally an embarrassment to the Leonean government itself, so it put them out of their misery."

"A and C is aware of all those reasons and more," Rajman said with a sharp glance at Glazer. He did not like playing the role of peacemaker, but he knew he had to if this meeting were to be kept under control. "We feel that none of them apply in this particular instance. The hierarchy in the Leonean administration—particularly Defense—has been stable for months, so they have no need to show off. And if this were a feint—if they wanted us to *think* something was happening there so

17

we'd concentrate all our resources on it and ignore something else—they almost undoubtedly would have left us some little hole to peek through, giving us tantalizing glimpses of their supposed secret. My staff and I are convinced that this crackdown represents a genuine effort to keep something from us, something happening at Defense."

Phyllis Rokowsky cleared her throat. She was a small but stately-looking woman, approaching her middle years with just a trace of gray in her elegantly coiffured black hair. "The question now," she said, "is, what are they trying to keep from us, and why?" Though she spoke in gentle terms, everyone paid attention; Phyllis Rokowsky reported personally to the director, who in turn reported to the primus.

Rajman cleared his throat and shuffled some papers around in front of him. "Whatever it is, we can be reasonably certain that it involves only Leone and none of its allies; all indications are that things are quiet along diplomatic channels. The immediate thought was that they'd developed some startling new weapons system. While we can't rule that possibility out entirely, our breakdown analysis shows less than a 5 percent probability. We've kept a careful monitor on all their ongoing projects, and none of them are close enough to completion. Even if they were, none of the new systems is advanced enough to justify a complete intelligence blackout of the sort they're using."

Rokowsky nodded and turned to Glazer. "Romney, as our expert on Internal Security, how long could *we* maintain such a blackout if we had something desperately important to protect?"

"Not all that long." Glazer was all business now. "I'd say two months at the outside. Working under heavy secrecy like that puts a big psychological strain on everyone involved. Plus, there's the fact that the opposition will be working triply hard to crack the outer shell. Entropy inevitably guarantees that little chinks will begin forming almost as soon as their screen is in place."

"It will also be expensive," added Marina Shekova, the Agency's budget director. "The cost of their own in-

18

ternal security will have to rise two to four times to handle the increased workload."

Rokowsky considered the input she was receiving from the department heads. "In other words," she said slowly, "whatever they hope to gain by this tactic must be a short-range objective. They know they can't keep us out forever. It would seem that this is something that must be kept secret in the developmental stage if it's going to exist at all; but once it's set in motion, it won't matter whether we know or not. Is that a fair hypothesis?"

Rajman looked down at his notes, then back at Rokowsky. "A bit simplified, perhaps, but it coincides with my department's diagnosis."

"Good," Rokowsky smiled. "Let me take my simplified theory a step further. What if they are planning a war, a surprise attack on us? That's something they'd want to keep very secret right now, but it wouldn't matter in two months because we'd know about it by then anyhow —the hard way." She turned to the military liaison officer. "Comment, colonel?"

Adaman Haiphez looked straight back at her. "From all the information available to me, Leone is not ready for a war." He glanced over at Rajman and, getting a confirming nod, continued, "There are certain preparations that must be made if you're planning a war. You have to make sure your troops are supplied—with arms, with fuel, with food, with clothing. You have to gear up domestic production so that critical materials can be both manufactured and distributed. You have to redeploy manpower in key positions. There are a thousand small, telltale signs, none of which are apparent on Leone. Leone is not ready for a major war today, nor—in my opinion— could it gear up for one in a mere two months."

Rokowsky nodded again. She was silent for a moment, then asked Haiphez, "What about us, colonel? Are we ready for a war?"

"We can easily defend ourselves against anything Leone can bring against us, now or in the foreseeable future."

"That's not what I asked," Rokowsky said—so gently that it hardly sounded like the reprimand it was. "Visualize our alternatives, colonel. The Leoneans have something so vital that they're going to a lot of trouble to keep it from us. We, therefore, have to find out what it is. Suppose the primus decides that this matter is so essential that all measures, including armed intervention, are justified. If we send a military expedition against Leone to crack their secrecy, all the independent planets will immediately resume hostilities against us. You know that as well as I do. My question, colonel, is whether we are prepared to wage all-out war on so many fronts."

Haiphez took a deep breath and looked away from her. "No, ma'am, we are not."

Rokowsky smiled—a cold, triumphant expression. "Thank you, colonel. That puts an upper limit on our possible response to this affair. Having thus eliminated the possibility of overt action, we are left with the covert methods. That is your responsibility, is it not, Ms. Karns?"

Joby looked the other woman squarely in the eye. She respected and admired Phyllis Rokowsky for the smooth, effortless way she was able to wield her power—but Joby refused to be cowed by her. "You're absolutely right. Since it was my department that first called everyone's attention to the situation, we have also been studying it more closely than anyone else—with the exception, of course, of Hakim's staff."

There was a slight chuckle throughout the room. Hakim Rajman's Assimilation and Correlation Department was by far the largest bureau within the Terran Intelligence Agency, with four times the manpower and six times the budget of any other single department. With data coming in continuously from sixty-three other inhabited worlds, there was an enormous need to sift it, evaluate it, and pass it on to those other sections of the government that needed to act on it. With so many people working inside, Rajman's department was also the least well organized. The joke in the other departments was that A and C stood for "Anarchy and Confusion."

Joby waited for the undercurrent of humor to subside before continuing. "Unfortunately, the timing of this whole situation could not have been worse as far as we're concerned. Our chief-of-station on Leone is a telepath

20

who we suspect is on the verge of going telepausal. One week ago—just a few days before this entire matter blew up in our faces—he boarded a ship to come back here for his routine biannual checkup. If he had waited a few days longer, I'm sure he would have been capable of penetrating the Leoneans' best screens. But as it is . . ." She placed both her hands on top of the table. "If we find what we expect to find, I suppose we'll have to replace him. And that, on top of this new development, puts us at a great disadvantage."

"Are you trying to build up a case for sympathy?" Glazer interrupted sharply.

Joby looked over at him. "What do you mean by that?"

Glazer gave one of his bitchy little smirks. While his eyes were fixed on Joby, his words were intended for the entire room. "I understand from your file that you attended the Academy with this agent and, in fact, had a very close relationship with him."

The bastard does his homework, Jody thought in a cold fury. "Close or not," she enunciated, "the rules governing telepausal agents are quite explicit and will be adhered to. One of my top assistants is handling the matter personally. I only express regret that a man of proven reputation—and I'm sure not even you could question Cheney's service record—will not be available to us in solving this current and urgent problem."

"I didn't realize you would be so touchy," Glazer said in mock apology. "If it would ease some of the burden from your mind, I could have some of my people take care of the Cheney problem for you."

Joby bristled. "Operations has always taken care of its own lame horses, thank you. When we need help from the goon squad, we'll ask for it."

Phyllis Rokowsky had but to clear her throat again and all eyes went to her. "I think we have strayed from the primary subject under discussion," she said in a soft voice. "Shall we return to the matter of Leone?"

Joby was furious at herself for letting Glazer ruffle her so badly—especially in front of Rokowsky. She tried to put the matter out of her mind, but it kept insinuating itself into her behavior, disrupting her train of thought and causing her to falter slightly in the wrong places.

As best she could, she outlined to the assembled department heads her contingency plans for restructuring the Leonean organization in the event that Cheney did need replacing. In addition, she promised to report within two days on a completely detailed strategy for piercing the Leoneans' shield of secrecy. Hakim Rajman pledged to have his staff work overtime to see if they could discover any clues about what might be happening there from previously known data.

The meeting dissolved as so many of them did, with no questions resolved, no actions decided. As Joby stood up to leave, Glazer tried to approach her. She brushed him off coldly with the excuse that she was expecting an important call and hurried back to her office.

"Has Morgan Dekker reported in yet?" she asked her secretary as she entered the spacious anteroom to her own suite of offices.

"No, ma'am."

Damn, what's keeping him? He's more than two hours late! "Well, buzz him through to me the instant he does, and keep the lines clear for him." She walked into her own office and closed the door against the world.

She tried to sit at her desk, but the combination of Glazer's heckling and Dekker's lateness made her too nervous. She lit up a drugrod, inhaling deep breaths and letting the effect flow into her. Within minutes she could feel the muscles at the back of her neck and shoulders starting to unknot themselves, could feel the easing warmth as the drug slowly worked its way into her brain, relieving some of the crushing burden she was carrying. On impulse, she stood up and walked to the wall control, dimming down the room's lights to a minimum. With a twist of a second dial, she changed the scene on her office's north wall from the gentle desert landscape it normally showed to a holographic map of the explored section of the galaxy.

Earth's solar system, naturally enough, was at the center of the map. Around it, forming an irregular globe, were the former colonies. And there, right up near the top of the map, was the small bit that was all men knew about the Dur-ill Empire.

"Empire." She was hardly aware she'd said the word aloud. Earth had had an empire too, more than a century and a half ago. The dominion of Terra had extended all around the mother planet in a sphere roughly thirty parsecs in diameter, including colonies on sixty-three inhabitable worlds. Nowhere had man found any challenge to his supremacy; the universe seemed his for the taking.

Then, within the space of a single decade, that dream of manifest destiny was shattered forever. Exploratory teams from the colony of Renna encountered the outer limits of the Dur-ill Empire. Scholars since that time had argued long and loud whether the ensuing war between widely disparate cultures had been inevitable. To Joby's mind, the argument was senseless; the war *had* happened, so of course it was inevitable.

Suddenly the dispersal of the human race throughout a vast volume of space became a liability rather than an asset. Earth's leaders found themselves tangled in an impossible logistical situation. They simply did not have the resources to defend and supply the colonies and, at the same time, carry on the war as it had to be conducted. A decision of priorities was made, and defense of the colonies was dropped in favor of devoting more resources to the development of technology and the growth of Earth's armed services.

The war raged on for eight years, and the government of Earth had to scrape the bottom of the barrel to keep itself going. With no intelligence about how the war was progressing for the Dur-ill, they were almost literally shooting in the dark at an enemy they hardly knew. Finally, when their resources were all but depleted, an armistice was reached whereby both humans and Dur-ill agreed never to violate the other's space again. Peace came once more.

Peace, that is, between humans and Dur-ill. Terra's former colonies were not overjoyed about the decision made eight years earlier to abandon them to their fate. In pure self-defense they had formed an alliance of their own, and desperation had enabled them to battle the Dur-ill to a standstill. But with that war over, old relationships were dead. The human planets were not about to resume their former dependency on a world that had been all too eager to sacrifice them when the chips were down. Earth now found it had a handful of enemies to face instead of merely one.

Relations between Earth and the other human-occupied planets seesawed drastically over the 150 years since then. Fortunately, with the Dur-ill removed, the various colonies had little in common with one another except for their hatred of Earth; the defensive alliance they had formed during the war quickly evaporated, leaving a situation of many autonomous worlds in conflict and competition.

The Terran Intelligence Agency had been formed shortly after the end of the war. It was cobbled together from bits and pieces of the old colonial administration, with some shiny new departments added to fulfill more current needs. Its avowed purpose was severalfold: to promote the interests of Earth among the other planets; to keep Earth's government apprised of affairs on the former colonies; and if it were not possible to make the other worlds receptive to Earth's interests, then at least to promote disunity among them so that they could never form an effective alliance against the mother planet.

The Operations Department had, since its inception, always been the elite outfit within the Agency. Other departments had more manpower, more funding; Operations had more glamour. It was the philosophy of Operations personnel that all the other departments were nothing but glamorized computer programmers; it was the agents in Operations who gathered the classified information and who engaged in the field work that made everything else the Agency did possible.

Joby Karns had worked long and hard to win her position as chief of Operations. There had been years of sacrifice, of long hours, of moving her way skillfully across the chessboard of office politics, of guessing whom to favor and whom to dump, whom to sleep with and whom to scorn. The world of politics within the Agency was every bit as cutthroat as the world of espionage outside. One little slip, one small mistake could bring the entire structure tumbling down around her head.

She had almost made such a slip this afternoon, when Glazer thought he'd spotted a trace of sentimentalism on her part for Alain Cheney. The mood of Earth's government these days was strictly utilitarian. It was sentimentalism that had caused the downfall of Joby's predecessor, Gunnar Tölling; Joby made a vow that the same fate would not befall her. She didn't think she still had any residual feelings for Alain—but even if she did, no one would ever see them. She would not give Glazer a clear shot at her back.

She didn't know how or why the fight had started, but Romney Glazer had hated her from the day she took over Operations. As head of Internal Security—in charge of making sure all regulations were obeyed and plugging any leaks within the Agency—he was a dangerous man to cross; his department was small, but it had an authority disproportionately large for its size. She had tried being friendly, but Glazer had snubbed her—and being homosexual, he was impervious to her physical charms. Joby had to treat him as a constant threat to her well-being—but at least he was a predictable one.

The intercom buzzed, startling Joby out of her reverie. "Morgan Dekker's call, ma'am," her secretary announced.

With a sigh of relief, Joby returned to her desk and punched the receiver button. "How did it go, Morgan?" she asked, hiding her anxiety behind a voice full of businesslike efficiency.

"Well enough. He was a few hours late getting off the ship, which is why I'm so late reporting. But once he showed up, things ran smoothly."

"Any traces of—" There was the barest of hesitations. "—of what we're looking for?"

"Hard to say. He seemed to be functioning well enough, but he was very quiet and reserved."

"Alain always was the introspective sort, always well in control of himself. That's why he's been such a good agent. We'll find out for sure tomorrow when he goes in for the examination. Do you think he suspected anything?"

On the screen before her, Dekker's face grimaced slightly. "Again, hard to say. He showed no signs, and I was careful to keep my thoughts under control—but it's always difficult to know with a telepath. There was a mild flicker of something across his face when I told him you had replaced Tölling. Would you know anything about that?"

Joby's political instincts sensed danger lurking in that innocent question. She knew Dekker harbored an infatuation for her, which could lead to feelings of jealousy if he felt she had any special interest in Alain. She was of two minds about his feelings for her. On the one hand, she had long ago made a personal rule never to sleep with anyone of lesser importance than herself, so she could not allow anything to come of her relationship with her aide; on the other hand, she did nothing to discourage him, because his feelings for her would make him more loyal to her—and loyalty was a rare commodity in the Agency these days.

In an attempt to defuse his question, she shook her head. "No, not that I can think of. We did go through the Academy together; maybe he's glad that an old classmate has risen so high. Has he been installed properly?"

"When I got him to the hotel he went directly to his room, lay down on the bed, and closed his eyes. He's either asleep or meditating. In any event, the entire room is monitored, so we'll know if he attempts anything unusual, and he'll be followed if he leaves. But frankly, I don't think he'll give us any trouble."

That could almost be the story of Alain's career, Joby reflected. In fourteen years with the Terran Intelligence Agency, Alain Cheney had been an exemplary agent. He had never disobeyed an order, never failed an assignment, never performed at anything less than a level of supreme competence. He was a constant factor in life, an eternal verity. And just because he was one of the top telepathic agents in her stable, she might have to kill him tomorrow.

The universe, she decided, *can play very perverse tricks.*

"Good," she said aloud. "I've got enough troubles without having to worry about him."

"Since he was an old friend of yours," Dekker said, a little too rapidly, "I was wondering whether you might, er, want to come out here for the decision tomorrow."

"I said an old classmate, not an old friend," Joby clarified carefully. "And I'm really too swamped with work to make a trip all the way out there for something that trivial. I have confidence in you, Morgan; I'm sure you'll handle the details just fine." She gave him her Number Three Smile: warm enough to make him feel a degree of solidarity with her, aloof enough not to make any rash promises. "Call me tomorrow when you learn the results of his tests." And without any formal signoff, she terminated the connection.

What she had told Dekker about too much work was quite true. This latest crisis would mean double or triple overtime for everyone on her staff having any connection to activities on Leone. She doubted she'd have a chance to leave her office until the reorganization and strike plans were all formalized and presented to the Agency Council.

Leaning back momentarily in her chair, she looked up at her star map once again. There, near the very top, was the pink dot that represented the class-K star Leone circled. Leone, being one of the systems nearest the Durill Empire, had suffered some of the worst damage of the war—and consequently, it held the greatest hatred of Earth. Relations between the two worlds were tranquil at the moment, with a fair amount of trade and unrestricted travel between them. But Leone was a world that could flare up as a trouble spot at any moment, which was why the better agents were usually assigned there.

Now, apparently, it had flared up—and her best agent was well on his way toward elimination.

She wondered whether the tests two years ago might have been mistaken, and whether Alain might still be all right for a while. But she recognized that for the wishful thinking it was. The tests were virtually foolproof. Alain

Cheney was either suffering from telepause now or would be in the very near future. Which meant he had to die.

Damn! With a frustrated shrug, Joby turned off the map and restored the lights in her office. She had plans to arrange and reports to write, and all her thoughts about the soon-to-be-late Alain Cheney would not alter that in the slightest.

chapter 3

Alain did not sleep well in his hotel room that night. In part, he told himself, it was because Earth's gravity was slightly stronger than he was used to on Leone, which tended to make the mattress feel lumpy and uncomfortable. But far more than that was the mental illness that was creeping into him. He was swallowing fistfuls of trimethaline at regular intervals, but they didn't even slow the pain down. Something was going badly wrong inside his head, and despite all his years of training and practice he could not keep it under control.

All night, as he lay in his bed, dreams assailed him. If they had been his own dreams, he might have coped with them somehow; but the dreams of people in the rooms all around his were more than he could handle. All their private hells, desires and needs, their personal symbolisms and problems were flying at his defenseless mind. By 3:00 A.M. he had buried his face in his pillow and was sobbing openly, clenching his fists in a futile attempt to brace himself against the telepathic onslaught.

Finally, as the sun came up and the other people were waking, he was able to doze off for a couple of hours of fitful sleep. His own dreams, however, were scarcely an improvement. They started with him in a graveyard, surrounded by a squad of skeletons. All the skeletons wore identical masks: the face of the man he'd been forced to kill a month ago, a young man scarcely more than a boy. The horror and pain on his face had sunk deeply into Alain's mind, and the telepathic projection of his death trauma had etched itself on Alain's psyche. The dead boy was now a continuing character in Alain's nightmares.

Eventually the skeletons tired of their game and were replaced by the succubi. Alain was amid a throng of sensuous, passionate women, all eager to consume him with the flame of their sexual desires. The wake-up call he'd left with the hotel's computer roused him from his unsatisfying slumber. He lay on the bed in a pool of sweat, with an erection that refused to go away until he'd masturbated to climax. Then, feeling ashamed and disgusted with himself, he rose and took a cold shower to purge himself of various guilts.

I'm glad I have that doctor's appointment, he thought as he emerged from the bathroom. *Maybe Dr. daPaz will know what's going wrong. Maybe he'll be able to help me.*

He could not face the thought of eating in a public place, so he had room service send up his breakfast. By the time it arrived he had dressed and made himself presentable for the day; as he ate, he read the latest news as it flashed on his room's telescreen. Immersing himself in external problems and focusing his mind outward eased some of the pain, but not to the extent he'd hoped. The news was too depressing.

Alain's mind had been trained for years to see the story behind the words, and he kept seeing—or imagining —the background behind everything he read. In this morning's reports alone, he counted two deaths and one resignation among governmental officials at varying levels and in different locations around the Earth. One of the officials had died in bed, the other in a pirt accident; the retirement was for reasons of failing health (the woman was fifty-two). Rallies in support of the primus's new agricultural proposals got widespread publicity; if anyone existed who disagreed, that fact somehow failed to draw the press's attention. There was great editorial

29

indignation over the planet Proserpine's charges that Terran vessels had willfully fired upon and destroyed their unarmed mining vessels in the interstellar dust region, which was theoretically free territory.

Elimination of political dissidents; suppression of opposing viewpoints; escalation of interplanetary tensions. *The world seemed so much better when I first joined the Agency,* Alain mused sadly. *Was it always this bad, and am I only seeing the corruption now because I'm so much more skilled at reading situations?*

He'd been more idealistic when he first enlisted. Earth was his home world; its interests had to be defended. He didn't think of the other planets as being evil, but they certainly bore Earth no good will. It was only right that Earth defend itself, and he was proud to be able to help.

He'd seen a lot of bad government on the other worlds he'd visited, and it had always been an immense consolation to think that his own world was so far superior. Suddenly, his government was looking as suppressive and dictatorial as all the rest, and it only added to the sickening feeling that bore down upon him. If he couldn't feel that his own cause was just, what was the point in going on at all?

Nonsense, he told himself sternly. *You're reading too much into trivial events, and you're letting your illness depress you too badly. At worst it's probably just a bad phase; even the best governments can go into declines every once in a while.*

He was just about to leave for the doctor's office when Morgan Dekker came to the door, saying that he would escort Alain personally to the doctor. This was puzzling; in all of Alain's previous visits for checkups, he had never been supervised as intently as this. *If I were paranoid,* he thought, *I could build a good case for being under suspicion of having committed some crime.* It was probably just a new procedure instituted under Joby Karns's regime. He scanned Dekker's mind to find out whether his supposition was correct, but Dekker was still keeping his thoughts well hidden behind a wall of lead, and Alain could not penetrate. Resignedly, he grabbed his shortcloak and followed Dekker out of the hotel to a pirt stop.

Alain paid very little attention to the ride today. The lack of sleep made him feel extremely groggy, and the pounding in his head from being outside, surrounded by so many people, only added to his malaise. It was actually a relief to be accompanied by a man like Dekker, who didn't talk and whose thoughts did not intrude on his own. Alain leaned back in his seat and did some meditation exercises to clear his mind during the journey.

Dr. daPaz's waiting room was empty as Alain and Dekker entered. Alain knew from past experience that the tests he would be undergoing were quite extensive and would take up most of the day. The doctor would have no other appointments scheduled.

DaPaz came out personally to welcome Alain. He was a little startled to see Dekker there as well. Alain introduced the two men, and daPaz asked Dekker to wait in the anteroom. Dekker obligingly sat down and turned on the telescreen, while daPaz escorted Alain into his office.

Alain could not read the doctor's mind, but that was not surprising. DaPaz was wearing a thin, almost invisible, crown of wires around his head—a telepathy interference cap. While he was wearing it, it would act as a baffle to the electromagnetic impulses being broadcast by his brain. While it did nothing to impede his thoughts, it generated a mental static for any telepath attempting to "peek in." It was required that any doctor doing research or checkups on telepaths wear one of those devices; otherwise, a telepath might be able to read the doctor's mind, see the anticipated result, and fake the test. The interference caps ensured objectivity.

Alain did not mind at all. In fact, in his present state of mind he wished everyone in the world were wearing such a cap; it would be far easier on him.

"How have you been these last two years, Alain?" daPaz asked as soon as he had closed the door behind them.

"The first year and a half were fine," Alain replied. "It's only in the last few months that there's been any problem."

"Could you describe the symptoms for me?"

"It started out as a series of occasional headaches. They'd go away with conventional medications, so I didn't think anything of them. They got stronger, though, sometimes incapacitating me completely for hours. It felt like knives jammed through my eye sockets into the sinuses. I found, though, that taking slightly larger doses of trimethaline stopped them. The last few weeks, though, absolutely nothing has worked, not even massive doses of trimethaline. It's like—well, imagine yourself trapped in a room with everyone around you yelling at top volume, except that they're all deaf so you're the only one affected. The trimethaline has always worked before to shut that stuff out; I was wondering whether I might have developed an immunity to it over the years. What do you think?"

"It's a *possible* explanation," daPaz said doubtfully. "Have you sought any other medical advice previously for this condition?"

"In the heart of enemy territory? Not likely. Besides, they don't even know telepathy exists; they certainly wouldn't know how to treat its disorders."

"Quite right. Sorry. Never having worked under field conditions myself, I tend to underestimate them."

"Do you have any idea what the problem is, doctor?"

"I'd like to run a few tests first," daPaz evaded, turning away so Alain could not see the expression on his face. "It's always easier to make a decision with all the facts at one's disposal."

"I understand."

"Step right into this room. You remember my assistant, don't you—Natalie Cellina?"

Alain nodded politely to the fortyish lady seated at the little table in the dimly lit chamber. He sat down opposite her as she skillfully shuffled her decks of cards. DaPaz left them alone and went into the next room, where he could observe them and comment over a loudspeaker system.

They started with the simplest test—a few runs through the standard Rhine deck—and worked their way upward. By the time Alain was at the point of reading more abstract concepts, the woman was sitting in the next room. Sometimes, in answer to daPaz's questions about what the assistant was thinking, Alain surprised himself by responding with complete sentences plucked from Natalie Cellina's mind. He was amazed at his own abilities. The reading of whole thoughts was almost unheard of; the best most telepaths could hope for was strong blocks of emotions, visual images of definite items, scattered bits of words or phrases. Part of the telepath's job was to play detective, piecing all these clues together to get a coherent picture of the subject's thoughts and feelings. *If I can keep this ability to read whole thoughts after I'm cured,* Alain mused, *I'll really be phenomenal.*

After the first simple series of psi tests, daPaz let Alain's mind "relax" awhile and gave him a standard physical examination. The conclusions were that Alain's body was in fine condition for a thirty-eight-year-old male, except for a slight abnormality in heartbeat and blood pressure—which was easily attributable to being under slightly heavier gravity than he was used to. Alain's only problems were in his mind—but they were serious enough.

DaPaz returned to testing Alain's mind. While the telepath lay back on the examining table, the doctor adjusted the receivers to take electroencephalogram readings. Four sets of EEGs were made: first, with Alain keeping his mind as blank as possible; second, while doing a simple series of arm-leg coordination exercises; third, while doing another basic series of psi tests; and fourth, after being given a slight dosage of a mind activation drug. Normally that final step was a routine one, but this time Alain felt his pain increasing dramatically as the drug took effect. Apparently his problem stemmed from the fact that his mind was already overactive, and the drug only added to the difficulty.

The final sequence was in the sensory deprivation chamber. Alain stripped down completely and waited impatiently as daPaz fitted monitors all over his body. Then he was given an oxygen mask and submerged in a darkened tank of warm water. The area immediately around the tank was cleared of people, so that not even thoughts could intrude on Alain's solitude. Sight, sound, taste, and scent were removed from him. The only sensa-

33

tion was the slight tickle of water against his body hairs—and as he remained motionless, even that vanished.

Alain drifted.

He was a little worried, at first, over what might happen. He knew from previous tests that, deprived of external sensory input, his mind usually conjured up images of its own. The murder of the young man a month ago haunted his dreams so badly that he was afraid his subconscious, now given free rein, would bring the incident up again with full force. Alain did not like killing—no telepath did, because they could sense other people's death traumas too thoroughly—and had tried to avoid it all through his career. This had only been the fourth person he had killed, and two of the others, like this one, had been due to unavoidable accidents. Many of his colleagues were, by now, hardened to death; Alain's philosophy was that if you had to kill someone, you were doing the job wrong.

But his worries were for naught. No such horrors bombarded his mind now. Instead, for the first time in weeks, he felt himself completely at ease. The pains that had been hammering at the inside of his mind all but vanished. Images did come to him, but they were innocent, restful, soothing. He was awash in a mental sea of greens and blues, remembrances of children and favorite toys; he was enthralled by the memories of women he had loved and the smooth feel of their skins against his own; he was carried away by the taste of chocolate and the scent of ozone after a spring rain.

Alain fell asleep while drifting in the tank and had to be shaken awake when the test was over.

While Alain was getting dressed again, Dr. daPaz locked himself inside his office to ponder the data. As he'd feared, the conclusion to be drawn from the tests was inescapable: Alain Cheney was already well into the first stages of telepause.

The symptoms were all there: the chronic headaches, which not even trimethaline could eliminate; the results of the blood tests, showing abnormally high concentrations of testosterone and of chemicals normally associated with psychic activities; the extremely volatile reaction to even a tiny trace of the mind activation drug; the sudden surges of sexual desire at odd moments; and most importantly, the phenomenal surge in Alain's actual psi abilities. He had scored 94 percent on today's Rhine tests; previously, his high score had been 79. His perceptions of actual thoughts were frighteningly acute. His EEG readings all had the high peaks and "ghost echoes" of telepathic activity, even when he was lying quietly on the table.

DaPaz sat down behind the desk and massaged gently at his forehead with the fingers of his left hand. He did not know Alain Cheney very well; seeing a man only one day every two years did not make for close relationships. But he liked what he did see. Alain Cheney seemed an intelligent, sensitive man, with both a sense of humor and some consideration for other people. DaPaz did not want to see him die because of some inexplicable hormonal imbalance. Further, he did not want to be an accessory to that death.

His problem was that he had no choice in the matter. Given the option, he would simply have lied to the Agency, told them that his earlier tests had been in error. But that simply would not suffice. He knew for a fact that all his instruments were monitored, their data fed instantly into the Agency's computers. The Agency—and probably in the person of that Morgan Dekker fellow—already knew the same things daPaz did about Cheney's condition. Their plans to kill him had undoubtedly already been drawn up; even at this moment they were probably being set in motion.

DaPaz could not lie to the TIA about Cheney. The only other option, other than to be a silent accomplice, was to tell Cheney about the Agency's intentions.

That path posed special problems in itself. DaPaz knew that his equipment was monitored, which made it possible, if not likely, that the rest of his office was monitored as well. He could not tell Cheney anything, not here, or he would only ensure his own death as well. Every word he spoke, and the tone in which he uttered it, must be completely proper, both medically and in terms of his own personality. But if he didn't tell Cheney anything, he knew he'd never have a chance again.

DaPaz stood up and walked around the room. The Agency had been good to him. It had underwritten his medical training, given him grants to perform the research that needed to be done in the field of medicine for telepaths. It had established him in a comfortable practice with high income and low risk. It had given him job security in a shaky world.

All it asked in return was an occasional human sacrifice.

There was a knock on his door. Alain Cheney would have finished dressing by now and would want to know the test results. With a deep sigh, daPaz opened the door and ushered his patient to a chair beside his desk.

"Well, what's the verdict?" Cheney asked as soon as daPaz had seated himself across the desk from him.

The doctor had to struggle not to wince at the other man's metaphor. This examination *had* been a trial, with judgment entered and death sentence pronounced. "Not as good as I'd like it to be," he said in a carefully clinical voice. "Have you ever heard of telepause?"

Cheney wrinkled his brow. "I don't think so."

"It seems to be a stage in the mental development of telepaths. The psi abilities become incredibly acute and somewhat unstable. The headaches you mention are symptomatic of the inability to shut out any mental processes that impinge on your mind. Something else you failed to mention, but which was obvious from the tests, is a strong increase in sexual desire. That, too, is typical of telepause."

Cheney's face looked progressively more somber as the doctor spoke. When daPaz paused, the agent spoke up once more. "Is there anything that can be done for it?"

"Oh yes," daPaz lied with what he hoped was the proper veneer of breezy confidence. "The Agency has seen this happen before—it usually only happens to the best telepaths, by the way—and they tell me they have a very effective program for treating it." *Sure, they kill you. The perfect cure, works every time.* "I'm not positive exactly what it entails; I'm only on the diagnostic end, I'm

36

afraid. What I'll have to do is make out a report for them, and they'll take it from there."

Cheney leaned back in his chair and closed his eyes. "That's a relief. You had me worried for a while."

DaPaz tensed. He would have to make his move now or be damned forever. "I wouldn't worry about it if I were you. Tell me, you mentioned something about having difficulty falling asleep last night, didn't you?"

"That's a mild way of putting it."

"Hm. I'd hate to punch in a prescription for you, because there's still so much trimethaline flowing through your veins that there might be adverse reactions. There is a good nonprescription sleep aid that I think I can recommend safely; I've used it myself on occasion. It's called 'Lites-Out.' Can you remember that?"

"I think so."

"They spell it an odd way. Maybe I'd better write it out for you just in case." DaPaz grabbed his memo pad and jotted down a quick note: *Your life's in danger. Meet me tonight 8:00 Seacrest Restaurant.* With his heart banging furiously, he handed it across the desk to Cheney.

The agent took the note, glanced at it, then looked up at the doctor, startled. DaPaz gave an almost imperceptible nod and said, "Don't lose that, now. They name these products so strangely that they all sound alike after a while."

Cheney looked at the note once more. "I won't," he promised, folding the piece of paper with excruciating precision and tucking it in his pocket.

The doctor stood up, indicating a formal conclusion to this session. "Other than that, you seem to be in perfect health. I'd better get busy on your report, so the higher-ups can get ready to treat you properly."

Cheney stood as well, and reached out to shake the doctor's hand. "Thank you very much," he said—and the look in his eyes as they connected with daPaz's was indeed one of gratitude. "See you in another two years."

DaPaz smiled and showed his patient out the door, then returned to the desk to write his report. It was more than fifteen minutes, though, before he could will his hands to stop shaking.

chapter 4

Alain took the paper from the doctor. It seemed to him that daPaz had written something longer than merely the brand name of a sleeping pill, so instead of sticking it immediately in his pocket he glanced at it to see what it said. He was expecting the traditional illegible scrawl of all doctors, but the note was clear, precise, and extremely troubling. Startled, he looked up at daPaz for confirmation, and the doctor gave him a slight nod to show that the message had indeed been the intended one.

A mass of thoughts crowded through Alain's mind simultaneously. The first priority was to establish the trustworthiness of the message. Ordinarily he would just have read the other's mind, but daPaz was still wearing the interference cap, which made that impossible. Alain had acquired enough sensitivity to other nonverbal signals over the years, however, that he was able to make a sufficient analysis even without telepathy. The doctor's hands were the slightest bit shaky, and as Alain looked at his face, daPaz averted his eyes. His jaw was tensed, his muscles tightened like springs under pressure. The man was clearly frightened about what he was doing.

Whether the information is true or not, Alain evaluated, *daPaz obviously believes it. He wouldn't be so scared otherwise.*

And that led him to an appraisal of the message itself. Was his life really in danger? And if so, from whom?

DaPaz worked for the Agency exclusively. He would have almost no contacts outside it—not unless the fellows at Internal Security were terribly lax, and Alain doubted

that. Which pointed to the conclusion that this was strictly an affair within the TIA itself.

The fact that daPaz had to be so secretive was also significant. He was obviously worried that his office might be bugged. If he suspected some foreign source, he would simply have requested that the Agency send some of their men over to fumigate the place. But if it were the *Agency* that had done the bugging, he would have no such recourse.

Alain remembered all the monitors he had seen at the Vandenberg terminal, the stringent precautionary measures in effect. His doubts of earlier that day were suddenly reinforced. The entire planet was like an armed camp, and people dared not speak freely in their own offices and homes.

But why? he wondered. *What have I done to single me out for this treatment?*

He could get no answers to those questions now. The only way he'd be able to find out what this meant—at least from the doctor's standpoint—would be to meet daPaz at the restaurant tonight as the note suggested. Continuing with the small talk, he folded the paper neatly and tucked it deep within his pocket, so that there was no chance of its falling out and being found by the wrong parties. At the soonest opportunity he would burn it, to ensure that there was nothing left to incriminate daPaz.

He let the doctor show him out the door, and when he said thank you, he meant it. Regardless of whether the information was valid, the doctor had performed a very brave act for Alain's sake, and Alain wanted to make sure his gratitude was evident.

Dekker was still in the anteroom waiting for him as Alain emerged from daPaz's office. The younger man was speaking quietly into his sleeve phone and watching the tiny screen intently. He looked up as Alain came through the door and said, "I'll be with you in a second. Just have some business to finish up." Then he went back to his previous phone conversation, in tones so low that Alain, even straining, could not pick up what was said.

This time Alain made a concerted effort to probe Dekker's mind, again with limited success. Dekker was a cold, emotionless man, a biological robot, and he used that fact to advantage. Trying to get beyond that solid exterior was like scaling a mountain of ice; every time Alain thought he'd reached the top and could see what lay beyond, he'd slip back down again and have to try once more. The little bit he could see did nothing to ease his mind. Morgan Dekker was a man of barely controlled violence and hard-edged fanaticism. Alain had seen the type before. They made the perfect soldiers: obedient, unimaginative, eager for the dirty jobs that more rational people would shun. They were useful in their own limited way, but whoever was in control would constantly have to remind himself of what those limits were—otherwise he would have a time bomb on his hands.

If they wanted to kill me, Alain thought, *they couldn't have sent a better man.*

Dekker finished his conversation and stood up. "All right, let's go," he said brusquely.

"Back to the hotel?" Alain asked, trying to sound casual.

Dekker hesitated a fraction of a second. "That depends. What did the doc have to say?"

He's testing me, Alain thought. *He already knows. That's what his phone conversation was about.* But he'd learned in his long career that this game was played by very precise, formal rules, and he adhered strictly to them, to drag out the process as long as possible. "He said I've got something called telepause. Do you know what that is?"

"Yeah, I've heard something about it," Dekker nodded. "It means that we won't be going straight back to your hotel after all."

The two men left the office and walked down the hallway out into the late afternoon sun. "Where are we going, then?" Alain asked.

"The Agency maintains a private reserve for telepause patients undergoing therapy. It's in the hills outside town; the doctors felt it was best to isolate the patients as much as possible from human contacts, so that their minds could be more at ease."

"I can understand that," Alain agreed. "The further away from people I am, the better this feels."

He could also understand why they would be leaving town if Dekker wanted to kill him. There would be no witnesses, and it would be easier to dispose of the body. "But all my things are back at the hotel," he continued.

"We'll send someone back for them, don't worry. Our chief concern is to get you over this condition."

"Awfully considerate of you," Alain said.

They walked to the nearest pirt station and waited while the people ahead of them dialed for their rides. When it came Dekker's turn, he had to spend a slightly longer time punching in his request, because he would need a car that was hooked into the state computer system rather than just the city grid. It took half an hour before such a vehicle was available, but eventually it did come sliding up to the curb and the two men got in.

This car was bigger than the ones that ran strictly within the city, with room for up to six people to stretch out comfortably. There was even a small snack and drink dispenser built in, in case the passengers should need any refreshment during long trips. The two TIA men took their seats with a gap of more than a meter between them, and Dekker punched out a code for their destination. His fingers moved too quickly for Alain to follow, but it wouldn't have mattered—he didn't know the local coordinate system anyway.

The car maneuvered through the streets of Lompoc and out into the hilly countryside surrounding it. Even out of the city proper, though, the hillsides were jammed with houses and apartment complexes, all filled with people, all emitting thoughts that bombarded Alain's mind. If Dekker wanted to kill him without witnesses, he would have to go a great distance indeed.

As on their previous rides together, the two men said little. In between his futile attempts to probe beyond the surface of Dekker's mind, Alain considered his situation carefully. If the Agency did indeed wish to kill him for some reason, it would explain why Dekker had been at his side from the moment Alain had arrived at the customs

41

desk. They'd never taken such thorough precautions on his previous trips back to Earth for checkups . . . but they would if they wanted to prevent his escape.

I could overpower him now, Alain thought. *The way he's sitting, he's not expecting me to give him any trouble yet. It would be a simple matter to . . .*

He cut off that line of thought abruptly. It was too easy to become paranoid in this business, too easy to see plots behind every bush. There were enough real threats without the added complications of inventing more.

The problem was, he just didn't *know*. Sure, he could overpower, and even kill, Dekker right now—but would that be the right thing to do? What if daPaz was crazy, and Dekker actually was taking him to a TIA reservation to be cured of this hideous illness? How would he then explain to Joby Karns exactly why he killed his escort? "Well, I *thought* he was going to kill me, so I had to get him first"? That would be asking for a quick one-way ticket to the nearest silly cell . . . if, indeed, they let him live long enough to reach it.

His situation was precarious. He dared not act until he was positive, which to all intents and purposes meant he had to let Dekker make the first move. On the other hand, he dared not wait too long, or the whole matter might become academic.

Alain sat and watched the hills flow past the car. On the other side of the seat, he could see Dekker doing the same thing. The other man's mind was as stony as ever. A bit of sweat broke out on Alain's upper lip. He wiped nervously at it, hoping Dekker would not notice.

It occurred to him that, if he could start Dekker talking, the man's mind might wander enough to give Alain a few glimpses inside. "Are they able to completely cure this telepause?" he asked aloud.

"I don't know," Dekker answered slowly. "I think so, in most cases. If not, I think they can reassign the person to a desk job somewhere, so there isn't as much strain on him."

The car had turned west, toward the Pacific Ocean. Houses were thinning out on either side, now, and the country through which they traveled was looking much

less civilized. *Soon, if at all,* Alain thought. "What sort of treatment does the therapy involve?"

"How should I know? I'm no doctor."

Still no break in the stone wall of Dekker's mind. "I just thought you might have heard something," Alain persisted. "You seem to know more about this than I do."

"Sorry. I'm afraid you'll just have to find out the hard way." Dekker's tone put a period to the end of the conversation—and Alain had not learned a single thing more than he'd known before.

He sat back, feeling frustrated. Once again fatigue washed over him—but this time he dared not close his eyes, for fear that he might not open them again.

The car veered off the main highway onto a small side road. From the look of it, this new path was seldom traveled; it was paved, but long neglected and in need of repair. Alain was surprised it was even tied into the state computer hookup that allowed guided travel. Of course, if there really were a TIA clinic at the other end, that would explain it. . . .

The car had barely gone a kilometer from the highway —just far enough to be out of sight—when it suddenly stopped. Dekker looked up; he appeared to be startled. Alain could read no such emotion in his mind, but that didn't prove anything. Dekker hid all his emotions well.

"What happened?" Alain asked.

"I don't know." Dekker began pushing buttons on the vehicle's console, but nothing happened. "Feels like the engine's died or something."

"We're not trapped in here, are we?"

"I don't think the situation's that desperate." As Dekker pressed another button, the door nearest Alain opened. "Why don't we get out and see what the matter is?"

Alain dared not leave the car first. If he did, he would be a simple target for Dekker to pick off with a gun— and even if Dekker missed him, Alain would still be on foot while his opponent would have the car, with its greater speed and mobility. "I really know nothing about these things," he said. "They don't use them on Leone.

43

Why don't you get out and check, and I'll wait for you in here?"

Dekker looked at him for a moment, trying to gauge his sincerity. It almost looked as though he were the telepath trying to read Alain's mind. Then he reached casually up with his right arm, as though to scratch the left side of his neck.

In that one instant, as he prepared to act, his mental shields dropped. All his thoughts were of necessity concentrated on his attempt to kill Alain, and it was like shouting his intentions to the telepath's mind. Alain, who had been waiting for some definite sign, waited no longer. Any hesitation now would be fatal.

From Dekker's mind, Alain knew that the younger agent had a Preston minibeam tucked up his sleeve in a spring-loaded holster. The specific gesture of reaching upward with his right arm allowed him to tense the muscles in the proper way for the spring to propel the gun into his hand. He then intended to whip his hand down quickly and fire before Alain could react. Dekker knew that Alain would see the plan in his mind once it was begun, but he didn't know that Alain had been expecting it.

Alain did not give Dekker time to fire. Even as the gun was sliding efficiently into the other's palm, Alain was lunging across the gap between the two men. His body collided with Dekker's, ramming the man hard against the opposite wall. Dekker's hand knocked against the door before he had gotten a proper grip on his weapon, and the minibeam dropped to the floor with a slight clatter.

As a continuation of his driving motion, Alain jabbed the knuckles of his left hand up underneath Dekker's ribs, taking a grim satisfaction from the other's gasp. As a final stroke, he brought up his right hand, jamming the heel of it hard against the underside of his opponent's chin. Dekker's head snapped quickly back and banged against the wall. He slumped in his position, unconscious.

Alain moved away from Dekker, bent down and picked up the minibeam. It was a deadly little toy, set to deliver a z-beam charge of killing intensity. Alain tucked it away in his pocket for future use while he sat back and considered what to do next.

Dr. daPaz had been right about the threat on his life, but now there were deeper questions to ask. Was Dekker acting on his own in this matter, or did he have the official backing of the Agency? If the latter, was the entire Agency supporting him, or had Alain stumbled into the middle of some war between two rival factions within his own organization? He was not naive enough to think such feuds did not occur; he'd seen three during his career, though he'd always managed to stay non-partisan before. He'd always felt that his job was to gather information, not to fight with his allies. But now that the fight had come to him, he could not ignore it.

In a struggle like this, which he had entered blind, all his conventional sources of information within the Agency were unreliable; he had no way of knowing *a priori* whether they would be for or against him. There could only be one trustworthy person from whom to get further data: Dr. daPaz, who had given him the first warning. DaPaz had asked Alain to meet him tonight for dinner, and that was an appointment Alain would have to keep.

That left the immediate problem of what to do with Dekker. The man was unconscious now and would remain that way for several hours at least, but once he came to he would alert the Agency that Alain was still alive and then the chase would be on. Alain patted the gun in his pocket. Should he kill Dekker or not?

His mind was aching as he tried to think through the scenario. Suppose he did kill Dekker. The Agency would know something was amiss in a few hours anyway when Dekker failed to report. They would probably know where he intended to kill Alain, so the search would begin. Even if Alain took the body to some other remote location and hid it, it would do no good because he couldn't carry Dekker very far by himself. He would have to use the car, and that was the weakest link in his entire strategy.

In order to make the car work, he would have to insert an identity card, so that central billing would know whom to charge. There were only two ID cards available to him—his own and Dekker's. The Agency could trace him by checking the computer records to see what charges had been made to either of those two cards. They could trace his movements exactly.

Killing Dekker would accomplish exactly nothing. The Agency would start checking records in a few hours whether Dekker was alive or not. Alain had constructed his entire career around an aversion to senseless killing, and he saw no reason to change that now.

On the other hand, he couldn't take Dekker with him, and he didn't want to leave him here as is. If Dekker should regain consciousness faster than Alain anticipated, he could report in via his sleeve phone and Alain would lose some of the time he needed so desperately. Something would have to be done.

Dragging Dekker's body out of the car, Alain removed the sleeve phone and stripped the other man completely naked. Dekker had been obliging enough to find an out-of-the-way spot; even if he came to in five minutes, it would take him quite some time to walk to a place where he could phone in. And even if the Agency got worried in a few hours and began their tentative searching, there would be some slight confusion until Dekker could give them his report. Alain estimated he would have a six-hour head start before the search for him began in earnest.

The car had a reference book in it, explaining the local grid system. Using Dekker's identity card, Alain punched in his destination: Vandenberg Spaceport. The car obediently lurched back down the road in the direction from which it had come, leaving Dekker lying naked on the ground behind it.

The ride back was frustratingly long, but Alain used the time to plan some strategy. Confusion was the name of the game now. As long as they knew what card number he was using, they would be able to trace everything he charged—so it was incumbent upon him to charge as many different things as possible, giving them more to trace and delaying them still further. The Agency would have the resources of computer facilities all over Earth to track his movements; he had merely his wits and his knowledge accumulated over fourteen years in the espionage game with which to counter their efforts.

The Vandenberg Spaceport, as one of only two on the North American continent, was a central linkup point for transportation all over the world. Suborbital flights linked it to all the other spaceports around the globe. High-speed shuttle tubes departed constantly for all cities in North America. Pirt cars were flowing endlessly in and out for destinations within the immediate area. It might be impossible to completely disappear, but in such a place he could lay so many false trails that the Agency would get as bad a headache as his own tracking down all of them.

He flashed Dekker's ID card about shamelessly, squandering that agent's credit as though it were grains of sand on a large beach. He bought passage on, and boarded, tube shuttles to more than twenty different locations from Miami to Seattle, only to get off again just before the shuttle departed. He booked passage on suborbital flights to Woomera, Gobi, and Canaveral, although he never actually boarded any because of the difficulty in getting off before they left. Finally, as the hour for his dinner appointment neared, he tossed both his own and Dekker's identity cards down a disposal chute and went into a men's room; when the room was vacant except for himself and one other man, he hit the fellow from behind and stole his card.

Using the stolen card, Alain summoned a pirt car and ordered it to drive him to a spot more than a kilometer from the restaurant where daPaz had said he'd be waiting. Leaving the card in the slot, Alain next instructed the car to go to a destination halfway across Lompoc. Then he jumped out before the vehicle started moving and slammed the door, watching it drive off into the night.

He walked the rest of the way to his rendezvous.

chapter 5

Joby Karns was sleeping on the couch in her office when the call came in. She'd been up late, trying to put the finishing touches on the report she had to turn in later today on how to cope with the Leone crisis. Her plans were all but complete, but a glance at the clock told her there was no point to going home for a few hours of sleep. She'd slept often enough on the couch here; it was merely one of the little annoyances that came with her position of power.

The buzzing roused her instantly; years of work in the field, with its attendant dangers, had taught her the value of sleeping light. Feeling unrefreshed by the amount of sleep she'd had, she glanced over at the clock. Four-thirty. Springing from her couch, she crossed the room and punched the acknowledge button, but turned off the visual transmit. It was bad enough having to talk to someone at this hour; she didn't have to broadcast her unkempt appearance to all and sundry at the same time.

"This had better be important," she growled into the line, ignoring more standard salutations.

The call was from Sector Police, California Division. A man claiming to be Morgan Dekker had been picked up wandering naked beside the highway outside of Lompoc. During routine questioning, the man had insisted that he was an employee of the Terran Intelligence Agency and demanded he be allowed to contact his superiors at once on a matter of great urgency. The police were skeptical, but fingerprint and voiceprint checks confirmed identity, and computer records listed all other information about the man as "classified."

Dekker had the special number and code phrases to be dialed straight through to her office. The police merely wanted her to verify his identity.

She demanded that Dekker be put on the line, and the police complied. In a moment, Dekker's face appeared on her screen, looking haggard. "Well?" she asked impatiently.

Dekker looked down, averting his gaze from the screen. "Cheney's gone," he said meekly.

Joby's fists clenched, but there was no other reaction as she stared ahead. When there was no response from her after several seconds, Dekker cleared his throat and continued, "Did you hear me? I said . . ."

"I heard you," Joby said coldly. "How?"

Slowly, painfully, Dekker told her of the encounter between himself and Cheney on the back road outside Lompoc. Joby listened impassively, speaking only when it was necessary to prod Dekker into further embarrassing revelations. "I could swear I kept my mental shields up all the time I was with him, so I don't think I inadvertently tipped him off. But something did, or he wouldn't have been able to react to me so quickly."

"Was he in contact with anyone else since he's been on Earth?"

"Just me, the doctor and his assistant, and room service at his hotel. I think we can discount the hotel people."

"Possibly." Joby's voice was remote as she pondered the problem. She was positive that something along the way had tipped Alain off to Dekker's intentions. It had to have been after he arrived on Earth, or he never would have walked right into the Agency's clutches.

She tended to believe her aide's assertion that Alain had not learned of the plan from any mental slips on his part. If Dekker had been that clumsy, Alain would not have waited until the last possible moment to attack him. She knew from Alain's record that he would have found the opportunity somewhere along the way to incapacitate her aide before he went for his gun.

That left only daPaz and his assistant as possible

sources—and neither of them had been told that it was Agency policy to eliminate telepausal agents.

"The problem now," she continued thoughtfully, "is that he's alive, armed, and aware we're after him. He knows no quarter will be given. All of which makes him extremely dangerous. Added to that is the fact that he's highly trained and experienced. He's been in this business for fourteen years; he's cagey, and he knows all the tricks. We let him slip away once, and he won't be that easy to catch again."

Even as she spoke, she was laying her campaign. According to all proper procedures, she was now supposed to report the incident to the chief of Internal Security and let him handle it. Most of Operations' manpower was located on other planets, probing for information; Internal Security had all its people right here on Earth, specially trained in the intricate art of ferreting out fugitives. They had the instant computer access which her department lacked.

But to do that, she would have to admit her error to Romney Glazer. The Internal Security chief had already made a special point about the Cheney case at the last meeting, and she had sworn she could handle it. Admitting her failure now would mean handing him an arsenal to use against her in the future. He could demand that henceforth, all matters regarding telepausal agents be handled through his department, diminishing the internal autonomy Operations had always enjoyed. She could not let that happen.

"I'm disappointed in you, Morgan," she said aloud. "I gave you this job because I thought you could handle it. I've been keeping my eye on you, hoping to groom you for higher things, but now—how can I recommend you for promotion when you let something like this happen?"

"But it wasn't my fault, I swear. . . . "

Joby believed him, but she had no intention of letting him off the hook. "Whoever's fault it was has no bearing. You were in charge, and you failed. You know the regs as well as I do; I have to report this whole mess to

50

InterSec. It'll go down as a black mark on your record, and you may never get promoted."

Dekker took her words stoically, staring straight ahead into the screen. Since she herself was not on camera, Joby allowed herself the luxury of biting her lip nervously. Had she overestimated his ambition and his intelligence? *Don't just stand there, stupid. Plead for help.* She wished at this moment that she were a telepath, even though she knew the mental powers would never work across a continent.

For a long second Dekker refused to react, pride and ambition warring within him. Ambition won. "Isn't . . . isn't there any way I can make up for this?"

Joby closed her eyes with visible relief. She had him now. But her voice was professionally level as she answered, "I don't see how. Even if you managed to catch Cheney again, it still couldn't erase from the record the fact that you let him get away in the first place."

"What if that never makes it on the record?"

"Meaning what?" Joby knew precisely what he meant —she had maneuvered him there herself—but she wanted him to say it first.

"Could you possibly pretend that this call never existed? If I can just have an extra day or so to rectify the error, I can then report in that the job was done and never mention that anything went wrong."

"I'd have to reprimand you for reporting late, in that case."

Dekker nodded. "I'll accept that—it's better than an official notice that I let Cheney get away."

"You're asking me to lie for you. That's a serious business. Not to mention destroying the record of this conversation, which would take some doing. I'm not sure I can risk it."

There was an air of desperation in Dekker's voice now. "I'll assume full responsibility. Just give me the chance to clear myself."

Joby smiled. It was nice to know that her underlings had the proper motivation for their jobs. "All right. I'll give you two days, no more. But it's only because I have faith in you. You'd better justify it. Is there anything else you need?"

Dekker hesitated. "Cheney has a several-hour head start. I'll need some help."

"Out of the question. I can't spare the manpower."

"What about a Code T authorization, then?"

Joby fretted. A Code T authorization would give Dekker the right to demand police assistance at a local level. With it, he could tap into computer records and have instant access to any information regarding Alain's movements. Any time Alain Cheney used his identification card to order a pirt car or buy a travel ticket, the police—and Morgan Dekker—would know about it. Code T authorization was an ideal weapon for tracking down fugitives and had been eminently successful for that purpose in the past.

There was only one problem. As chief of Operations, Joby did not have the right to issue a Code T authorization. Her department was supposed to deal exclusively with matters on other worlds. There were only three people within the Agency who could grant a Code T: the director, the chief of Internal Security, and the chief of Counterintelligence.

Joby took Dekker's number. "Stay there, I'll get back to you," she said crisply, ringing off in disgust. She hated being in a position where she was being squeezed, yet that was exactly what was happening here.

Dekker would need a Code T if he wanted to catch Alain. The telepath was simply too experienced to leave an easy trail, and it would take all the police resources to catch up with him. InterSec had the manpower and the training, but the whole point of this exercise was to keep Glazer as far from this case as possible.

Obviously, she could never ask Glazer to give Dekker the authorization. Similarly, she didn't know the director well enough to presume on him for a favor. Joby debated the idea of working through Phyllis Rokowsky, the department chiefs' liaison to the director, and having her apply to the director for the authorization. Rokowsky was a woman Joby respected, and she'd always seemed friendly enough to Joby's cause.

But something made her hesitate. Like herself, Rokowsky was a totally political animal—and she owed Joby no favors. By going to her, Joby would be exposing a weakness, putting herself on the block. If Rokowsky did her the favor, Joby would become *her* woman, aligned irrevocably with Rokowsky's side in any struggle. Joby preferred to stay loose, drifting with the political breeze wherever it might blow; that was how she'd managed to rise this high this fast. And if Rokowsky did not do the favor, Joby would have handed her the perfect weapon to be used against her.

She shook her head. Phyllis Rokowsky was ruled out, now and for the foreseeable future.

That left Karl Junger, chief of Counterintelligence. Joby smiled. Although her tenure as Operations chief was short, she'd already worked closely with CI on one major case two months ago. Karl Junger was a man built out of rectangles, tall, broad shouldered, graying at the temples, with a European flair for gallantry. She remembered their long private meetings, the after-hours meals they had consumed while discussing the case, the little ways he had of brushing against her body to make it seem like an accident. Though he protested vigorously that he was deeply in love with his wife, the way he patted Joby's hand was more lecherous than paternal. As an experiment, she had treated him to dinner upon the successful conclusion of the case and made attempts at physical contact. It hadn't been hard to pry him from his pose of marital fidelity, and his hands had been most eager to explore her body. She hadn't followed through completely, though; it was always best to leave some resources untapped in case of emergency.

Now that emergency was here, and the resource would be ready.

She called Junger at home and had to let the phone ring for a while before getting an answer. "Karl?" she said, letting just the faintest hint of desperation leak into her voice. "This is Joby."

"Hm?"

"I know this is a dreadful time to call, but I'm in a terrible bind and I need your help."

"What's the matter?"

"I can't discuss it over the phone. Security, you know."

"Where are you?"

"At the office. Could you come down here right away?"

Junger looked at his bed clock. "Can't it wait a few hours?"

"That may be too late. Some things break quickly."

After a pause, the man sighed. "All right. I'll be there in half an hour."

"Come straight to my office. And Karl . . ." Joby gave a short hesitation, then injected a trace of Pitiful Little Girl into her voice. "I . . . I want you to know how much I appreciate this. I've always thought you were the most helpful man on the staff; this confirms it. I'll make it up to you for the inconvenience, I promise."

After hanging up, she quickly began straightening out her appearance, adjusting her makeup so that she would seem harried but not panicked, needy but not desperate. As she worked, she thought of the story she would tell him: that there were some misplaced funds she'd been trying to track down for ages, and she didn't want to bother Budget because she suspected one of her own people at a lower echelon was padding his pocket; it would look better if she handled it quietly herself, and she needed the Code T authorization to run a thorough check. That should work, if Junger did not have the opportunity to examine the story too closely.

And when Joby Karns went to work on a man, he paid little attention to what she was *saying*.

DaPaz sipped slowly on his drink, then checked his thumbwatch for the third time in ten minutes. It was now almost eight-thirty, half an hour past the time he'd asked Cheney to meet him here. An army of ugly scenarios was marching through the doctor's mind as he waited. Perhaps Cheney had been killed after all, despite the warning. Perhaps he had gotten away, but was prevented by circumstance from coming to the restaurant; even now he might lie wounded in some alleyway, needing medical attention and unable to trust anyone. Or—the worst scenario of all—perhaps he had tried to save his own life by making a bargain with the Agency. He could inform them that daPaz knew their secret and had tried to help him escape their trap. A team of assassins from the Internal Security Department could be converging on this restaurant at this very moment, their sole purpose being to snuff out the life of a traitor to their organization. . . .

He burrowed himself a little deeper into his seat. Fortunately the restaurant was dimly lit, and his eyes were well accustomed to the light level by now. He could probably spot anyone before they saw him—provided, that is, he knew what he was looking for. His eyes kept darting around the room, looking for anyone or anything the least bit suspicious.

I'm a doctor, not a spy, he thought. *I'm not used to all these intrigues. I should never have gotten involved in this business in the first place.* He took another deep gulp of his drink and made a mental vow to leave if Cheney did not show up within the next ten minutes.

"You were right, doctor," said a man who abruptly sat down across the table from him. DaPaz's heart nearly stopped at the unexpected approach, until he realized that this was indeed the man he'd hoped to meet. He'd thought he'd kept a watchful eye all over the room; how had Cheney managed to slip in without his noticing?

"I'd almost given up hope," he said, fighting to keep the anxiety out of his voice. "You were so late, I thought . . . *something* might have happened to you."

Cheney gave him a cold smile. " 'Something' very nearly did—and would have, if it hadn't been for your warning. I owe you. I had to get rid of the scent, at least temporarily, which is why I'm so late. It would have been lousy repayment of your favor to lead the trail straight back to you. Do you mind if we move to another table? You've got lousy taste in position; I prefer my back to a wall in situations like this."

"Of course." DaPaz called the waiter over, and Cheney explained that, because of his headaches, he preferred a table in an even darker portion of the restaurant, preferably tucked away in a quiet corner. The waiter was quite obliging, escorting them to a booth that was much more to Cheney's liking. The agent, after a brief glance at the menu, ordered the seafood variety plate. DaPaz belatedly ordered the same thing, though he was too nervous to eat.

"What happened?" the doctor asked as soon as they were once again alone.

"Dekker tried something, I stopped him."

"You didn't . . ." DaPaz hesitated; he didn't want to use the word "kill" in a public place for fear of who might accidentally overhear them.

"I didn't stop him *permanently,* if that's what you're worried about," Cheney said. DaPaz sighed with relief, and Cheney continued, "I don't really believe in that sort of thing. But the fact that Dekker is still active means that time is of the essence. You invited me here to tell me something. Please do, I need the information."

"What I told you about telepause is true; you do have it. But if there's any cure, no one's told me about it." DaPaz wanted to take another sip of his drink but discovered his glass was empty. He placed it unhappily on the table. "Except for the final cure, of course."

"Why do they do that? Is there some power struggle going on within the organization?"

"Not that I know of. And this has been going on for years—ever since I've been working for the Agency, I suspect. They've never told me anything officially, but I've pieced it all together from little clues they've dropped . . . and from all the patients who developed it and never returned."

Cheney closed his eyes and took a few deep breaths. "Bad for repeat business, eh?" He leaned back in his seat as the waiter arrived with their dinner order, and waited until the man left before continuing. "What exactly is there about the disease that prompts them to do this?"

"I'm not sure," daPaz said. He picked halfheartedly at his food. "We know that telepathy seems to be hormonal in nature, that there are certain trace chemicals in the bloodstream that enhance the phenomenon. Telepause seems to be a natural stage in the life of a telepath where the hormone imbalance increases drastically. Sexual drive is intensified, all the reception and perception is sharpened, and the ability to shut out the rest of the world is atrophied."

"In other words, the victim faces the hell that I'm going through now." Cheney was very matter-of-fact as he ate. He attacked his plate of fish with steady persistence; if what he'd said was true about narrowly escaping death, daPaz could understand why he was hungry.

"More or less," the doctor agreed. "The odd thing is that it seems to hit only the very best telepaths; the ones with minor or borderline abilities never seem to be affected at all."

Cheney gave a small, mirthless laugh. "Life is full of these little ironies, isn't it, doctor?" When daPaz did not answer, Cheney continued. "All right, what happens then?"

"When?"

"After all these headaches, the increased sex drive, the inability to shut out the world, the mental thunderstorm I'm having to cope with. What do I have to look forward to?"

DaPaz fidgeted, and the answer flashed through his mind before he remembered he was dealing with a telepath. Cheney stopped in midbite and looked at him, so daPaz figured he might as well say it aloud. "Eventually, insanity and death."

Cheney started chewing again—slowly. "Eventually. Nothing more specific than that?"

"It's . . . it's hard to say for certain, the data are all so sketchy. Maybe five years, at the outside."

"Five years of agony like I'm going through now?"

"I . . . from what I'm told, it gets worse."

Cheney stopped eating, leaned back in his chair, and let out a long, deep sigh. "Then what in hell did you warn me for? I could have been blissfully dead by now of a nice, quick z-beam burn." He shook his head. "Never mind, I know the answer. You're a doctor. You think about saving human lives without considering the cost. Forget I said anything. I am grateful—at least now *I* have the option, not someone else."

And under his breath so daPaz could barely hear it,

he muttered, "Five years of this or worse. No wonder they go insane."

"There is another reason for my wanting to save you," daPaz said indignantly. "I want to find out what telepause is all about, so that maybe, someday, there'll be a cure for it. The Agency is dead wrong on this matter. Hell, if society had gone about killing everyone who ever caught smallpox, no cure could have been developed. We know so little about telepathy as it is. We don't know what causes it, why it appears in some people and not in others, how to control it. We doctors are left with almost nothing to experiment on. Anyone who shows the least sign of the ability is snapped up by the Agency and sent off on missions to other planets. We're lucky to know this much."

"I'm afraid you won't have me as a test subject, either," Cheney said. "I'll be moving along after dinner, and quickly."

"But . . ."

"Really, doctor, do you think they're going to give up because they failed once? That only makes them more determined. I have knowledge now, and I'm dangerous. As long as I'm on earth, they'll be able to track me down and try again, as many times as it takes. I've got to get away as quickly as possible."

Cheney finished his meal and wiped his mouth with the napkin. "I'm afraid I'll have to impose on you to pay for the dinner; I seem to have misplaced my identity card. But since you did save my life with a timely warning, I feel it's only right that I return the compliment. I'd advise you to get off Earth immediately."

The doctor's eyes widened. "I'm not as free to move as you are. I've got patients, commitments. Do you really think it's necessary to . . . ?"

"Right now, tonight, you could get away with it. They're after me at the moment; they won't start wondering about who warned me for a little while. You're not under any suspicion yet. Liquidate as many of your assets as you can tonight, and abandon the rest. Buy passage on the next outbound flight to anywhere, the further the better. Once you get there, change your name and occupation—anything but a doctor. Manual labor is always good, it's easy to remain anonymous. Be sure to . . ."

DaPaz was shaking his head slowly. "You don't understand. I can't live that way."

"You can't live this way—not much longer, at least."

"I can't just abandon my whole life. I'm sorry."

"I'm sorry too." Cheney looked directly into his face, and daPaz turned away. The telepath continued, "Well, if you can't follow Words of Wisdom Number One, let me offer you an alternative set. You will be questioned about this matter—that is a certainty. Stick to your story of innocence."

"Of course."

"Not of course. It won't be that easy. You don't know how thorough they can be when they're questioning you. If they want to go to all the trouble of a full-scale inquisition, they'll be able to drag anything out of you they want, using a combination of drugs and torture. I don't think they'll go to all that trouble just for you, you're probably not worth it. They'd probably just stick to the torture, figuring you'd crack under that if anything. Don't believe a word they say. The minute you admit your part in this, you're a dead man. No matter what promises they make about forgiving you if you confess, they're lying. I don't think they'll kill you if they're not positive about you—not unless the political situation here has changed even more drastically than I think."

"You don't paint a cheerful picture," daPaz said slowly.

"I don't feel very cheerful at the moment. I think you're a fool not to leave tonight." Cheney pushed his chair back to stand up, then hesitated for a moment. "Look, I'll tell you what. It'll take me at least a day to clear my trail enough to get offworld. I presume your home phone is listed in the public directory." When daPaz nodded, Alain continued, "I'll give you a call between eight and eight-thirty tomorrow night. You can let me know if you've had any second thoughts. If you have, I'll do my best to help you get away, though it'll be harder than tonight."

DaPaz looked down at his still-full plate and said nothing.

"Promise me you'll think over what I said."

"How can I not think about it?" daPaz asked. He continued looking at his dinner for a long moment; when he looked up again, Cheney was gone.

DaPaz sat at the table alone for an hour before he finally paid the bill and left the restaurant for home.

chapter 6

Alain was feeling dead on his feet as he left the restaurant. Despite the throbbing agony of his telepause, he felt he could sleep for a full day straight through. It struck him as only one more irony in a long chain that now, when he *could* sleep, he dared not do so. He still had a couple of hours left on his estimated head start, and he had to use them to maximum advantage. There would be time enough for sleep if and when he reached a place of relative safety.

Walking was the only truly anonymous activity left on Earth, he reflected. When you did anything else, you had to present an identity card to someone and could thereby be traced. But there was still no way to track the movements of an isolated pedestrian.

The city closed its impersonal cloak of night around him. Pedestrian traffic in Lompoc at this hour was light, but there was enough that he didn't stand out as unusual. Pirt cars glided silently through the streets beside him as he walked; the vehicles moved in their carefully defined lanes, almost a world apart from the pedestrians. The walkways were well lit by glowing panels set overhead, and buildings rose into the dark sky on either side of him. The light panels blocked out any chance he might have of seeing the stars, but he knew they were there. They had to be; they were the only chance he had.

And always, there were people. Their thoughts hit him from all directions, bombarding his brain with a cacophony of sensory impressions, spurious emotions, burdensome anxieties. He needed the people around him; being one face among so many ensured his survival. But the toll was staggering. Other people's thoughts intruded on his own, breaking his concentration, ruining his chain of thought, making it impossible to plan his strategy as clearly as he ideally should have.

Five years, he thought. *Five years of agony more excruciating even than what I've got now. Nothing to look forward to but a lingering death. Wouldn't I be better off just letting Dekker find me and put me out of my misery before it really gets bad?*

The thought was comforting in its simplicity. No more pain. No more worry. No more lies, cheating, or falsehood. Just quiet resignation to his ultimate destiny. *Everybody dies sooner or later. Why go through all the pain just to end up dead when there are simpler methods?*

He'd come close to death on a number of occasions during his career with the Agency. Looking back on them, they didn't seem all that terrible. Crossing the ultimate threshold did not hold the same mystique for him that it held for those less acquainted with death.

But beneath the blanket of pain, beyond the fog of mental oppression, something within him rebelled at the thought. No matter how hopeless daPaz told him the struggle was, a small part of him refused to believe it. *Maybe they don't have a cure yet,* this segment reasoned, *but it could happen next year or the year after. Am I so weak that I'd cheat myself out of several decades of productive life just to avoid a little pain? What's the point of ever having lived at all, if it's to end so meaninglessly?*

When he came right down to the decision, he knew he could not willingly go to his death. He had spent all his adult life hiding away in corners, striving to be unnoticed, perfecting his anonymity for the sake of his planet. His only reward, if the Agency were to have its way, was to be exterminated like a cockroach. If he were to die now, there would be nothing to mark his passage, no indication on the face of the universe that he had ever existed.

I won't let them do it to me, he decided. *I refuse to let my life be snuffed out without having accomplished something. Maybe my name will never be blazed across the history tapes in golden letters or written in fiery script, but I'm damned if I'll go without leaving a trace. Somewhere, in some corner of the universe, there's going to be a small sign to let people know Alain Cheney was here!*

With the decision came an extraordinary inner peace. The throbbing pain did not abate, the mental intrusions and sexual desires brought on by the telepause did not stop; but there was a banishment of uncertainty, a commitment to something greater than himself. His commitment to Earth had been eroding so gradually that he himself had been unaware of it. Now, for the first time in more than a decade, he was driving rather than drifting. It felt good.

With a goal set, he turned his thoughts toward achieving it. Obviously, he could not survive long here on Earth. The Agency was too powerful here, it had too many connections. Police on Earth would automatically cooperate with the TIA, and it would be a matter of days, at best, before he was tracked down.

Offworld, his chances would be greatly improved. The other inhabited worlds harbored no great love of Earth, and the TIA was considered their enemy. There would be no cooperation from the local authorities; if the Agency wanted to kill him that badly, they would have to divert some of their own manpower and scanty resources to do it. It could still be done, he knew—he'd directed a couple of searches like that himself. But it was a much more haphazard process, and there were enough holes that an enterprising man could slip through. His chances would be infinitely greater away from this planet.

But getting away would not be easy. The first thing the Agency would do upon learning that he was free was to clamp down on all outgoing flights. Passenger lists would be screened, and no one even vaguely resembling him would be allowed to pass without a thorough inspection. Even leaving tonight, while they still suspected nothing, would be chancy; he would have to steal someone else's identity card to buy the ticket, but even an ordinary emigration check would show he wasn't the person the card claimed he was.

It all boiled down to a question of identity. In this computer-ruled age, if your identification was not consistent all the way down the line, you would be spotted as a phony instantly. On the other hand, if you did have consistent identification—no matter how fraudulent— you could get away with anything. As an experienced spy, Alain well knew the value of a solid ID.

As he pondered the problem, his first ray of hope emerged from the gloom. Six years ago, just before his promotion to chief-of-station on Leone, he had spent some time under cover on the planet Rhisling, working as a ship's mate. When that particular case was through and the ship Alain was serving on returned to Earth, Alain had turned in all his papers, as was required. Gunnar Tölling, his old boss, handed them back to him. "I hate to 'kill' anyone useful," he'd said. "Put our friend in safe storage for a while. He might come in handy someday."

I don't think old Gunnar quite had this in mind at the time, Alan thought, *but that old identity could never be handier.*

The identity package had contained an identity card, passport, entry permit, astrogator's license, a substantial line of credit—enough documentation to prove to all but the most careful scrutiny that Alain was indeed a citizen of the planet Rhisling. Alain had stashed the bundle in a safe-deposit box at a bank right here in Lompoc, close to the Vandenberg Spaceport in case the identity ever needed resurrection in a hurry. He would not be able to pick up the package until tomorrow after the bank opened. Everything depended on how alert the Agency's trackers would be, and whether they'd notice the minute entry on his file saying that this identity had not been turned in.

But it was a chance—at this point, one that was better than any other possibility open to him.

He quickened his steps. Even though he couldn't pick up the identity package until tomorrow, there was still some groundwork he could lay tonight. With a fair amount of luck, by tomorrow at this time he could be well on his way from Earth to safety.

Morgan Dekker spent a humiliating night. At first, the police who had picked him up had been most solicitous—a man abandoned naked in a deserted spot without his identification was no joking matter to them. They took him to their local station, got him into some ill-fitting clothes that were handy, and tried to get a story out of him. At first he refused to talk, but when they pressed him for details of how he had ended up in that predicament he finally admitted to being an agent of the Terran Intelligence Agency. He demanded that they verify his identity with his superior.

Joby did confirm his story, but that was when Dekker's trouble began in earnest. The TIA had always considered itself an elite organization, looking down on the ordinary police forces much as a starship test pilot regarded his cousin the bookkeeper. Now, with the tables momentarily turned and Dekker at the mercy of these police, they took the opportunity to gather subtle revenge.

Since he did not as yet have his Code T authorization, they were required to show him no more than bare civility. They apologized profusely that the only clothes they had for him were old workclothes they'd found in a back cupboard. No more would be available until the stores opened tomorrow morning. They would try to get him a new ID card, but paperwork took time, they said. Meanwhile, police were coming from all parts of the station to look him over and snicker silently at his predicament.

Dekker knew what was going on, and he hated it. It was humiliating enough to report his failure to Joby, to crawl to her pleading for a favor like some spineless weakling—but to have to endure the indignities heaped upon him by what he considered his inferiors was almost more than he could bear. Dekker sat in the police station as the morning hours lengthened, growing madder by the minute. His anger was directed at the man who'd caused all his problems in the first place—Alain Cheney.

The Code T authorization finally came through at a little after six in the morning, Pacific Time. Immediately the atmosphere formalized, and his tormentors were once again—properly, to his view—his slaves. New clothes, supposedly unobtainable, were brought to him at once, as was a new temporary ID card. Dekker was furious at all the time that had been lost on formalities—Cheney could literally be on the other side of the globe by now, if not completely off the planet.

Dekker's first step was to check on all interstellar departures from each of Earth's spaceports since the time Cheney escaped yesterday afternoon. It took half an hour for data to creep in from the farther points of the globe, but they were all encouraging: no one answering Cheney's description had bought a ticket off Earth or departed on any outgoing vessel. In order to keep it that way, Dekker immediately put out an order to all spaceport officials to keep an eye out. Departure desks were supplied with a complete description of the suspect, and the notation, "Dangerous, shoot to kill."

With that step accomplished, Dekker breathed a little easier. Cheney would be trapped on Earth, now, and it was only a question of time before Dekker could tighten the noose.

Even while waiting for information from the distant spaceports, Dekker had not been idle. Already he had been tapping into the police computers for credit readouts on two identity cards—his own and Cheney's—since the time of Cheney's escape. Cheney's record was nil, but Dekker's produced a long list of charges, virtually all for methods of transportation, all leaving from Vandenberg for locations scattered widely around the globe.

He wants me to spend my time tracing down all those false leads, Dekker thought. *That could take me days, or even weeks. There are quicker ways of finding out what I want to know.*

He asked the computer for a time readout as well, to

correlate it with the previous list. Obviously the last charge Cheney had made would be the only one that mattered, and all the rest would be decoys.

The final charge was to purchase a ticket on the sub-orbital flight to the Gobi Spaceport—but there was no record of the ticket's having been turned in, which meant that Cheney had never boarded the flight. Nor had there been any further charges to either identity card for nearly twelve hours. That was only logical—Cheney would have ditched both as soon as they'd served to lay his smoke-screen. From this point on, the trail would be much harder to follow.

As Dekker considered the problem, he realized one factor that was working to his advantage. Because space-craft were constantly landing and taking off from Vandenberg, the actual port was a good distance from the surrounding community. Unless Cheney wanted to walk better than twenty kilometers, he would have to find another ID card there at the port to go anywhere. Dekker couldn't completely rule out the walk, but he considered it unlikely; Cheney would not want to lose his head start, and would be moving as quickly as possible.

It did not take long to turn up a new lead. A computer check showed three reports of identity cards lost or stolen at the spaceport terminal within the past twelve hours. Two of those had not been used in the intervening time, which was natural—thieves usually sold such cards to forgers, who would alter them slightly and, in turn, sell them to fugitives in need of new identities. The third card had been used twice, to charge a ride in a pirt car from Vandenberg into Lompoc, and then from that spot to another across town. The card had been found abandoned in the car by the next person to use the vehicle and had been turned in to the police.

That had to be Cheney's doing; no ordinary criminal would have used the card in that manner. Dekker was narrowing the field; he could now pinpoint Cheney's position between eight and nine last night to one of two points within the city of Lompoc. He had every expecta-tion of continuing his success.

His lips twisted into an ugly grin. Cheney had shown

him up once, but he would not get away again. And when Dekker caught up with him this time, Cheney would have to pay for the night of humiliation. Dekker was going to make Cheney wish he'd died cleanly the first time he'd had the chance.

chapter 7

Joby Karns made very sure she was early for today's meeting, even though it meant rushing. Fortunately, she had finished the presentation she would need before Dekker's call came through, so that was ready, though there was no time to rehearse her spiel. Junger had turned out to be a maudlin sentimentalist, and she'd had a hell of a time chasing him politely out of her arms and her office once they were done with their rendezvous and she had the Code T authorization for Dekker. She barely had time to brush out her hair, freshen her face, and pick up her notes before dashing to the meeting room. But she was the third person there, so there would be no commotion today about her tardiness.

So what if my clothes look like I've slept in them? she thought. *It just goes to show how industrious I've been.*

Slowly the room filled with the same cast as the previous meeting two days ago. There was the low-level social chatter as the department chiefs settled in, exchanging pleasantries as a warmup for the serious session they knew lay ahead of them. Karl Junger arrived and sat down at the other end of the table. He avoided looking at Joby so studiously that as far as she was concerned, he might have been carrying a placard advertising their activities of a few hours before. Joby smiled. Junger would be her ally from now on; she had all the right keys to unlock his soul.

Hakim Rajman, of Assimilation and Correlation, came in looking quite excited. He glanced quickly around the room, spotted her, and came to her side. "A breakthrough of sorts on the Leone matter," he said in low tones. "I've got a target for you to aim at."

Before he could discuss the matter with her further, Phyllis Rokowsky walked into the room and sat down toward the back. "I've got a long series of meetings today," she said brusquely. "I see our principals are here, so let's get started and be done with this as quickly as possible, shall we? Ms. Karns, I believe you had a report to make on the reorganization of the Leonean contingent."

"Yes, I do," Joby said efficiently. "But Hakim has just informed me of some sort of breakthrough that might affect what I have to say. I'll yield to him, for the moment, so we can all hear what it is."

Rajman stood up and shuffled through his papers, trying to sort them into the proper order. After a few seconds, Rokowsky cleared her throat and Rajman took the hint to start speaking regardless of his disarray. "Uh, we at A and C think we've uncovered the area where all the secrecy is centered. Up until two weeks ago, Leone's Ministry of Spacial Resources operated and funded a small project called Cepheus. It was classified at the Secret level, but they never bothered to take any special precautions, so we took a quick glance and filed the information away. Basically, Cepheus appeared to be a project to locate rich mineral-bearing deposits in interstellar regions. Since Leone is so far away, such deposits would not be of much economic concern to our own mining interests; we presumed they were trying to keep the project secret from the other nearby worlds, rather than specifically from us. Small scout ships were repeatedly sent out on one- and two-week missions, with few if any reportable results. The low level of funding was consistent with such an operation, so we more or less ignored it.

"Two weeks ago, however, the entire picture changed. Project Cepheus was abruptly canceled. All its personnel, instead of being fired or absorbed within the supposed parent agency, Spacial Resources, were transferred en masse into the Defense Ministry. The same is true of all their equipment, all their records . . . everything that was ever connected with Cepheus is now the property of the Defense Ministry. And then, a few days after that consolidation, Defense made their big clampdown that startled us so badly."

"You think, then," Rokowsky interrupted, "that one of the pilots for Cepheus, while out searching for asteroids, found something so big that the Leonean government is willing to go to these lengths to hide it?"

"Not at all." Rajman shook his head for emphasis. "Once we knew what we were looking for, we went back over our records and took a closer look at Cepheus. Its small budget and seeming insignificance were a ruse, and a damned good one. Organizationally speaking, Cepheus was located at the bottom of a funnel. Funds were reaching it from all over the Leonean government. Personnel supposedly working on other matters were often 'on loan' to Cepheus—and not just clerks; I'm talking about some of their top scientific talent. There were special flurries of activity whenever one of those scout ships would come back, including hundreds of hours of computer time—and as you know, computers are a much less developed resource on Leone than they are here. For Cepheus to steal that much computer time away from other projects is a very significant sign. Whatever those scout ships were looking for, it wasn't rocks."

There was silence in the room as Rajman sat down abruptly. Rokowsky shifted her weight in her chair and tapped a finger on the desktop a couple of times before she spoke. "Food for thought," she said at last. "A veritable banquet, in fact. Any idea of exactly what Cepheus *was* looking for?"

"Not yet," Rajman admitted. "We're still correlating the data. We hope that by finding out exactly which specialists donated their time, in what order and to what extent, we may find the general outlines of the puzzle emerging. Of course, any new information Operations can give us would be greatly appreciated."

All eyes turned now to Joby. Like the others, she had listened with fascination as Rajman unfolded his tale. Sometimes the detective stories that came out of A and C made even the exploits of her own department look tame —but then, she told herself, A and C could do nothing if her people didn't get the information to them in the first place.

"Based on Hakim's work, I now know where to aim my agents for best results," she said aloud. "Thanks, Hakim, for pointing the way." She was genuinely grateful, and Rajman blushed at the acknowledgment.

"As we feared," Joby continued, "Alain Cheney was found to be telepausal, and that necessitates a slight reorganization of our Leonean team." She used her pocket projector to throw an image on the wall. There were two charts, before and after, showing the new structure compared to the old. "As you can see, I've had to redesign the grouping, because Cheney was the only telepath we had on Leone of a high enough ranking to perform in that way. Instead of simply replacing him, I've had to redistribute his duties among three other people. In addition, five more agents will be transferred to Leone from other posts within the next week—the theory being that if the government there knows some of our old familiar faces, we might be able to catch them up with some newer ones.

"I'll need a little time to assimilate what Hakim just told us, of course, but speaking off the top of my head I can see a few avenues open to us. If we regard those scout ship flights as military reconnaissance missions, then the former Project Cepheus will probably now be under the direct control of the military intelligence unit— which will obviously be the toughest nut to crack under any circumstances. Not impossible, however. I noted, looking over the old reports, that one or two people within that particular agency have been successfully subjected to pressures in the past; we can try hitting them that way again. We'll draw up plans for several possible strikes to penetrate the MI offices; fortunately, our team has already got a good background for us, and we have detailed plans of the layout. I'm thinking, too, that for something this urgent we might even want to go with a capture-and-interrogate of one or more of the project officers involved; that drastic a step, though, would require the director's specific okay."

Phyllis Rokowsky nodded as she listened to Joby's plans. "Draw that up as a contingency measure, at least," she agreed. "We should have a full spectrum of options available. I'll expect a detailed set of attack charts no later than noon tomorrow. You'll be coordinating your efforts with Mr. Rajman, of course, so that we don't end up duplicating knowledge we can already infer." She looked at her watch. "Other than that, I can't think of any other business to discuss here . . . and I have another meeting to attend." She rose and walked quickly from the room, effectively adjourning the meeting.

As Joby was gathering her papers together and preparing to return to her office, Romney Glazer approached. She ignored him as long as she could, but she had to acknowledge his presence when he spoke.

"I noticed," he said, "that one subject passed over very quickly was the disposition of your telepathic agent, uh, what's his name?"

"Alain Cheney," Joby said, barely looking up. "I saw no need to rehash that matter, since we went into it at such length last time. Besides, Rokowsky was in a hurry, so I wanted to get to the important stuff."

"Cheney's been eliminated, then?"

"I said I'd take care of it, and I have."

Glazer gave a slight smirk. "I think it's time you and I had a long talk about a few subjects."

Joby looked up, allowing herself to exhibit a carefully controlled anger. "Look, in case you didn't hear her, I have to prepare some detailed reports and hand them in by noon tomorrow. This affair has us all running around in circles, and I don't have time. . . ."

"You'll make time," Glazer warned. "I want to talk about late-night incoming calls and possible misuse of Code T authorization."

Joby twitched for just a fraction of a second, then continued stacking her papers neatly. "I don't know what that would have to do with me," she said. But she could not bring her eyes up to meet Glazer's.

"Then you'd better have that talk and find out. Shall we say my apartment, seven tonight? You can get the address from my secretary." He started to walk away, then turned back for emphasis. "Don't be late. The consequences might be dire."

Joby did not answer. Inwardly she was furious for letting herself be caught so easily in this attempt to cover up the Cheney problem. But in her heart, she knew she would meet Glazer tonight; she had no other choice.

Dr. daPaz had had a rough day. He'd gone home after his meeting with Alain Cheney and tried to sleep, but found that impossible. The agent's warning of doom kept floating ominously through his mind and would not let him rest. He prescribed a few late-night drinks as a sedative and ended up drinking himself into a stupor.

He woke in the morning with a terrible hangover, feeling not the least bit refreshed. He went to his office more out of habit than out of conviction, and spent the day floundering through trivial examinations and meaningless paperwork. Each new face he saw was a threat; could this be someone sent by the Agency to torture him into revealing Cheney's whereabouts?

He drank heavily with his lunch, and most of the afternoon was just a blur to his memory. The only coherent thoughts he could recall were ones of abandoning his practice and his life here on Earth, of fleeing to the stars for sanctuary. The idea was both frightening and romantic at the same time. Every man dreams of being able to cut all ties and escape to a new existence, but the practical considerations keep most from following through. In daPaz's case, though, practical considerations almost necessitated such a move.

He rode home, still uncertain what he'd say when Cheney called later tonight. More and more he found himself wishing he'd never gotten involved; he could have saved himself all this anguish by just letting Cheney walk out of his office unsuspecting. Trading security for principles was a lousy deal all around.

He opened the door and stepped inside his house—and suddenly he was grabbed and spun around. His right arm was twisted high up against his back and the inside of an elbow was locked around his neck. He was dragged all the way into the room and slammed up against a wall so hard that the air was driven from his lungs.

"Where is he?" a voice asked in his ear.

DaPaz suddenly found himself coldly sober as he struggled to regain his breath. "Where's . . . who?" he gasped.

The doctor was spun around now to face his attacker, and was not too surprised to see that it was Morgan Dekker. "Cheney," Dekker said in slow, deliberate tones. "I want you to tell me where he is."

"Don't you know?"

Dekker pressed a hand to daPaz's throat and pushed him even tighter against the wall. "If I did, would I be asking you?"

"Glg . . . I guess not. But I don't know where he is. The last time I saw him was when he left my office yesterday. I thought he went with you."

Dekker backed up suddenly, releasing his grip. The doctor bent over, gasping for breath. "Somebody tipped him off," Dekker said, watching daPaz dispassionately. "You were the only one he had any real contact with. It had to be you."

"Tipped him off about what?"

Dekker hesitated. "About what was going to happen to him. You told him, didn't you?"

DaPaz was regaining a little of his composure. "Yes, of course," he said. "I tell them all, when they ask. Why should I lie about it?"

This was not the response Dekker had been expecting, and it threw him slightly off balance. "What did you say?"

The doctor straightened up, trying to calm his racing heart. *Be cool, logical,* he told himself. *If he had any real evidence, he wouldn't be questioning you.* "I told him that the Agency has a clinic where they handle the telepausal patients. What's the matter, didn't he like it there? Did he run away?"

"I'm asking the questions," Dekker snarled. He slapped daPaz across the face with a backhand blow. "You warned him I was going to kill him, didn't you?"

DaPaz let his eyes widen in surprise. "Kill? You were going to *kill* him?"

Dekker's only response was another slap.

DaPaz shook his head and shot his tormentor a glare of hatred. "How could I warn him of something like that? I didn't even know it myself."

"Stop playing simple, doc. You'll only make it rough for both of us." Dekker was doubling his fists, and menace filled his voice.

"Be reasonable. How was I supposed to know you were going to kill him? You didn't tell me, nobody did. How do you know *you* didn't tell him?"

Dekker delivered a solid blow to the solar plexus that made daPaz double up once more and slump to the floor. "I don't want to waste my time with silliness," Dekker said.

DaPaz gagged, and struggled to keep from vomiting. "I'm . . . I'm serious. Cheney's a telepath, right? He could have read it from your mind. And he's telepausal now, which means he's more sensitive than ever. I'm not saying you told him deliberately, but you might have let it slip in your mind."

The other man was hesitating; clearly, that thought had occurred to him as well, but he didn't want to admit it. He had to have someone to blame; daPaz was the most likely target around.

"It couldn't have been from me," Dekker said at last. "If it had, he wouldn't have waited until the last possible second to get away. It was from some source he wasn't positive about, someone he couldn't trust 100 percent. You're the only one who could have told him."

DaPaz was starting to feel very lightheaded. The pounding he was taking from Dekker, on top of all the alcohol he'd consumed in the past twenty-four hours, was making him more than slightly nauseated. *Cheney was right,* he thought. *I should have left last night. I could have been safely away from here by now.*

He clung desperately now to the rest of the agent's advice. He would admit nothing to Dekker; it was the only way to survive. "I didn't tell him," he said weakly. "I didn't know."

Dekker stood over him, looking unconvinced. "I can see we're going to have a long night ahead of us," he said, kicking the doctor in the face to emphasize his point. "A very long night."

Alain Cheney's night was a busy one. Following his meal with daPaz and his stroll to think out his strategy, he walked fifteen kilometers across Lompoc to get to the "spacetown" area. This was the section of town closest to the spaceport, where crewmen on leave from vessels in port could stay and entertain themselves. Like similar neighborhoods throughout human history, spacetown was not well kept up; because it was used primarily by transients, there was no need to. Bars, brothels, and boardinghouses were the three institutions that thrived in the area, roughly in that order. More than any other single place, spacetown would afford a fugitive the maximum possible shelter from the authorities.

Alain's first step was to find a drunk and roll him for his identity card. That accomplished, he proceeded methodically to search out the information he needed. It was surprisingly easy. Buying a round of drinks usually won him instant friendship and loosened the tongues of other spacemen at the same time. Even on those few occasions when a man refused to answer one of Alain's questions verbally, the correct answer invariably flashed through his mind, and not knowing Alain was a telepath, the man would make no attempt to suppress it. The raucous atmosphere and drunken, wandering thoughts that bombarded Alain only made his head throb worse, limiting the amount of time he could spend in any one place before he had to leave. But he learned enough to lighten his spirits.

There were currently three Rhislinger ships in port, one of which, the *Bakalta,* was due to leave in two days. It was on a very tight schedule and could not afford any delays. It was fully manned at present—but Alain had plans to take care of that.

Stopping at an all-night market, Alain picked up some gloves and a jar of insecticide from the gardening department. Diluting the insecticide sufficiently, he spread the poisonous mixture on the exterior of the middle finger of the right-hand glove. He then returned to his round of the bars, until he found one of the crewmen of the *Bakalta,* an assistant astrogator. He got into a conversation with the man, and found an opportunity to rub the special mixture onto the other's skin. Within hours, the man would develop weakness and a high fever. Doctors, having no reason to suspect the crewman had been in contact with insecticide, would be baffled at his mysterious "illness." The man would recover eventually—but his place on the ship would have to be filled by someone else.

First thing next morning, Alain used his "borrowed" identity card for the last time, buying himself some clothing appropriate to his new station in life as an able-bodied spaceman from the planet Rhisling, after which he went down to the bank where the safe-deposit box was kept. His thumbprint correlated with the one on record, and he was given the box and its contents. Everything he remembered was intact. He left the building firmly ensconced as Kurd Alders, astrogator.

He had an interview two hours later with Captain Bergstrom of the *Bakalta.* He explained that he'd been living on Earth for the past few years but decided now that he wanted to go back to his native world. His Rhislinger accent was a trifle rusty after all this time, but that was only to be expected of a man who'd lived so long among foreigners.

His astrogator's license was now out of date, but his answers to a few practical questions assured the captain that Alders still knew his job. As it happened, the captain had an opening for just such a man, his own assistant astrogator having come down with some mysterious illness. Bergstrom offered a ridiculously low wage for someone with Alders' background. Alain looked offended, but took the job; he would gladly have paid for the berth.

He was taken to his post and spent a couple of hours familiarizing himself with the equipment and his companions. He then received permission to return ashore to straighten up his affairs overnight, with the strict understanding that he would be aboard ship by two o'clock the next afternoon.

He left the ship with a profound thanks to the Academy advisor who'd made him take the optional courses in spaceship guidance and control. He had needed an additional year of hard classes to master the art of running an interstellar spaceship, but this was not the first time that knowledge had paid dividends.

He was now so tired he could hardly stand—but for the first time in a day, he felt safe. He found a convenient flophouse, checked in, and fell on the bed in a state of utter exhaustion. Despite the mental pressures brought on by his telepause, he fell instantly to sleep with all his clothes on and slept deeply for six hours.

His internal clock woke him. It was dark in the room, and he experienced a momentary disorientation about where he was and why. When that cleared through his brain, there was a persistent itch of something left undone. He went out and got himself a hot meal, and while he was eating, it came to him what he had omitted. He'd promised Dr. daPaz last night that he would call between eight and eight-thirty to find out whether the doctor needed any help getting offplanet. It was nearly eight-thirty now.

Was it worth it? he wondered. DaPaz seemed firmly rooted in this world, the sort that needed explosives set under him before he'd move. Maybe he *would* be safe; Alain had to admit he didn't understand the full situation here on Earth, and it could well be that the doctor knew of some protection Alain didn't.

Alain looked at his watch again. *Can't hurt to try,* he thought. DaPaz had taken a large risk to save his life; Alain would be taking a slight one in return to try to save the doctor's. Alain owed him at least that much.

There was no answer at daPaz's home number. Alain tried the office but got only a recorded message.

There were at least a thousand reasons why there would be no answer. Maybe daPaz thought so little of the threat to himself that he was disregarding Alain's offer. But Alain knew from his peek inside the other's mind last night that the doctor was frightened something might happen to him. Or daPaz might have been unavoidably detained by some medical emergency or other perfectly acceptable circumstance. But Alain was worried.

The man who'd saved his life was very possibly in trouble. Alain was a great believer in paying his debts; it was one quality that had helped him build a superior team on Leone. He had the night free before having to report to the *Bakalta* tomorrow afternoon; he could afford to go investigating. If it turned out to be no problem, he would have lost nothing. If, on the other hand, there was trouble . . .

He patted the minibeam in his pocket. He would be able to sense trouble coming before it reached him, and he was well enough armed for most situations. He could handle himself.

chapter 8

Joby approached the door to Romney Glazer's apartment nervously. This command invitation to visit him was not at all in keeping with what she knew of the man. Romney Glazer was considered a private individual who kept his personal life guarded and very much to himself. If he at least had heterosexual designs upon her body, she could have understood his motivation a little better; but given his known proclivities in the other direction, his reasons for having someone whom she viewed with obvious dislike visit him in his inner sanctum were murky at best.

The apartment building was a lavish highrise, far more luxuriously appointed even than the building in which she lived. But then, she'd only had a few months since her promotion to chief of Operations to accommodate herself to a higher style of living; Glazer had been head of InterSec for six years.

Joby glided along the thick carpet, admiring the original oil paintings on the walls of the hallway, stalling for time before she reached the door. But she could not put it off forever; eventually she found herself facing the portal, a large ebony door, elaborately carved with the ugly impish faces of gargoyles and a wrought-iron dragon for a latch. She reached out and touched the heat-sensitive plate on the wall, signaling her arrival.

After a few moments the door was opened by Glazer's houseboy, an attractive lad no older than fifteen, with dark hair and a dusky complexion. He was barefoot, his slender body outfitted in a tight red bodyshirt gaping open to the waist and sleek black knee britches that emphasized every curve and muscle of the young man's lower anatomy.

"I presume you're Joby Karns," the boy said before she could introduce herself. At her nod, he continued, "Come in. Mr. Glazer is expecting you."

The carpeting was, if anything, thicker inside the apartment than in the hall. The interior was brightly lit, and the scent of a musky cologne permeated the air. The walls were decorated with carved wooden bas reliefs of figures engaged in athletic pursuits.

The houseboy ushered her into the spacious living room, where a leather-topped black walnut desk, a long black leather couch, and a black leather easy chair rested atop a red Persian carpet. The entire far wall was a picture window with a superb view of the river, and by one corner of the window a fully-bloomed cactus, reaching almost to the ceiling, stood in a weathered bronze pot. On the desk and on the walls were pictures of Glazer with various athletic teams, surrounded by his teammates. Three whole shelves were crowded with trophies, plaques, and loving cups, all attesting to Glazer's prowess in sports.

Romney Glazer himself was seated in the easy chair, his feet tucked up under him, reading a report. He wore a casual black-and-white kimono and, like his houseboy, was barefoot. Joby was at least thankful that her own dashiki would not seem too informal in these surroundings; she'd seen no point in changing from her work outfit just to visit Glazer.

The chief of InterSec looked up as she entered the room, nodded at her, and rested the report he'd been

79

reading on the arm of his chair. "Quite punctual, Ms. Karns," he said.

"I usually am."

"I suppose so. We all take pride in our minor virtues. Would you care for a drink?"

"Just some white wine."

Glazer turned to his houseboy. "Rafael, a glass of Pinot Chardonnay for the lady." As the boy left on the errand, Glazer gestured toward the couch. "Please make yourself comfortable."

"Thank you." So far, everything had been scrupulously polite—and that, too, was not characteristic of Romney Glazer. The man was noted for his bluntness. Joby was doubly on her guard, waiting for some sign of the knife she was sure Glazer was preparing to stick between her ribs.

Rafael returned a few moments later with Joby's drink. She took the glass of straw gold–colored fluid and thanked him. Glazer dismissed his servant, saying that the two wished to be alone for a while.

"You have a very elegant apartment," Joby said. This conversation was turning rapidly into a duel of wits, to see which of them could force the other to bring up the unpleasant matter first.

"Thank you. It's sufficient for my purposes." Glazer was staring at her, hoping to rattle her confidence.

Joby took a long, deliberate sip of her wine and paused to consider it. It had a fruity taste—apple, she thought—with a slight overtone of vanilla. "My compliments, too, on your taste in wine. It's a superb vintage."

Glazer merely nodded and continued staring. After a moment of silence, Joby took another calculated sip and returned his stare.

Tiring of the game at last, Glazer broke first—a minor victory for Joby. "I presume you know why I asked you here."

"You presume too much. You gave me some dark hints, that's about all."

"I don't like you, Ms. Karns."

"The sun rises in the east, Mr. Glazer. If that's going

to be the level of our conversation, I might point out that I still have a lot of work back at my office."

"You don't like me either," Glazer continued undaunted.

"You never gave me the chance. From the instant I took office, you've been openly hostile. The few friendly overtures I made were rebuffed with disdain. A person gives up trying after a while. What did you expect?"

"I've progressed beyond the point where I care what my coworkers think of me as a person. I do my job the best way I possibly can, and I don't give a damn for office politics. I've found where I wanted to be, and I've spent all my efforts to make it a solid, secure home. You, on the other hand, reek of ambition. That is dangerous, and that is why I dislike you."

Joby snorted. "You feel there's something wrong with my wanting to better myself?"

"That depends. There is constructive bettering and destructive bettering. If you tried to do it by becoming a superior Operations chief, I would have no objections. But your method, which I could smell from the outset, is to tear down everything around you, making you only relatively higher."

"What gives you the right to sit in moral judgment?"

Glazer smiled. It was not a pleasant smile, and Joby could draw no comfort from it. "As it happens, Ms. Karns, I am a patriot. I suppose that makes me old-fashioned, an idealistic anachronism in this world of pragmatic efficiency. I happen to love my native planet, and I will do everything in my power to make it secure. Everything and anything."

Joby's anger flared for real. "And you're accusing me of being unpatriotic? Of not loving Earth? Why the hell do you think I got into this business in the first place? If all I'd wanted to do was visit exotic places and order people around, I'd have opened a travel agency."

"There's a difference in quality. You, my dear Ms. Karns, are a patriot by convenience; I am one by conviction. Your first love is, and always has been, Joby Karns, and all your thoughts and schemes are directed toward her betterment. I, on the other hand, have no interest but that of Earth and, as a corollary to that, the interest of the Agency. That's why I will not tolerate you. Given your way, you would tear down everything I cherish to make yourself look more important. I won't allow that."

Joby was silent for a minute, stewing within herself. She knew the value, however, of not speaking when she could not control her voice, so she waited for her indignation to die down a bit before opening her mouth again. When she did speak, her voice was level and controlled. "I didn't come here to listen to sermons. If all you want to do is some cheap moralizing, I'll be getting back to the office. My work *for the Agency* is more important than this."

"Ah yes, I lured you up here with veiled threats, didn't I? Threats not to the Agency, but to the possible reputation and future career of Joby Karns. Very well, let's go into those charges; I'd hate to be accused of luring you here under false pretenses."

He picked up the slender report he'd been reading when she came in, and set it on his lap. "This makes some fascinating reading, although it's very sketchy at the moment. There is a record here of a phone call coming into your office early this morning from the West Coast. Unfortunately the tape of the call seems to have been erased before I could determine its contents."

"I have agents all over the explored galaxy. Calls come in all the time. If you're going to routinely tap my phone and use that to accuse me of impropriety . . ."

Glazer waved his hand in dismissal. "The call in itself is nothing. And I routinely monitor everything that goes on at the Agency. That's my job—Internal Security. To remain secure, I have to know everything that happens— such as the fact that after receiving this call, you put in another call to Karl Junger, and that he came to your office for an excessively private session."

Joby was about to speak again, but Glazer raised a hand to silence her protest. "Don't worry, I have no intention of publicizing that meeting. You and Karl are both responsible adults, and your personal affairs *are* personal. But the actions resulting from that rendezvous are not personal. Immediately afterward, Karl put through a Code T authorization, which he has every right to do. The authorization was not for one of his people, however, but for one of yours."

"That's hardly unprecedented."

"True, but it is unusual, and not at all standard procedure. You probably are not aware of it, since I never publicized the fact, but every Code T authorization is reported to my office as a matter of course. That's so CI and InterSec can coordinate on matters of mutual concern without working at cross-purposes.

"This incident was just unusual enough that I decided to pursue the matter further. Would you care to see the record of information your agent has requested so far? To my poor, befuddled brain it looks very much like a search pattern for a fugitive—a fugitive, in this case, named Alain Cheney. Isn't that the agent you said had gone telepausal, the one you said had been dealt with already? It hardly looks that way, from the evidence."

"All you have are inferences and suppositions. If you're going to charge me with impropriety, I'd suggest you have more substantiation than that."

"I intend to, when the time comes. But that will not be for a little while yet."

"Why so generous to someone you admit you hate?"

"Patriotism," Glazer answered simply. "At this particular moment, the Agency is facing a very severe problem—the Leonean crisis. It unfortunately falls within your sphere of influence. If I were to bring my charges now, it would cripple Operations past the point of efficiency. There would be a short period of readjustment while the hierarchy shifted, and the question of finding out what is happening on Leone would be shoved to the background temporarily—perhaps until it was too late to do anything about it. I won't let that happen. I'd rather allow you to remain in charge a little while longer, until the matter is resolved, than risk having the affair bungled due to administrative shake-ups."

"How generous."

"That's the second time you've used that word. Don't confuse practicality for generosity. None of this is for your sake. I'm serving notice right now that, as soon as the Leonean affair is concluded, I'll destroy you. I blame myself for letting you rise as high as you have, and this is where it will end. Not because you made a mistake and one of your men messed up his assignment—that could happen to anyone. But because you decided, for the sake of your career, to cover up the mistake, to compound it, rather than to call for help from the people whose job it should properly have been in the first place."

Joby took another sip of her wine. "Aren't you afraid that, by warning me, I might be able to stop you, maybe topple you from your own throne?"

For the first time since she'd known him, Romney Glazer laughed. "You're welcome to try, my dear. But you'll find you can't touch me. Unlike you, I'm not constantly reaching for newer horizons; that leaves one exposed. I've concentrated on defense, on digging in and preserving my domain. Any move you can try has already been anticipated and can only boomerang on you. I'd suggest you put your affairs in order and start wearing a parachute—you're in for a long fall."

Joby mused on the conversation all the way back to her office. The worst thing about it was that Glazer was right: she couldn't touch him. He played no politics, made no mistakes. He was always on the side of the Agency, and there was no way to fault him.

But I will weather this storm, she knew. *I'll eliminate Alain, solve the Leonean puzzle, and even overcome whatever obstacles that sodomizing little bastard can throw against me. Joby Karns is a survivor; nothing is going to change that!*

DaPaz's house looked dark as Alain approached it cautiously. Perhaps the doctor had chosen to go out somewhere tonight. Perhaps he'd taken Alain's advice after all and fled the planet. Or perhaps he'd been dragged bodily away by Dekker and the boys from Inter-Sec and was even now being grilled somewhere under treatments so intense that even a saint would crack.

If the latter were the case, Alain knew he wouldn't be able to help any further. Not only had he no idea of where they could have taken daPaz, but even if he had, it would be suicide to go charging in there alone. All he could do was save himself and hope they'd be merciful with the doctor.

He went up to the door but, mindful of a trap, did not knock. Instead, he closed his eyes and extended his mind as far as he could inside the house, trying to read emanations that would tell him whether anyone was alive inside. The telepause was actually a help for once, extending his powers considerably, but he could detect no minds functioning within his range. Quietly, he slipped around to the back door of the house and "listened" again.

There was something, very faint. It was not a conscious flow of continuous thought, nor was it the jerky, haphazard pattern he associated with dreams. This was unconsciousness, a black, steady buzz to indicate that the brain was working but not thinking.

The back door was locked, but after a short exploration Alain found a window he could force open with a pocketknife. Climbing through, he found himself in daPaz's small kitchen. He did not turn on a light, but instead used his mind as a homing device to track down the person he knew was unconscious somewhere in the house. He could not pick up direction with his powers, but he could tell distance from the strength of the emanations he received. He just kept moving in the direction where the thoughts were strongest.

He found daPaz slumped in a chair at the entrance to the hallway leading from living room to kitchen. This was close to the center of the house, and Alain could detect no other thoughts around him, so he decided to risk turning on a light.

The doctor was a mess. His face was a battlefield of cuts and bruises; both eyes were puffy, as were the cheeks, and the nose had been broken. DaPaz's clothes were quite rumpled, as though subjected to repeated blows. Whoever had interrogated daPaz—probably Dekker—had not availed himself of the neater, modern methods of investigation, but stuck to the tried and true techniques of torture.

Alain went to the bathroom to check the medicine cabinet. He found it well stocked—not surprising for a doctor's house—but settled for some damp compresses and antiseptic to clean away the blood from the wounds, and smelling salts to bring daPaz around.

After sponging the worst of the blood from the doctor's face, Alain waved the smelling salts under the man's nose. DaPaz's head jerked back violently, then fell forward again as he gave a low groan. Alain tried again, and the head jerked even more violently; in addition, there was some body reaction this time. Encouraged, Alain made a third pass with the smelling salts.

DaPaz began coughing up blood and made a feeble attempt to push the bottle away with one hand. "Wake up, doctor," Alain whispered. "It's me."

DaPaz squinted, as though straining to see him through a dense fog. "Cheney?" he croaked.

"Yes. What happened?"

"You were right. Dekker came . . . asked me . . . didn't, I didn't tell him. . . ."

"Good. Good man, doctor. I'm proud of you. Let's see if we can move you to someplace a little more comfortable."

Alain draped the doctor's arm around his shoulder and started lifting the man out of the chair, with the intention of moving him to a couch. As he did so, a small piece of metal dropped from inside daPaz's shirtcollar and fell to the ground. Alain set the doctor back down and bent to examine the fallen object.

It was a shiny rectangle, only three millimeters long and flat as a chip of mica. Alain was quite familiar with it—he had placed any number of similar devices himself. It was a tiny transmitter with a range up to one kilometer. Everything they'd said so far had been broadcast to someone waiting outside the house.

Alain cursed himself as all sorts of a fool. This setup had been a trap, with poor daPaz left in the center as bait. Dekker must have lost the trail and figured that this would be one way of drawing Alain back—and it had worked. Every word he had spoken—few and trivial though they were—had gone directly to Dekker, telling him exactly what he wanted to know.

Alain crushed the transmitter underfoot and looked quickly around, gauging his alternatives. Dekker would not have stayed in the house; knowing that Alain was a telepath, he would be afraid his thoughts might give him away prematurely. But the transmitter only had a range of one kilometer, which meant Dekker would have been waiting nearby—and he'd be well on his way back here this instant.

There was no time to run; he wouldn't be able to get far enough away in time to avoid being spotted— particularly if he took daPaz with him. The man was in no shape to do anything at the moment, least of all flee for his life. Alain would have to make a stand here. He had no idea whether Dekker would be alone or with a party of friends. Alain would just have to plan his defense as best he could.

Reaching into his pocket for the minibeam he'd taken from Dekker, he pulled it out and aimed carefully at the electrical socket. He pulled the trigger and a bolt of energy shot from the barrel, humming seductively as it hit its target. The lights flickered for a split second and went out; Alain hoped the charge from his gun had been sufficient to overload the circuits in this house. He didn't want his adversary to have the chance to turn on a light in here.

He turned his attention to the still-groggy daPaz. "Get down behind the sofa," he said, pushing the man roughly in that direction. "Stay there and don't come out until I tell you to. We're about to have company."

He himself took up a position in the hallway, just out of sight of the front door, able to defend himself from attack originating from either the living room or kitchen. He held his gun at the ready and waited in the quiet darkness.

Thoughts came to him—sharp, dark, and deadly. They were unmistakably Dekker's, filled with a mixture of hatred and cold rage, with half-formulated promises of what he would do to Alain when he caught him. Alain could not get a directional reading on the thoughts, but he didn't have to. Dekker's own mind provided the clue, as he visualized the front door and thought about kicking it in.

The door exploded inward, and for a fraction of a second, Dekker was framed in silhouette against the street lights outside. But then the younger man dived forward and rolled into the darkness of the house, as he had been trained to do. No one else came in behind him. For some reason, Dekker had chosen to come alone rather than with a squad from InterSec.

Alain did not pause to marvel at his good fortune; he merely accepted it. His hand tightened on the gun, but he didn't want to use it. His telepause was making him so sensitive that killing Dekker would etch the man's death trauma deeply into Alain's mind. It could conceivably incapacitate him, maybe even kill him on the rebound. In the dark, he had a natural advantage over his adversary anyway because of his telepathic ability. It should be enough.

Dekker rolled to a kneeling position, his thoughts darting and elusive. Alain could feel the tension in the other's fingers as though they were his own, clamped on Dekker's own gun, ready to fire at the first thing that moved. Dekker was making no attempt to shield his thoughts from Alain now; he knew he could not do that and, simultaneously, react to danger as quickly as the situation required.

Dekker's mind was a fascinating amalgam of present and past, of reality and fantasy. While the dominant item was the current problem, other factors were slyly insinuating themselves. Memory flashes, very quick ones, of previous encounters, of training classes and teachers' advice, of hours at the Academy's target range and in the confrontation simulator—all these went streaking through his mind at just above subliminal level. Also intruding into his thoughts were old childhood fears of the dark, fairy tales of monsters, the death-fear and other primal motivations with no direct connection to the present circumstance. They served merely as components of the man Alain was fighting. Alain felt that if he could understand all of them, he could predict every move Dekker would make.

But that was an impossible ideal. Alain abandoned that speculation in a fraction of a second and concentrated on the business at hand.

He didn't have to see to know where Dekker was—Dekker was doing the seeing for him. The younger man was kneeling to one side of the door, just inside the entrance to the living room. Alain would have had to move to get a clear shot at his antagonist, had he wished to shoot at all, and movement was the last thing he wanted at the moment. He must do nothing to let Dekker know where he was until the other would have no chance to react in time.

Dekker crept cautiously to the switchplate, but the light did not turn on. Alain could tell from his mind that he was not really surprised; he'd half expected this to be a duel in the dark and was resigned to the fact.

Keeping his back to the wall as much as possible, Dekker made his way around the perimeter of the room, stepping away from the wall only to avoid bumping into furniture. His pace was slow and deliberate. His eyes continued darting back and forth through the darkness, searching for any faint signs of movement that would give Alain away. Alain did not move.

Dekker was coming closer to where he stood. Another few steps and the man would be within reach; Alain could try to fight him without gunplay. Almost as if sensing that, Dekker stopped moving. Alain could read his motivation—there was a doorway coming up, the entrance to the kitchen hallway. Such portals were to be approached with extra caution.

For a long, silent moment both men waited, each hoping the other would make some decisive move. The war of nerves dragged on. Dekker was a naturally cold and emotionless man; Alain, on the other hand, had the experience. He'd faced similar situations many times and had a patience born of confidence. They waited.

A noise from the couch on the other side of the room. Still only half-conscious, Dr. daPaz groaned feebly as a slight movement brought him a sharp, stabbing pain. He had been the forgotten man in this situation, but he was suddenly the decisive one.

Dekker's reaction was almost instantaneous. His arm raised, his fingers tightened on the firing button. A bolt of energy streaked from his gun, parting the air and setting the sofa afire. At the same moment, Alain flung his gun halfway across the living room, so that it clattered noisily to the floor. This caught Dekker in a conflict of desires. He wanted to spin instantly and fire in the direction of this new sound as well, but at the same time he had to cover himself in case his initial shot had not fully destroyed whatever threat came from the first direction.

The split second of hesitation was all Alain needed. As Dekker stood poised with doubt, the telepath sprang out from his hiding place toward his foe. Dekker tried to turn in this new direction as well, but his reflexes betrayed him. Hie neural circuits overloaded, and instead of moving quickly to cover himself, he froze.

Alain's first move was to grab the other's outstretched gun hand, holding it with a strong grip to prevent the pistol's being aimed back in his direction. As soon as that was accomplished, his other hand lashed out in an openhanded blow to Dekker's throat. The other man began reacting belatedly, but not nearly in time. He tried pulling away, and the throat blow landed imperfectly. He staggered backward but could not get away from Alain's tight grip on his right wrist.

Alain moved in closer, following up on his initial advantage. Without loosening his hold on Dekker's gun hand, he rained a series of blows and kicks upon the other's body. In a reaction of self-defense, Dekker released his grip on his weapon in order to free his right hand. That was all Alain had been waiting for. A few quick strikes left Dekker writhing on the floor in agony, helpless.

"You'll have to learn, one of these days, not to antagonize your elders," Alain panted as he stood over him. He picked up the other's gun, then went across the room to retrieve his own. Dekker could make no move to stop him. On the way back, Alain looked for daPaz and found, much to his relief, that the doctor was safe. He'd been behind the couch when Dekker fired, and the furniture had absorbed the bulk of the charge.

The flame-retardant material of the couch had ended the short blaze begun by Dekker's blast. Alain reached down and helped daPaz to his feet. "Do you have a flashlight in the house?" he asked the doctor.

DaPaz still had trouble verbalizing, but the answer was clear in his thoughts. Alain went to the visualized location, found the flashlight, and brought it back to the living room. Neither of the other two men had moved.

"By all rights," Alain said, looking down at Dekker, "I should kill you. You'd do it to me quickly enough if the situation were reversed. And without you in my way I'd have a better chance of escaping.

"But I've been doing a lot of heavy thinking in the past twenty-four hours. I've lived my whole life without making a ripple on the surface of the universe. From now on, that's going to change. People will know I've been here—starting with you. I hope you live a good long time, Dekker—and you're going to remember me every day of it."

For starters, he kicked Dekker in the balls.

chapter 9

Dekker's pain made itself felt telepathically as Alain administered his "remembrance" lesson, but the younger man was soon mercifully unconscious and the pain eased. In addition, beating his opponent had relieved Alain's aggressions and frustrations tremendously—and while the feeling raged through him, the anguish of his telepause abated almost completely. Much as Alain hated to admit it, it felt good to beat up someone completely at his mercy.

Maybe if I become a full-time sadist I can get rid of the telepause, he thought sourly.

Doctor daPaz sat silently by while Alain inflicted his treatment on Dekker. Although the doctor said not a word, his thoughts were abundantly clear to Alain. DaPaz disapproved of human suffering—that was why he had become a doctor in the first place—but he could not feel the least bit of sympathy for the man who, only a few hours before, had been torturing him in much the same way. Alain sensed a vicarious enjoyment as the doctor watched him abuse the hapless Morgan Dekker. *If he dared, and had the strength,* Alain mused, *I do believe he'd be licking his chops.*

By the time Alain had finished, daPaz was fully conscious and, while in a great deal of pain, capable of moving around on his own. "How are you feeling?" Alain asked.

"Dreadful. My entire face feels numb, which is probably for the best. My body is covered with bruises. I think I've got at least two broken ribs."

"Feel like running a little?"

"I don't have much choice, do I?"

Alain looked down at Dekker's unconscious form. "I'm afraid not. He'll be out for hours, and sick for a while after that. But he'll be back on your trail sooner than you'd believe—and next time he won't be as pleasant as he was today."

DaPaz winced, both from the pain and from the thought of what Dekker might do to him if their paths ever crossed again. "It'll be as you said last night, won't it? I'll have to leave Earth for good."

"Well, good or bad, it'll be permanent," Alain nodded.

"Can we at least stop and bind up my ribs? The pain is terrific, and I don't want to do any further damage. It won't take too long."

"Okay, we can spare a few minutes. But we can't take you anywhere for major help, only what we can do ourselves. Any serious medical treatment will have to wait until you're at least in space and well out of Dekker's reach. That clear?"

"Perfectly."

The two men went into the bathroom and Alain helped the doctor bandage the battered chest. DaPaz winced as the dressing was pulled tight and fastened, but he had to admit that he felt a lot more capable of sustained activity than he had a little while ago. "What now?" he asked Alain.

"Now we tie up our friend and get away from here as quickly as possible. Do you happen to have any rope or cord around the house?"

In the end, the best they could manage was the rest of the roll of surgical dressing. They used it to bind Dekker hand and foot and left him lying on the floor. As they walked out of the house, daPaz turned for a silent look back, even though there wasn't much to see in the dark. Alain could tell from the doctor's thoughts that he was bidding a final farewell, not only to his house, but to all that was familiar and comfortable for him. Alain felt suddenly sad himself . . . and strangely, the sadness held a touch of self-pity. He had never built up permanent attachments to anything in his life, had never had a true home since before attending the Academy. No person or place had ever held him down or tugged at his emotions in quite this fashion. He had never known any sad good-byes, and that in itself was sad. He allowed daPaz his moment of reflection before urging him onward.

"The first thing we have to do," Alain said when they'd walked a respectful distance from the house, "is find you a new identity. I don't want you using your card again, is that understood? Dekker has probably already left orders that it's to be traced—and if you turn up at the spaceport, you'll be taken for sure." He paused. "But getting you one that will see you past the next twelve or twenty-four hours is going to be a bit of a problem. We can't just steal one—it would be reported and tracked too easily. You'll need an exit permit too." He stopped talking and started considering the possibilities as the two men strode along the street.

They came to a pirt post, and daPaz stopped, thinking

that they'd call for a car. Instead, Alain walked right past it, and after a moment, daPaz caught up with him. "Aren't we riding? My ribs . . ."

"Your ribs will have to wait, I'm afraid. Even though Dekker probably doesn't know the number of my new identity card, any pirt car summoned to this area at this time will arouse his suspicion and may lead back to us. We'll have to walk several kilometers before we can be sure of safety. Sorry, but that's the way it has to be."

"I understand," daPaz said. Alain could see from his mind that the doctor was in pain but was resolved to bear up under it.

After walking another block in silence, daPaz spoke up. "Couldn't you get me a new identity the same way you got one for yourself?"

"Hardly. Mine's a special case. If we were still in the Agency's good graces, their documentation department could fix you up with a beautiful set of papers in no time—but if we were in the Agency's good graces, you wouldn't need them.

"I know a couple of people who used to work in that department. One of them retired a couple of years ago and lives not too far from here, just down in Mexico."

"Then let's go see him."

Alain shook his head. "I can't afford to go near any old acquaintances; we may find to our regret that their loyalties are more to the Agency than to me. We'll have to go through channels outside the Agency."

"What channels are there?"

"I don't know yet. But I know they exist. We'll just have to find them—tonight."

After more than an hour of walking, the two men arrived at a pirt substation crowded enough for Alain to consider safe. They took the car to the cheap room Alain had rented for the night. "You'll be safe enough here for a while," Alain told the doctor. "Stretch out on the bed, get some rest. You'll need it. I'll go out and ask a few questions around the local bars. You'd be amazed at the amount of information a telepath can pick up, even if no one answers his questions."

When Alain returned near dawn, daPaz was lying

asleep on the bed in a position Alain would have considered singularly uncomfortable—but Alain had not been tortured the night before. DaPaz had merely sought the arrangement of his body that caused the least amount of pain.

Alain woke his companion gently. "I think I've found our forger," he said after the doctor opened his eyes. "She comes highly recommended from several sources. We've got an appointment with her in three hours, which should be just enough time to change your appearance a bit and have breakfast."

While he was out, Alain had purchased a wig, new clothes, and some makeup for daPaz. With an expert's touch, he began to remake the doctor into someone else. The new daPaz looked older, with more forehead creases and lines around the corners of his eyes; a slight squint added to the appearance of age and changed the entire look of his face. His hair was longer, blacker, but with streaks of gray at the sides and temples. The clothing was stylish, but far more conservative than daPaz normally wore.

With that accomplished, they went out to a local restaurant. DaPaz was still feeling somewhat squeamish after his ordeal of the night before and did not feel like ordering much food. "You'd better have a big breakfast anyway," Alain advised him. "We're both in for a long, arduous day. I hope by the end of it we'll both be safely out in space, and we'll be able to behave more or less as we choose—but in the meantime, we'll need strength to do what has to be done."

They ate in a leisurely manner, but Alain was all too aware of the pain daPaz was feeling. It flowed across the table toward him like an electric current, adding to the intensity of his own mental anguish. There were moments it became so strong that he just wanted to drop his fork and flee the room, trying to shut out the rest of the world. But he could not do that, any more than he could make the Agency disappear. He forced himself to put on the same brave front as daPaz, and make believe nothing was wrong.

When they finished, Alain called for a pirt car and the

two men drove across town. This was a newer section of the city, devoted to offices and fancy commercial enterprises. The architecture was of the curvilinear school that the new resilient materials had made achievable at relatively low cost.

DaPaz was frankly amazed that they would be coming to this neighborhood for the help they needed. "I must admit I was picturing some sleazy room over a spaceport bar, and an unshaven man with a cigar and a squinty look."

"There are some of those around," Alain told him. "But I wouldn't go near them. They're more of the cut-and-run philosophy; the cards you'd get from them would fool candy machines and department store clerks, that's about all. We need an expert, someone whose work will pass a very thorough scrutiny. Who better than someone who makes her living with computers? I had to search all night to find her, but she comes highly recommended."

They came to a building labeled Metricomp, Inc. and entered an air-conditioned, carpeted office with oil portraits of Rubenesque nudes on the walls. A receptionist asked them whom they wished to consult, and Alain gave the name of Hoshi Brooks. They were escorted into the back of the suite of offices and introduced to their contact.

Hoshi Brooks was a small, middle-aged lady with Oriental blood somewhere in her ancestry. She was dressed conservatively, all in black, and had sharp, piercing eyes that fixed on the two men the instant they walked through the door and never entirely forgot them. She bade them sit down and then asked, "What can I do for you?"

Alain was going to do all the talking. "My friend here seems to have an identity problem. Somehow, his card number got mixed up with that of a highly wanted criminal, and now the police are harassing him constantly."

"That is a shame," Brooks sympathized. "I presume he's applied for a change."

"Oh sure, but you know how the bureaucracy is. You fill out thousands of pages worth of information in quadruplicate, and then they tell you to wait—and you're still lucky if you ever hear from them again. His position is particularly sensitive since he has to leave today on an important offworld business trip. You can just imagine all the complications and hassling *that* will entail."

"Indeed I can. I've seen it happen entirely too often, to other people."

"I've heard that you're sometimes able to cut through the red tape and get the new identity papers much faster."

"Sometimes," Brooks admitted. She nodded her head slightly and eyed daPaz even more carefully. "Like all specialized services it is, of course, expensive."

"We realize that," Alain said. "This is, though, a *very* important business trip."

"Aren't they all? Well, let's see what we can do for him."

Brooks took some essential information on daPaz's physical characteristics. The doctor stuck his hands in a small machine that not only took his fingerprints, but also his Kirlian patterns and a small sample of his blood, which it analyzed in under a minute. His retinal pattern was recorded and attached to the record. He read the standard test pages to obtain voiceprint ID as well.

Then they came to the question of money. It was obvious that daPaz would have to surrender all his old identity papers—meaning, potentially, his entire fortune. In return, his new identity would require some operating capital. Brooks would not be able to touch daPaz's belongings at present, lest she draw police suspicion on herself. There were subtle ways to alter computer records and assign daPaz's credit to herself, but that would take time. In the meanwhile, the money she assigned to daPaz's new identity would be a loan. The amount of the loan would depend on the doctor's current net worth, minus her fee. Using the small terminal built into her desk, Brooks tapped into the central finance files and obtained a credit rating for daPaz. She nodded and took from her safe a series of blank documents and cards. She excused herself from the room, going into a back room to change the blanks into the required documents.

Within an hour, everything had been arranged. DaPaz was now Roberto Pasqual, a bank vice-president from Santa Barbara with a fictitious wife and two children. He had a new identity card, complete with photo and thumbprint, exit visa, passport, and certificate of fund transfers so that his credit could be established on some other planet. Pasqual was also far poorer than daPaz had been—but Brooks had warned it would be expensive.

"Don't use the new card before noon," Brooks warned. "Anytime after that will be fine." She stood up to show them to the door. "It's been a pleasure meeting you, Mr. Pasqual."

"Thank you, Ms. Brooks," daPaz muttered. He and Alain left the office and walked out of the building, onto the street.

"She sure took a big enough chunk for herself," the doctor complained when they were far enough away.

"She earned it, don't ever doubt that."

"But she only did a couple of things. . . ."

"I've heard people say the same about doctors; why should they charge so much for an operation when all they did was make a few simple cuts? The trick lies in knowing which cuts to make. Besides, Roberto Pasqual doesn't need that much money—just enough to take him to his destination. After that, he has to disappear too, and he won't be able to take any of his money with him. Don't worry, though; a lot of the outer planets are far less sophisticated than Earth, and a man without any ID isn't at that much of a disadvantage. You'll be able to build a new identity and a new bankroll fairly easily."

The two men went shopping, and Alain bought the doctor a new suitcase and some changes of clothes. "You'd look pretty strange going on an interplanetary trip without them," he explained. "You want to do as little as possible to call attention to yourself."

They went to a café for lunch, and Alain talked continuously, imparting little hints he had learned over the years that would help daPaz remain alive. "When you get to the spaceport," he advised, "buy a ticket on a ship that's going to make at least two stops outward bound. Make sure that the ship is not of Terran registry, and that the first stop will be on a reasonably civilized world, with plenty of traffic. Buy a through ticket to the end destination, but when you reach the first stop, change it in on a ticket to Leone. That way you'll avoid hassling with funds on that first world, and it may provide some misdirection for anyone trying to follow your trail. Someone will, believe me, but it may take them some time."

"Aren't you coming with me?" daPaz asked, suddenly very frightened.

Alain tried to reassure him with a smile. "No, I'm afraid not. I have my own means of getting off this planet. Besides, the two of us traveling together would only make us more conspicuous; it'll be harder for Dekker and company to zero in on two separate individuals."

"What about a gun? Shouldn't you give me one of the ones you have?"

"Absolutely not. There are detectors all over the spaceport. They'll spot you in a second and the whole charade will collapse in a puddle at your feet."

"But I'll need something to protect myself."

"Try an unshakeable conviction in your own innocence. That's the only thing that has any chance. In every other category they'll have you outgunned and outmanned."

He paused and laid a hand gently atop the doctor's. "If we both make it to Leone, I'll look for you and try to help. I've been living there six years now, it's almost home turf. If you make it and I don't . . ." He shook his head. "Well, Leone is not too bad a place to live. The government is repressive if you stand up and make trouble for it, but you'll be avoiding that on general principles. They don't have a computerized identity system, so it won't be too hard to start a new life. As I told you before, stay away from doctoring. Move out into the country; from what I'm told, they're always looking for help on the farms, in the mines, and in the logging camps. They pay more attention there to what a man is than to what he's done. You won't be as comfortable as you used to be here, but you will be alive."

He stood up and, belatedly, so did daPaz. The two men shook hands solemnly, and Alain smiled. "I'll see you there," he said.

DaPaz tried to return the smile as the handclasp ended. Alain turned and, abruptly, walked out of the café, down the street.

But despite their pretenses of confidence, each man knew instinctively that he would never see the other again.

chapter 10

Joby Karns spent the night in a fit of feverish activity. A great deal of that time was spent on the Leonean problem. Joby had to make herself an instant expert on everything the Agency had ever known about that world. Her staff had been working overtime, preparing summaries of reports to let her know what methods had succeeded on Leone in the past and which were likely to be a waste of time. The intelligence resumé of the past thirty years included biographical profiles of all top Leonean officials who might have any bearing on the present situation. The Assimilation and Correlation department added to her load by sending over piles of their own data, both on the Defense Ministry and on the mysterious Project Cepheus, that they thought might be of help.

After returning from her troublesome meeting with Glazer, Joby spent another few hours sifting through the reports, until she was heartily sick of the entire subject. At 2:00 A.M., she called in her top planning staff—who had also been staying up and reading similar reports, in more detail—for a bull session on strategies for assaulting the wall of silence thrown up by the Leoneans. The meeting lasted two and a half hours, with everyone popping pills to keep themselves awake. Some good ideas emerged, and the meeting broke up with individuals returning to their own offices to write their mission proposals. Joby would serve to coordinate their efforts—and to mediate between people whose tempers, after so much continual strain and effort, were likely to flare at the slightest disagreement.

As she sat in her office, feeling the load of her job more than she ever had before, she allowed her mind to forget Leone for a moment and return to the problem of Glazer. She had no doubts that he would carry through his threat to destroy her career—it was just the sort of mindless vengeance for imagined slights she expected from such a petty person. Despite his blathering about patriotism, she suspected deeper motivations behind his actions —jealousy at her rapid rise, perhaps coupled with sexual undertones. She and he would be competing sexually for the same targets, after all, and she was having markedly better success.

But knowing his motivations did nothing to alleviate the threat he posed. She dared not sit around and wait for him to attack; she would have to take positive steps of her own to ensure her safety. Glazer had been foolish enough to give her warning, through whatever twisted motives he was serving; her own actions now would determine his success.

The Leonean problem was one part of her counterattack. If she could pierce their armor and find out what Project Cepheus was all about, she was sure she'd be able to write her own ticket. It would be Operations' biggest success of the decade, and she would receive the lion's share of credit. Let Glazer bring his puny charges against her then; she could laugh them off as trivial intradepartmental matters and issue countercharges that he was interfering in the efficient performance of her own department. The air would be so thick with confusion that any investigating board would prefer to drop the entire matter.

But that was all dependent on a quick solution of the Leonean question. In the meantime, it would be rank foolishness to leave her rear unguarded. The Alain Cheney matter had to be resolved immediately, in a manner that was, if not totally flattering, then at least as minimally unfavorable as possible. The affair had already dragged on far too long, and she was painfully aware that Dekker had not reported to her in almost twenty-four hours.

What was happening out there on the West Coast? Granted that Alain was one of the best and most-experienced agents she had, Dekker was very promising himself—and with a Code T authorization, he had the resources of the police behind him. Why hadn't he managed to catch Alain by now?

Alain had taken Dekker's sleeve phone after their encounter in the car, and unfortunately it took a while to requisition a new one. That meant her aide would be out of personal contact until his phone could be replaced. But there should be other points of contact.

To free her mind temporarily from thoughts of Leone, she placed a call to the Lompoc police with whom Dekker was working. They filled her in on some of the general details of the investigation to date but reported that they hadn't heard from Dekker themselves in more than six hours; he had said he would be tracking down a possible accomplice of his fugitive and had declined their help. Feeling frustrated by her inability to learn anything substantial, Joby clicked off in disgust.

The matter was pushed to the back of her mind as Leone once more intruded. Plans were starting to come in from her aides, and she had to marshal her concentration to deal with them. As the different strategies came in one by one, she coordinated them into what she hoped would be a united effort on several fronts and began writing an overpolicy that would encompass the entire attack. She sent preliminary orders to Leone concerning the reorganization, now that Alain Cheney would no longer be in charge—but without giving the local people any reason for his removal. For all they were to know, he was being promoted for a job well done.

The planned intelligence assault on Leone would be threefold. First, there would be a concentrated effort to obtain information on Cepheus from the normal informants at the Leonean Ministry of Spacial Resources. The Leonean wall of silence had been selective, concentrating specifically around the Ministry of Defense, where Cepheus was now located; there might still be a few cracks at Spacial Resources, a few people who remembered what was going on at Cepheus and could be induced to talk about it.

Second, additional pressure would be applied to the normal informants within the Defense Ministry. Many of the TIA's sources had been transferred to other departments when the security crackdown came; others had been eliminated outright. But there were still a few well-placed informants within the ministry who had merely shut up completely when the tightening hit, frightened by the brutal examples of what had been done to other leaks. These people must be persuaded to reveal what they knew, regardless of the cost.

Third, an all-out series of covert operations would be targeted against the Defense Ministry itself. These missions were designed to obtain information directly, either from papers or computer files. Given the Leoneans' security-conscious attitudes at the moment, these covert operations were high-risk ventures. Joby had to expect to lose a large percentage of her best agents on that planet—but in this particular case, that risk was justified by the high potential gain.

Strictly as a backup plan, should other avenues prove futile, there were outlines for three different capture-and-interrogate missions against the three project officers who probably could give the TIA the most relevant data. Joby hated the thought of actually ordering such a mission, because they were of the highest possible risk, provocative, and more than likely to backfire; but she had promised Phyllis Rokowsky she would consider such plans, so she had to have them listed.

In addition to these direct actions, Operations would also engage in a series of indirect steps to procure the desired information. TIA agents on worlds other than Leone would be instructed to pay special attention to the activities of Leoneans on their worlds, particularly in diplomatic and military circles. Governments friendly to Leone would be carefully investigated to learn how much they knew of Project Cepheus. The governments on planets hostile to Leone would be discreetly approached with an invitation to pool resources and share any resultant knowledge of Cepheus that might be to the mutual interest. As always, the gathering of intelligence had to be considered on a galaxy-wide scale.

Joby finished her rough draft at the ungodly hour of 7:00 A.M., read it over quickly once more for any major mistakes, then gave it to her secretary—who'd been called in early—to make the final copies. With that temporarily off her hands, she tried putting another call through to Morgan Dekker on the West Coast but was told there was still no word. In frustration she asked for a complete copy of the Agency's dossier on Alain Cheney and began reading through that.

This is being blown out of all proportion, she thought, *but it looks like I'll have to take a hand in it myself just out of self-defense.* She decided that as soon as her report on Leone was in and approved, she would personally fly out to Lompoc to supervise the Cheney situation. If, that was, Alain had not already been dealt with by then.

The finished report came in shortly before ten, two hours ahead of her deadline, and she gave it a quick skim. In its neatly printed form it had much more the air of authority and self-confidence. Joby only wished she were as sure of her plans as the report appeared to be.

She took copies of her report over to the office of the director, where she was admitted immediately. She spent an hour giving a verbal summary of the report to the director, Phyllis Rokowsky, and the rest of the administrative staff, at the end of which time her report was unanimously adopted and she was given the go-ahead to implement it. Joby was congratulated on both the speed and excellence of her report, and she found herself smirking inwardly. *I wonder what Glazer would have to say about that.*

As the meeting broke up, Phyllis Rokowsky approached and offered her own private congratulations. Joby thanked her with genuine gratitude—Rokowsky's opinion counted for a great deal with her. Rokowsky also invited Joby to lunch with her that afternoon, but Joby reluctantly had to beg off, claiming that other urgent matters awaited her. Rokowsky, nodding, agreed to a raincheck.

Joby made a quick stopover at her section, but there was still no word from Dekker. She called her staff in for a brief pep talk, thanking them for their all-night efforts. She left instructions for implementing the plans they had devised and dismissed them again, letting them leave with a justifiable pride in their accomplishments. She dashed into her office to tuck the Cheney dossier into her briefcase, told her secretary she could be reached via sleeve phone if anything dire came up, and made a brief trip to her apartment to change clothes. She discarded her standard dashiki in favor of a sturdy navy blue jumpsuit; if she were going to be chasing all over California after Alain Cheney, she might as well wear something practical for the occasion.

Then it was off to the airport, where she caught a supersonic jet bound for the Lompoc Spaceport. Her eyes were now so tired that she thought she'd need toothpicks to prop them open, but she forced herself to read through Alain's file in detail. She read his numerous citations and commendations, the list of classes he'd taken at the Academy, his list of numerous field assignments and cover identities up to the point where he'd been assigned as chief-of-station on Leone six years ago. She fell asleep, finally, with the secret file propped open in her lap.

She woke with a start after only an hour. She'd had a vivid dream about spaceships and crewmen, and that in turn had triggered an alarm in her brain. Rubbing her eyes, she flipped back through the pages of the Cheney report until she found what she was looking for.

Six years ago, just before accepting his promotion and assignment on Leone, Alain had worked on Rhisling under the cover identity of Kurd Alders, an astrogator. Despite the successful completion of that mission, the identity papers for "Alders" had never been turned in, and the case still had a small circle beside it, indicating an open file.

He has another identity all prepared, she groaned with dismay. *He could be light-years away by now, while we fiddle around looking for an identity that no longer exists.*

She used her sleeve phone to place an urgent call to the Lompoc police once again. This time she was told that Dekker had reported in, received emergency medical treatment, and asked for information concerning local ID forgers. After that he had raced out again and was once more out of contact.

Joby fumed. Dekker had botched this case from the beginning, and now he was following the wrong trail again. He could trace forgers from now till doomsday; Alain had no need of them, and the trail would only grow colder. She would have to see to it that Dekker drew a severe reprimand and a demotion for his handling of this affair.

God save me from incompetents! she steamed. *It looks like, if I want to get something accomplished, I'll have to do it by myself!*

When Morgan Dekker opened his eyes again, it was still dark. For a long while, perhaps an hour, he lay on the floor bound hand and foot, his body racked with pain—the aftermath of the torture Cheney had inflicted. Dekker prided himself on his toughness, but even so he could not completely stop the involuntary groans he would make every time a muscle twitched.

Finally, as his mind climbed higher toward self-awareness, he pushed the pain down into the background enough for him to think. Cheney and daPaz would have left long ago, losing themselves somewhere in the city. DaPaz was injured, though still capable of some movement. Unless he, Dekker, were missing some vital piece of information, there were no other members of that conspiracy, so the two fugitives would have no further reason to stay on Earth. They'd be leaving as soon as they got new identities.

Dekker closed his eyes. The physical pain he felt was nothing, he knew, compared to what Joby Karns would do to him when he reported this failure. The Agency was not lenient toward those who did not succeed.

He struggled against the tightly wound surgical dressings that bound him, but the material had been designed to be tough under stress. Finally he crawled, in a hump-backed worm fashion, into the kitchen and turned on the burners of the stove. Struggling to his feet, he turned around and thrust his wrists into the flames. The pain, coming on top of what he'd already been through, was enormous, and he almost fainted again. But his trick worked; the dressing material burned, freeing his hands. He fell to the floor for a time and lay there, panting, before untying the rest of himself.

Daylight was just starting to filter through the windows as he pulled himself to his feet and staggered to the phone. His call to the police station was answered quickly; within five minutes a special patrol car arrived to take him back to headquarters, and a police doctor was standing by to treat the worst of his injuries.

Even so, the process seemed incredibly slow to Dekker. He chafed as the doctor examined him, gave him injections, and taped his bruised and broken body. All he could think about was that Cheney and daPaz were using all this time to move further and further from his grasp. He asked that a new computer analysis scout for any use of either of their identity cards in the past few hours while the doctor was tending his wounds. He also asked for a readout on calls for pirt cars within a ten-block radius of daPaz's house. The first analysis turned up blank, and the second yielded little that looked promising.

I'll have to find the new identities they're using, he thought. *That's the only chance I have now. And I'll have to do it this morning, or they'll be so far away it'll be impossible.*

The police doctor wanted to recommend that Dekker be sent to a hospital for X rays and observation over the next twenty-four hours. Dekker vetoed that idea instantly. Instead, he demanded from the police to know the names and addresses of suspected ID forgers in this area. When he had that, he put out a notice to apprehend Dr. daPaz as well as Alain Cheney, with complete descriptions of each, and made certain the notice was particularly seen by spaceport officers. Then he left the station once more to find out what he could from the suspects on his list.

It was twelve-thirty before he hit paydirt. He arrived at the office of Metricomp, Inc. and asked the receptionist whether she'd ever seen either of the men in the photos he showed her. She denied it, but only after a slight hesitation that told him what he needed to know. Dekker stormed into the back area until he found Hoshi Brooks's office, where that lady was currently eating her lunch. She barely had time to register her surprise before Dekker came around her desk, lifted her bodily out of her chair, and slammed her against the wall.

"You'd better listen carefully," he said through gritted teeth, "because I don't have the patience to say this twice. I'm not some buzz-sticker making a polite little roust on suspicion of forgery. I'm with the TIA, and we're dealing with matters of planetary security. I don't make deals, and I don't waste time being pleasant. If you won't tell me what I want to know, you'll fry for treason right alongside the men I'm chasing."

Brooks looked at him coldly, saying not a word. She had a professional reputation to consider and was not about to talk lightly to the authorities for fear that future customers would not trust her.

That was fine with Dekker. He had a lot of aggression to let out of his system, and it mattered little to him whether the target was Hoshi Brooks or Alain Cheney. He set about the same relentless routine of questioning he had used on daPaz, but found that Brooks broke more easily. After only ten minutes, she was willing to tell him what he wanted to know.

Dekker copied down daPaz's new name and ID number, but drew a blank when it came to Cheney. No matter what threats or pressures he applied, Brooks's story remained the same—she had supplied ID only for daPaz, not for Cheney. Finally, with time passing all too swiftly, Dekker gave up on that line of questioning.

I'll be able to pull in one fish, at least, he decided. *When I have daPaz in custody, he'll lead me to Cheney soon enough.*

108

chapter 11

Javier daPaz felt nervous as he got out of his pirt car at the Vandenberg Spaceport. Despite having lived in Lompoc for fifteen years, this was only his third visit to the big interstellar terminal. He had an orderly mind, and even had he not been in fear for his life, the chaos throughout the spaceport would have instilled in him a feeling of uneasiness.

He knew that his best chance for safety lay in anonymity. He joined the surging crowd, flowed with it as it pushed through the brightly lit corridors and past the flashing electric signs with their incongruous advertising slogans. His body joined the press of people on their way to or from some destination of greater or lesser urgency.

Despite the mob, he felt naked and exposed. Everywhere he looked were security guards, well armed and scanning the crowd for . . . for what? His face, almost certainly. He wished Alain had not been so adamant on the point of not bringing a gun along; even though daPaz was totally inexperienced in the use of weapons, it would have given him a more comforting feeling to know that he was armed, that he had a chance to fight back if an emergency should arise.

After wandering aimlessly throughout the vast complex for half an hour, he decided it was time to make his move. As he passed one of the automated routing booths, he slipped from the safety of the crowd, waited beside the booth until its current occupant was finished, entered and seated himself before the readout screen.

He sat, almost mesmerized, for fifteen minutes as the long series of alternatives flashed across the panel. Each planet name conjured up images of exotic locales, and each made him more aware of how completely cut off he would be from his native world. Finally he shook himself out of his reverie and forced his mind to concentrate on the job at hand. Time was the big factor; he needed a flight that would leave as soon as possible, to get him out of the Agency's clutches.

The next outbound flight listed would be departing in one hour. Its ultimate destination was Perdakesh, with stopovers on Millings and Farway. The ship was run by a Perdakesh company, with no allegiance to Earth at all. It fit perfectly all the criteria Alain had laid out for him, so daPaz informed the booking computer that he would like to purchase passage on that flight, second-class, all the way through to Perdakesh.

The computer asked for his identity card, passport, and exit visa, which daPaz supplied by sticking them in the appropriate slots. The machine sat there, staring blankly back at him while it checked the documents. DaPaz felt his muscles tensing as the seconds ticked past without any response. It seemed like an eternity, but in reality no more than half a minute elapsed before the machine hummed to life again. The computer spit daPaz's papers and card back at him, along with a small plastic certificate of booking which he was to take to the boarding gate in half an hour. He was now officially registered as a passenger on the flight to Perdakesh.

DaPaz let out a large sigh of relief. Thanking Ms. Brooks silently for the quality of her work, he rose on two very shaky legs and left the booth. He could have ID-tagged his suitcase and sent it down the baggage shaft for stowing aboard his cabin, but he felt so dazed at his victory that the thought didn't even occur to him.

I need a drink after an ordeal like that, he decided. He had thirty minutes to kill anyway, and instead of wandering aimlessly through the corridors he might as well spend the time anonymously in a crowded bar.

He ended up having three drinks. They helped soothe the pain in his ribs, which had by this time degenerated into a constant dull throbbing. As he sat, he listened to fragments of a dozen conversations around him. Some were concerned with the wonders of interstellar travel, others over such minutiae as whether a person had packed warm enough clothing. The dangers and the tension of his upcoming voyage faded into a pleasant blur around him as it came time to leave the bar for the boarding gate. Soon the whole ordeal would be over and he would be well on his way to freedom.

A series of subtle signs told him he was in trouble. The line in front of his boarding gate seemed longer than any of the others, as though the passengers were being screened more carefully. All electronic surveillance in the area was focused on that one gate. There was a slightly higher percentage of armed security guards standing around the entrances, pretending to look nonchalant.

DaPaz took a deep breath to clear his head of the alcohol he'd just consumed. It was probably just his own imagination building the situation up worse than it really was. In any event, he had no choice but to play the charade through to the end. Resolutely, he waited in line, and when his turn came, he walked up to the desk and handed in his plastic token.

The clerk took the token and deposited it in his comp slot. DaPaz could not see what reaction that caused on the board, but the clerk responded by pressing a button. "I'm sorry, Dr. daPaz, but we'll have to detain you," he said.

DaPaz's heart stopped for a chilling instant. "I'm afraid you've made some mistake. I'm no doctor. My name is Pasqual, Roberto Pasqual."

With his peripheral vision, daPaz could detect the guards slowly converging upon this point from their positions throughout the room. He wished more than ever he'd been allowed to bring a gun. He steeled himself to rely on the defense Alain had told him would be his best bet—an unshakeable conviction in his own innocence.

"Please, doctor." The clerk was summoning the two guards who stood behind and to either side of him. "We know where you got the false ID. Things will go easier with you if you cooperate."

"I'm telling you, you're making a mistake. I don't even know anyone named LaPaz, or whatever it is. My name . . ."

Dekker stepped up beside him, seeming to appear out of nowhere. "Go on, doctor. I'd be fascinated to hear your story."

In that instant, daPaz lost all hope. There would be no fooling Dekker with false cards, a cheap wig and some makeup. This time the Agency man would pull out all the stops, and the doctor could not count on Alain's timely intervention to save him again.

With the knowledge that his fate was sealed, daPaz reacted with uncharacteristic abandon. In a sudden, violent motion he brought up his suitcase with all the force he could muster, swinging it at Dekker's head. The agent automatically moved a step back to get out of the way, and the suitcase went sailing through the air just centimeters from his chin.

The instant he let go of the suitcase, daPaz broke and began running in the opposite direction. He had no idea where he was going, but it didn't matter. Away from Dekker was his only choice.

Two guards stood on either side of the entrance to the corridor leading from this chamber. As daPaz ran toward them, pushing frantically to get past the milling mob that stood in his way, they converged to block his path. DaPaz ran straight for them anyway, and they nervously began to draw their guns.

"Don't shoot!" Dekker's voice bellowed over the confusion of the crowd. "I want him alive."

The guards hesitated, and daPaz barreled into them full force. All three men went sprawling on the ground, but the doctor, armed with desperation, was the first to scramble to his feet. The clatter of pursuing boots on the hard tile floor behind him filled his ears as daPaz threaded his way through the crowded corridor to the large terminus beyond.

Overhead, the loudspeaker was blaring something. DaPaz was beyond making sense out of the individual words, but it was clear that the spaceport police were mobilizing their forces against him. It seemed that everywhere he looked were police, drawing their guns and looking about, trying to pick him out of the crowd. The fact that he was the only person running for his life made him easy to spot, but he dared not slow down.

He edged along a side wall. The crowds were thinner along the edges, and he could make better time. If he had any conscious plan at all, it was merely to outflank his pursuers and make a break for the pirt stands outside—though what good that would do him, he could not have said.

There was a door on his left, marked "For Employees Only." He grabbed for the handle, fearing it would be locked, but it wasn't. Opening the door, he ducked inside and found himself facing a long empty corridor, narrow and brightly lit. There was a series of doors on either side of the hall, an encouraging sign. The door daPaz had come through closed automatically behind him. He looked, but there was no way to lock it.

He started down the corridor. His broken ribs were a stabbing pain in his chest now, throbbing with each labored breath he took. His bruised body protested every step. He could not go much further. He prayed fervently that one of these other doors, each with a name painted on it, would open and give him a new avenue of escape.

His luck ran out completely at this point. All the doors were securely locked. He rattled each as hard as he could, but they would not budge. As he came to a dead end in front of the last one, the door through which he had come opened once more. Morgan Dekker and two policemen stepped through.

As the pursuers assessed daPaz's situation they relaxed slightly and began walking confidently down the corridor toward him. Trapped, the doctor backed as far as he could, until he was right against the wall and could go no further. His eyes widened with fear as he watched the other men approach.

"You've led us a rough chase, doctor," Dekker said, a cuttingly cold edge to his voice. "We'll have to see that you're paid back accordingly."

The look on Dekker's face was demonic. At that moment, daPaz did not need Alain's telepathic ability to read Dekker's mind. The agent was recalling all his efforts, all his humiliations, all the pain he'd suffered at the hands of Alain Cheney and, indirectly, Javier daPaz. The doctor already knew what a merciless tormentor Dekker could be—and that had been when he only *suspected* daPaz of being in league with Cheney. Now that he *knew,* now that he'd suffered more, there would be no controlling him. A quick death from a z-beamer seemed positively blissful by comparison.

I'm sorry, Alain, daPaz thought. *I should have believed you. I should have left that first night, while I had the chance.*

As the three men came closer, daPaz made a sudden move, reaching into his coat pocket as though to pull a gun. One of the police, seeing the threat, reacted instinctively by firing his own weapon. The z-beam hummed through the hallway before Dekker could yell a countermanding order. The doctor screamed and crumpled to the ground, dead.

"You idiot!" Dekker shouted at the guard. "I said I wanted him alive. I needed to question him and find out about his friend."

Ignoring the other's protestations, Dekker knelt beside daPaz's body, which was still twitching with galvanic reflexes. He pawed briskly through the other's clothes, but could find no clues to Cheney's whereabouts.

Muttering about "damned incompetents," Dekker stood up again, looking down on the body. His frustration at being cheated out of his revenge against the doctor, and at losing Cheney's trail once more, was building to monumental proportions. He gave the corpse a sudden vicious kick in the face, then turned to storm out of the hallway. "Clean that mess up," he told the two policemen. "I've still got things to do."

chapter 12

Joby arrived in Lompoc amid a cloud of complications that left her feeling more frustrated than ever. The Lompoc police chief had told her, politely but firmly, that the Code T authorization was only for Dekker; no matter how important she was within the TIA, she would have to get a separate authorization for herself if she wanted him to turn over his facilities to her. After the warning she had drawn from Glazer about her first misuse of such an authorization, Joby was reluctant to phone back to Karl Junger and ask for a second one. Morgan Dekker, she was told, was somewhere at the spaceport, but locating him was next to impossible, so she could not use his authorization.

If she'd had the time, she was sure she could have gone down to the station personally and browbeaten the police chief into giving her all the assistance she needed. But time was the one commodity she didn't have. Alain might already have gotten off the planet by now, but if he hadn't, she didn't want to give him any additional hours by arguing with the local cossacks. There would be, she knew, other ways to achieve her goals.

Still, as her jet touched down on the runway, she felt she was strangling in red tape.

The Lompoc airport was located in one corner of the vast facility that was the Vandenberg Spaceport, and Joby actually had to take a quick shuttletube ride to reach the main service area. She used the time well to map out her strategy, and when she finally arrived, she went directly to the traffic scheduler.

The woman in charge of this department was far more impressed with Joby's credentials than the police chief had been, and it took almost no badgering to get full cooperation. Joby was given a complete list of all vessels of Rhislinger registry currently in port, as well as those that had left within the past forty-eight hours.

There was only one in the latter category, and it had left so close to the time when Alain had first escaped from Dekker that Joby ruled it out as a possibility. There was always the chance that Alain might seek passage on a ship of some other nationality, but she doubted that. Alain was bound to use his supposed Rhislinger citizenship as a sympathy ploy to attain a position on an outbound ship. A Rhislinger captain would be the most logical target.

One Rhislinger ship, the *Bakalta,* was due to lift off in forty-five minutes. That would be Joby's first choice. Rather than give herself away by going aboard the ship, she had the traffic controller summon the *Bakalta*'s captain to the tower on a last-minute technicality.

Captain Bergstrom was furious with the possible delay; his schedule was already tight enough as it was. He stormed into the controller's office, but confronted an equally strong-willed Joby Karns in place of the woman he expected to find. Joby introduced herself and asked him to be seated.

"What's the meaning of this?" Bergstrom demanded.

"I represent the Terran Intelligence Agency, captain. We have some evidence that you are harboring a fugitive who is of great interest to us. We want you to hand him over before you leave."

"That's ridiculous. We're a cargo vessel, not a passenger ship. The only people we have aboard are spacehands, all native, loyal Rhislingers. We've been on Earth less than a week, hardly time for them to have gotten into much trouble."

"The man I want is named Kurd Alders. Is that name familiar?"

"It could be. It's not all that uncommon a name." The man was hedging, which gratified Joby immensely. At last, something was going right.

"You may have heard it within the past day or two. Here's a photo of him."

Captain Bergstrom looked at the picture of Alain she handed him, and studied it for an overly long time. Finally he shrugged his shoulders and handed it back to her. "What is there about this man that makes him so important?"

"That's the TIA's business, captain, not yours."

"I'm not a citizen of Earth. I have no allegiance to your TIA, and if you persist in harassing me I'll file a formal protest with the Rhislinger Embassy."

"Let's stop pretending we're children, captain. You have this man; we want him. Don't force me to get nasty. I have the authority to forbid you to take off, to send a squad of men aboard your ship, to charge every member of your crew with spying against the government of Earth. I could tear your cargo hold apart looking for stolen secrets. You could fight it—I'm sure you would —and you'd probably win . . . but you'd lose a week, possibly two, off your schedule. I'm trying to settle this matter as one civilized human being to another. Help me, and I'll see that you have no more trouble."

Joby was far overstepping her bounds, and she knew it. She had no authority to do any of the things she described; the most she might have accomplished was to use her influence with the traffic controller to delay the takeoff, and even that would be countermanded if the captain appealed to higher authorities. She was betting, though, that the captain would not realize that. He was a foreigner, unfamiliar with the rules of the bureaucracy under which she operated. What was more, if the captain was like the pilots of other cargo vessels she'd known, he would be operating on a thin margin, and the threat of delay could mean enormous penalties that would take bites out of his profits.

Her bluff worked. The captain sagged visibly in his chair and nodded. "Yes, he's aboard my ship. I hired him yesterday as assistant astrogator when my own took ill."

Joby flashed him a gracious smile. "Thank you, captain. See how easy it is when we all cooperate? I'm

117

genuinely sorry to hear about your assistant astrogator, but I'm sure your astrogator is competent to fill the void until his aide recovers. Let's go aboard now, so I can recover my fugitive and you can be on your way."

The design of the bridge for any ship built to land on planets is a matter of awkward compromise. For the vast majority of the time, the ship will be under freefall, and the temptation is to design the chamber to utilize all available bulkhead space. Some of the most important moments in ship control, however, are performed under gravity conditions, which impose strict limitations on the planners. The most workable solution seemed to entail lacing the controls in a ring all the way around the room. Small stools were attached to the walls so the crew members could sit while they worked; in space, these stools slid easily into compartments within the walls.

Alain was seated at his station, conferring with the chief astrogator. He was striving to concentrate on his calculations despite the agonies of his telepause, and he did not detect Joby's thoughts until a moment before she entered the room. He stood up suddenly and spun around, but by then it was too late—the door had opened and Joby entered the bridge with the captain, a z-beamer clutched firmly in her hand.

Her eyes quickly scanned the thirteen men in the room and picked him out instantly. "You've led us a merry chase," she said, pointing her weapon directly at him. "But it's over now."

Alain felt dismay at his discovery but was not about to give up yet. He was using his last resource, his mind, to find some way out. Joby's thoughts were an open book to him, but it was a book with the pages scrambled and out of order. Feelings of triumph were strong, but they competed with anger, frustration, and even—tucked way down in a corner—regret. Overriding everything, though, was fatigue; Alain could see with some surprise that Joby had gotten even less sleep in the last two days than he had. There might be some way to work that to his advantage. He also noted that she was alone now—a fact that offered still more hope.

"Do you really think you can take me?" he asked.

"I'm the one with the gun. Let's not make a scene here in front of all these nice people. I promised Captain Bergstrom I wouldn't make any more trouble for him; you wouldn't want to make a liar of me, would you?"

"God forbid," Alain said, starting forward resignedly.

Captain Bergstrom spoke up. "I want you to fulfill your end of the bargain, Ms. Karns. Call Control and tell them our flight is again cleared for takeoff at its scheduled time." Alain could easily read the captain's resentment of Joby as a smoldering red glow that covered the rest of his thoughts. Would the captain be an ally if he were to act? It was hard to judge what was going on beneath that layer of resentment; some people were inherently more passive than others.

Without taking her eyes off Alain, Joby took the radio transmitter in her left hand. When the ship's radio man reached Control, Joby informed them that she'd gotten her prisoner, and the ship could leave on schedule. She handed the set back, and her aim never wavered. Alain realized that, tired or not, Joby was an experienced agent; she would not give him the opening he needed. He'd have to provide that for himself.

"Captain," he said, "it might interest you to know that the reason she's so interested in capturing me is that I possess some of Earth's secrets that are vital to the interest of Rhisling. I'm a member of the Rhisling Intelligence Command. If you let her take me, you'll be doing our world a vast disservice."

A pattern of hesitancy formed in Bergstrom's mind. He was a devoted Rhislinger and had been unwilling to turn one of his compatriots over to Earth on general principles. If it would hurt his home world, he was even less willing to do so.

"I warned you against scenes," Joby said, a tightness in her voice. She recognized the ploy for what it was, and knew it stood a good chance of success. She dared not let him talk any more and raise emotions further against her. Whatever conflicting feelings she might have about Alain's death, her agent's instincts told her not to hesitate any longer. Her finger tightened on the firing button.

Alain had been monitoring her thoughts carefully and knew her intentions the instant she did. Even as she pressed the stud to kill him, he was in motion, diving forward and slightly to the side to avoid being hit by the z-beam from her gun. Her beam struck an auxiliary control console and sent a shower of sparks flying harmlessly through the air. She started to swivel to get a better shot at her moving target, but she never had a chance. Captain Bergstrom's fist clipped her alongside the jaw, and she staggered backward into the arms of the first mate, who held her while the captain hit her again. Joby sagged in the mate's arms, unconscious.

Alain picked himself up off the floor, looked first at Joby and then to the captain. "Thanks," he said, but the word sounded all too simple to convey the depths of what he felt.

"Was all that true?" Bergstrom asked. "Are you really with the RIC?"

"Yes," Alain lied. "Why else did you think she wanted me so badly?"

"Why didn't you say so when you signed on?"

"I didn't want to make any trouble for you. If she had come an hour later, we could have avoided this whole scene and no one would be the wiser. As it is, you've now gotten a record for yourself, captain, and you may never be allowed back on Earth again. I'm sorry."

Bergstrom waved a hand. "Who cares about coming to Earth? It's much too crowded and dirty for my taste, anyway. I'd much rather be of service to my own world. As for getting in trouble," he gestured at Joby's still form, "we could take her along with us, dump her out the airlock, and no one would ever know."

Alain shook his head vigorously. "No, I don't operate that way. Even though she's an Earthwoman, even though she tried to kill me, I wouldn't do the same to her. I've killed on a couple of occasions, but only when it was unavoidable. If we could just tie her up and gag her, then leave her behind in a storeroom—somewhere she won't be found for an hour or two—that should suit our needs. Believe me, it'll be the best way."

Bergstrom nodded slowly and delegated two crewmen to help Alain with the task. Joby was bound and gagged and dragged off the ship; the three men emptied the contents of one packing crate sitting in the unloading warehouse and dropped the still-unconscious woman inside when no one was looking. She would be found eventually, but only after it was much too late.

Less than an hour later, the *Bakalta* lifted majestically into the sky, and Alain Cheney left Earth behind him for the last time in his life.

chapter 13

When Joby returned to TIA headquarters in New York, it was in ignominious defeat. She had risked not only the good name of her department, but also her personal reputation, in the gamble to recapture Alain Cheney without help from the more experienced Internal Security Department, and she had failed—miserably. What was worse, she was sure the story of what happened to her would be all over the building long before she set foot in it again. She'd made enough enemies during her rapid rise to power that there was bound to be a sea of smirking faces throughout the complex—and chief among them would be Romney Glazer.

She gave strong consideration to not returning at all. It would have been comparatively simple just to board an outbound ship and vanish along with Alain. She would never have to face her critics. The mood of the Agency was tough right now, and she knew she faced an inquisition the instant she set foot in the building.

But to do that would be admitting defeat, and she hated to let a worm like Glazer have the last laugh. Even though she faced an uncertain fate, the situation was not hopeless. She still had resources and allies to back her up, and she would not yield all she'd worked for without a struggle. What was even better, she had a scapegoat—Morgan Dekker, a convenient tool to pry her way out of this tight situation. There were no strong threats to her from within her own department—she'd always been extra careful about that—so Operations would be a wall to brace herself against when confronting foes from outside.

She went home first, took a long bath, and planned her defense. She spent an hour making herself up, seeing to it that her face was composed and looking perfect. There could be no sign of weakness here, no scent of blood to attract the predators further. She dressed in one of her most compelling outfits, a navy blue jumpsuit with red diagonal stripes. When she was finally ready, she returned to her office.

As she'd feared, there was the smell of a lynching in the air. A few people gave her a brief hello as she walked down the halls, but most of those she encountered studiously avoided her. Word of her arrival traveled quickly; she barely had time to sit down behind her desk and look at one of the latest reports on the Leonean problem before word came that she was to report to the director's office immediately. Steeling her nerves, she walked proudly to her inquisition.

Phyllis Rokowsky met her in the anteroom. "I hope you've got a good story," she said. "The prevailing mood is for crucifixion."

Joby was pleasantly surprised by this show of concern. Up until a couple of days ago, Rokowsky had stayed impersonal and aloof—but after Joby had submitted her Leonean policy, there had been the invitation to lunch. And now there was another indication that Rokowsky cared about Joby's safety and ultimate fate. *I don't know what I've done to earn it,* Joby thought, *but an ally this powerful can't be refused.* She smiled confidently. "Thanks. I can but do my best."

Rokowsky led her into the conference room. Officially, this was not a trial, merely an "inquiry" into the events surrounding the Alain Cheney affair. But the verdict reached here would affect her entire career; it could even be a matter of life and death. Joby was not about to be lulled by the false sense of cordiality that pervaded the room.

Seated at the far end was the director, dictating a few notes into his portable secretary. Phyllis Rokowsky sat on his right, another assistant on his left. Romney Glazer sat on the other side of Rokowsky, his face a mask of impartiality. Joby could only guess at the jubilation he felt.

The director started off by thanking her for coming and cooperating with the inquiry. Her aide, Morgan Dekker, had already testified for them; could she add any information to what he had told them?

Joby would be shooting in the dark. She had no way of knowing exactly what Dekker had told the committee, or whether he might have tried to weasel out of the charges *he* faced by blaming something on her. Her best line of defense was to stick strictly to events on the record, but presenting them as favorably to her cause as possible.

The picture she painted was not flattering to her subordinate. He'd started the mission off badly by reporting late to her, and that mistake had compounded itself as his mission went along. He had been careless enough to let Cheney get away from him, and had come whining to her for help. She said she'd wanted to report the matter to InterSec immediately, but he'd pleaded with her to give him another chance. She arranged for him to have a Code T authorization—through the very kind intercession of Karl Junger, who, she emphasized, was in no way to blame for what happened. Dekker had only fumbled further, letting Cheney's accomplice escape as well. Eventually, he'd had to resort to killing the man, thus losing all the useful information they might have obtained. In the meantime, seeing her aide's incompetence, Joby herself had personally intervened to uphold the reputation of Operations. She was thinking solely of her department, she said, when she acted. She'd caught

Cheney, but had been overpowered by the crew of the *Bakalta* before she could kill him.

As she finished her testimony, Glazer leaned forward. "You admit, do you not, that you disobeyed standing regulations by not reporting to InterSec the instant you were aware of Cheney's escape?"

"If you will examine Morgan Dekker's file, you will see that he had been, until this incident, a most competent agent. I had faith—misplaced, as it turned out—that he would continue—"

"You're not answering my question," Glazer insisted. "The regulations are quite specific on this point, yet you willfully ignored them."

Joby was silent for a moment, her sharp mind calculating different strategies. She could not hope to outbluster Glazer on this point, because he was absolutely right and would cling to that fact with bulldog tenacity. Perhaps humility would sway the jury more effectively.

"I cannot deny that," she said evenly. "Nor can I deny that I, as chief of Operations, take responsibility for the entire fiasco. I take great pride in my department, Mr. Glazer—and justifiably, I think. Remember, Alain Cheney was also a product of our training, and admittedly one of our best agents. He was also, not incidentally, a telepath. Even so, were it not for the totally unpredictable intervention of Dr. daPaz this case would have been wrapped up silently without any fuss. Dekker obviously cracked under the strain of the situation, and I will have to reevaluate his performance ratings. By the time I intervened, it was just a hair too late to save the situation. I will stand on my record and that of my department. Surely you don't believe that one bungled case can outweigh all the successful service my agents have performed throughout the years."

"Ignoring, for the moment, the question of blame," Rokowsky interrupted, cutting off another potential harangue by Glazer, "the fact remains that Alain Cheney—a man on intimate terms with most of our procedures, a man capable of disrupting our network on what is currently the planet where our most sensitive work is being done—Alain Cheney is at large and knows we are after him. He represents a very serious threat to our organization. Since he is now offworld, he is beyond the jurisdiction of InterSec." She did not look at Glazer as she said that, but the point could not have been lost on him. "What, if anything, do you intend to do about the matter now?"

This was it, the crucial moment. Rokowsky was handing her the opportunity to either save or damn herself. *It's all up to me now.* "It's become apparent to me," Joby said carefully, "that Alain Cheney is not a man who can be treated lightly. As I said before, I take full responsibility for the way this matter has been handled so far, and I will continue to do so. I realize I cannot turn the matter over to subordinates, who might only foul it up again. The only person whose talents I can absolutely rely on are my own. Therefore, I will make it my personal duty to see that Cheney is eliminated."

She could see by the reactions plainly visible on people's faces that her bombshell had had the desired effect. She did not give them much time to recover, but continued relentlessly on.

"Despite the fact that Cheney now has a Rhislinger identity and is aboard a Rhislinger ship—and despite the fact that he knows we are likely to track him back to Leone—I consider it 95 percent certain that he will return to Leone anyway. As the chief-of-station there for the past six years, he knows the planet well, so it is the only place where he can feel he is on familiar territory. All his contacts are there, all his resources. He'll return to Leone, even knowing we expect him to, because that's where he'll stand the best chance of combating us.

"I therefore propose to travel to Leone personally to oversee the effort to eliminate him before he can compromise our operations there. The trip will actually serve a double purpose; while I'm there I can also supervise the operation to penetrate Project Cepheus. The urgency of both these missions compels my presence on Leone."

She leaned slightly back in her chair, feeling rather pleased with herself. Her proposal had taken everyone by surprise, and an off-balance enemy is less of a threat. She had exhibited a strong enough will that she needn't lose any face, and yet the nature of the trip could be interpreted as penance for her sins, which would placate her enemies—in part, at least.

There was a moment of silence following her conclusion. The members of the inquiry board exchanged glances, and finally the director spoke. He thanked Joby for appearing and telling her side of the story, and told her the panel would consider her proposal carefully. She was then dismissed to return to her regular work.

The only one of the board members who would meet her eyes as she rose to leave was Romney Glazer—and his feelings for her had obviously not changed in the slightest.

Joby went back to her office and tried to take her mind off her fate by immersing herself in work. But no matter how hard she concentrated, the reports on her desk were just abstract symbols on paper, totally meaningless. After she found herself reading the same sentence over for the fifth time without understanding it, she gave up and tossed the report to one side. Lowering the lights in the room, she changed the wall to the three-dimensional star map and leaned back in her seat, watching the restful patterns of the constellations and, in particular, the class-K star near the top that served as Leone's primary.

Hours passed, while her fate was debated by others. Joby was acutely conscious of the passage of time but considered the long wait a positive sign. If they were going to eliminate her outright, it would be a simple decision: sometime within the next few days, some anonymous assassin would pick her off from a window and that would be the end of it. But she had given them some alternatives to think about, and they needed time to choose. *Let them take all the time they need. I can wait.*

Near the end of the day, she received a call from Phyllis Rokowsky, summoning Joby to her office. Encouraged, Joby made the long hike back to the administrative section of the complex. She had to fight to keep her stride steady, and refrained from breaking into a run. That would not have been seemly for a woman in her position.

Rokowsky's office was decorated in shades of pale blue

and green. The large desk faced a long couch that was up against a wall. Rokowsky bade Joby be seated on the couch, then stood in front of her, leaning back against the desk. The two eyed each other for a short while, but finally it was Joby, much as she hated to do it, who broke the deadlock. "What's the verdict?" she asked.

"It was decided," Rokowsky said, "that from now on, InterSec will have the responsibility for eliminating telepausal agents. Such duties are, at best, peripheral to the major function of Operations, and your department is not equipped to handle that task as efficiently as InterSec. This will allow you to return your full attention to the field work for which your department is justifiably noted."

Joby nodded. Though she hated the concept of Operations losing any of its autonomy, she recognized that some sacrifice would have to be made to appease the critics. If this was the worst part of the board's decision she could live with it for now and try to recoup her losses at some future date. But there was one aspect of the situation that would have to be cleared up immediately.

"What about the Cheney matter?" she asked. "Does that still come under my jurisdiction? InterSec has no expertise in offworld operations, and that's where my people excel. Surely they're not going to take that away from me too."

"Ah yes, that." Rokowsky closed her eyes. "We went around and around on that for most of the afternoon." She opened her eyes again and stared straight into Joby's face. "You really tossed us a curve on that one."

"Sorry. I didn't mean to."

"The hell you didn't," Rokowsky said pleasantly. She crossed the room and sat down on the couch beside Joby —a little closer than Joby had expected. "But you did win that battle. Operations—meaning you, in particular —will still be responsible for eliminating Cheney. Your proposal to go personally to Leone is being accepted. The orders are being drawn up now and you'll leave sometime late tomorrow."

Joby sighed with relief and slumped down on the couch. She had won! As she leaned her head back, it came to rest on Rokowsky's hand; the other woman had slid an arm around on the top of the couch behind her and had inched even closer to Joby.

"I want you to fully realize exactly where your support is coming from," Rokowsky said, using her free hand to turn Joby's head so that it stared straight into her own. "I was the one member on that board who insisted you be given the extra chance."

"I'll bet Glazer didn't want to let me go," Joby said, slightly wary of Rokowsky's behavior.

"Surprisingly, no. He was quite willing to send you to Leone—but he did want to strip you of your title as Operations chief. If it had been up to him, you'd have been given a new designation, something that would be completely meaningless once the Cepheus matter was dead. I fought that, too, on your behalf. I spent all afternoon sweating to keep your position relatively intact. I hope you appreciate it."

The emphasis in that last sentence left no doubts at all in Joby's mind. Rokowsky had used all her influence to save Joby's neck and her job. She would be wanting something in return. To Joby, the direction of this conversation was clear: Rokowsky was seducing her.

Joby almost laughed at the unexpected twist. She had used her body flagrantly in the past to gain her goals, and now a demand was being put on it from a new source. She eyed the other woman more carefully—short but dignified, with an air of middle-aged grace about her and a look of deep-set power in her eyes. Rokowsky was used to getting what she wanted—and right now, she wanted Joby.

I've been to bed with worse, Joby thought, *for even less gain.* The point was, she had no choice. If she said no, Rokowsky could reverse the board's decision, have her stripped of her job, possibly even killed. Saying yes would save her, but it would brand her forever as one of Rokowsky's clique. Joby had always tried to avoid alliances with one side or another, so she could jump whichever way was most advantageous. Now that neutrality would be gone, and her fortunes would rise or fall with Phyllis Rokowsky's.

Well, she gave a mental shrug, *can't remain a virgin forever.*

Reaching out a hand, she put it gently on Rokowsky's knee and returned the woman's gaze. "I do appreciate it, Phyllis," she said softly. "I only hope I'll have the chance to show you how much before I leave for Leone tomorrow."

Morgan Dekker walked into the office of Romney Glazer, outwardly calm but inwardly in turmoil. A summons from the chief of InterSec was never a good thing, although Dekker was not quite sure what he had done to bring himself to that department's notice. There were probably enough errors in the Cheney case, though, to make his name common knowledge throughout headquarters.

Glazer came right to the point. "I want your help."

Dekker was startled. "I'm afraid I don't understand."

"I intend to bring down Joby Karns. She's momentarily wriggled out of my grasp, and I think you would be the best tool to get her back again."

"She's my superior. I can't—"

"She's perfectly willing to crucify you on the Cheney affair. She's trying to place the whole burden on your shoulders. I'd say you owe her no allegiance at all."

"But it was my fault. I said that in my testimony. You heard me."

"What I heard was the end result of some of the shrewdest manipulation I've witnessed in some time. She's playing you for a class-A chump, Dekker, and you're letting her."

Glazer stood up from behind his desk and began pacing the office. "Listen. If, at the moment you reported Cheney's escape, Ms. Karns had gone through the proper channels and told me, the matter would have been finished by now. Cheney would be dead and you might have ended up with a reprimand, perhaps a transfer to other duties—nothing that a bright career officer couldn't have overcome in time.

"But it did not suit Ms. Karns's purposes to call Inter-

Sec into the case. She will not allow anything that would interfere with her personal power. Instead, she *let* you convince her to handle the rest of the job yourself—a job you were not completely trained to handle. As a result, Cheney is still alive and you've gained an indelible black mark on your record and a reputation for incompetence—undeserved, in my opinion, but it *is* there. If the Agency really wanted to be nasty, there are charges that could be brought against you, and you could be dismissed in disgrace. Ms. Karns lost no opportunity during her own testimony to smear you, and she has emerged relatively unscathed. I do not feel that justice has adequately been served."

Dekker listened to the harangue in stony silence. He dared not allow himself to believe that Joby would do such a thing to him.

Glazer could almost read his mind. "If you need some more convincing, I can play for you a recording of Ms. Karns's testimony, in which she practically blames you for everything that has ever gone wrong in the Agency for the past two years." When Dekker still did not answer, Glazer pushed a button on his desk, and Joby's voice filled the air around them.

Dekker listened in horror to his boss's recitation of the story. While he could not fault her on the facts, she lost no opportunity to cast aspersions on his character and ability. Things that he considered honest misjudgments she painted as gross stupidity. On the basis of what she said, he could be liable for severe disciplinary action, perhaps outright dismissal from the Agency. As he listened, his emotions ran the gamut from disbelief to dismay to outrage. Was this the woman to whom he was giving so much devotion? Glazer was right—he owed her no loyalty at all.

"I see your point," Dekker said when the recording was through. "But how can I help you? I'm hardly in a position to help myself anymore."

"Joby Karns will be leaving tomorrow for Leone, to track down Cheney herself and to spearhead a drive to penetrate a Leonean project called Cepheus. That would be all very well, but I distrust her motivations—and I dislike having her beyond my reach if something should go wrong. I would send one of my own men out there to keep an eye on her, but my people aren't specifically trained for work offworld. Unlike Ms. Karns, I believe in choosing the proper person for a job from the very beginning—and I'm not averse to picking someone from outside my own department, if that's what it takes. As an agent from Operations, you've been trained to handle conditions on other worlds; if you agree, I can have you temporarily transferred to InterSec and given the assignment of watching over Joby Karns—discreetly—while she's away. Or," he waved a hand, "you could refuse my offer and take your chances with the charges that are certain to be filed against you."

Glazer grinned like a crocodile. "The choice is entirely your own."

When it was put in those terms, Dekker clearly saw the light.

Unable to sleep, Joby tossed aside the covers, got up and crossed the room in darkness. Without turning on the light she paced over the thickly carpeted floor to the picture window that overlooked the city. The window, of one-way transparency, took up the entire west wall. Joby stood there naked, looking out thoughtfully at the shimmering lights below her and the twinkling of the few bright stars that penetrated the haze from above.

On the bed behind her, she could hear Phyllis Rokowsky stirring, reaching out for her and finding her gone. "Joby?" the other asked sleepily.

Joby did not turn around, but continued staring out at the lights in the darkness.

"Joby, dear, come back to bed. It must be cold out there."

When Joby still did not answer, Rokowsky sighed, threw back the covers and got out of bed herself, padding across the carpet to stand behind Joby. She put her arms around Joby, her hands delicately caressing the smooth skin of Joby's belly. "You're thinking about Leone, aren't you?"

Joby nodded. "Can you blame me?"

"I suppose not." Rokowsky started a series of small kisses around Joby's back and shoulder blades. "I had hoped to keep your mind off such things, for tonight at least." Her hands began wandering upward along Joby's body.

Joby closed her eyes, but did not pull away. "It's not you, Phyllis, I have no complaints there. . . ."

"I'm glad to hear that." Rokowsky's hands were now cupping Joby's breasts, stroking them with a loving, expert touch.

"But I'm facing my entire future life, my whole career. There's a million possible things that can go wrong on Leone."

"They won't. You're one of the most talented women I've ever encountered, Joby. You'll be the equal of any situation."

"But what if I'm not? What happens if just one of those million possible things goes wrong and keeps me from doing my job?"

For just an instant, Rokowsky's hands tightened painfully on Joby's breasts, then relaxed again. "In that case, my dear," she said, "I suggest you not bother coming back."

Joby sighed. She had already reached the same conclusion herself.

Putting her hand in Rokowsky's, she let the older woman lead her back to bed.

part ii:

leone

chapter 14

Alain's flight from Earth to the *Bakalta*'s next port of call—the planet Panjow—took four days. The crew treated him almost reverently; none of them had ever met a member of their world's intelligence service before, and they were thrilled at the prospect of aiding their government in a top-secret mission. They allowed him to do hardly any work and insisted on treating him as a celebrity. Alain was not used to such attention and basked in its glow. In payment, he regaled them with stories—some only slightly fictionalized versions of the truth—about the espionage business in general and some of his own exploits in particular. He refused, though, to give them any details of his current "mission" to Earth.

"It's for your own safety," he explained. "If you don't know anything, it's not worthwhile for TIA agents to capture you and torture you for the information. The TIA will already be keeping a close watch on everyone aboard this ship because of me; I'd hate to repay your kindness by getting you into further trouble."

Every chance he could, he tried to get away from the rest of the crew to ease the growing pain in his mind. A cargo ship was not the same as a passenger liner, however; quarters were much more cramped, and it was impossible to be completely alone. His telepathic powers seemed to be getting sharper every day, and the impinging thoughts of the others, even through several thicknesses of bulkhead, threatened at times to split his skull apart. The sexual fantasies and dreams grew stronger as well, with the added macabre twist that Joby Karns now held a starring role in many of them. On those occasions when he could sleep at all, he would wake up in a feverish sweat. Nocturnal emissions increased to as many as three per sleep period.

Again, in private, he would wonder whether his desperate clutching at life was really worth this agony. A z-beam from Dekker's gun might have been far more merciful. At those times, he reminded himself of a higher goal. He was not surviving just for the sake of mindless survival; somewhere, somehow, he was going to make his mark on the universe. Then too, thoughts of revenge crept in; if for no other reason, he had to live merely to spite Joby and the impersonal hierarchy that ran the Terran Intelligence Agency.

When the *Bakalta* landed on Panjow, Alain took his leave. He thanked Captain Bergstrom and the crew for their help, but said he'd brought them enough unwanted attention and would best be able to complete his mission by going through his regular channels. He left the ship amid a group of other crewmen, in case any TIA assassins were watching, and stayed with the group until he could quietly slip away in a crowded bar.

Panjow was still a relatively backward planet, not computerized to nearly the same extent as Earth. Cash was still very much in use here, for which Alain was profoundly grateful; it would enable him to move about freely without leaving a trail of identity behind him. He exchanged a sizable amount of his credit as Kurd Alders for local currency and lost himself in blessed anonymity.

There would be a ship leaving for Leone in two days. Alain had a long debate with himself whether to risk going back there. It was certainly the move Joby would expect him to make, and the possibilities were good that he'd be walking straight into a trap. But there were other reasons for going. He knew that world better than any other—all the hiding places, all the tricks it could offer up to the unwary. The best strategy, if one was on the defensive, was to take a stand on familiar territory. He had contacts there, with the local citizens as well as with other agents. He might be able to find some outside help in his flight from persecution.

There was also the fact that he had steered daPaz to

Leone. If the doctor did manage to make it there, he would need Alain's help in establishing a new identity. Alain had made him a promise and felt honor bound to keep it.

Now that he was back among people again, and not quite so fearful for his life, the sexual urges became overwhelming. He had the time and cash to squander and indulged himself with a series of prostitutes. There were three in the first day, but instead of slaking his thirst the sexual activity actually increased his desire further. He purchased the services of four different women the second day and felt exhausted but still unsatisfied.

The trip from Panjow to Leone took three more days. This ship was less luxurious than the one Alain had ridden from Leone to Earth, but it mattered little to him. He stayed in his cabin almost the entire time, having even his meals brought to him and avoiding contact with the other passengers. Even so, the throbbing pain of being in the enclosed vessel with so many others was almost paralyzing. Mostly he lay on his bed, moaning from the combination of pain and repressed sexual urges, trying as best he could to get some sleep.

Leone. The small orange sun in the sky never looked so beautiful to him as it did when he disembarked along with the rest of the passengers. Leone had only the one spaceport, and it looked tiny compared to the enormous complex at Vandenberg Alain had left not so long ago. His eyes were busily scanning the crowd ahead of him, looking for any familiar faces or anyone too preoccupied with him. He opened his mind wide too, despite the pain, hoping to detect any stray thoughts indicating danger.

If there was anyone at the spaceport with an unusual interest in Alain, though, that person kept himself out of sight and his mind under control. Alain breezed through Immigration and Customs without any problems and within half an hour found himself standing on the street outside the terminal, preparing for his next step.

Leone's capital city, Port Mombarra, was still a relatively young town, built on the ruins of the old capital that had been destroyed during the war with the Dur-ill. Buildings had a newer, livelier sparkle to them than did their terrestrial counterparts. Even the attitude of the people seemed younger, fresher. They went about their errands with more enthusiasm, as though impatient to move on to other things. In some ways this was charming, in other ways annoying, but Alain found it a welcome change of pace after his horrible visit to Earth.

Leone had been settled largely by Africans and the predominant skin color was black. White people were not so unusual, though, that they attracted special attention. Alain had worked on this world for six years, operating a large import shop as his cover identity, and had experienced no problems because of his race. His obviously Terran background tended to be a social handicap, but not an insurmountable one. His store and his reputation had flourished.

He dared not go anywhere near the store now; that was certain to be under surveillance. But there was an emergency route that he'd planned out for himself, refining it over his six-year tenure. It had originally been intended for use if the Leonean government discovered his identity; it would serve him almost as well now.

He hailed a cab. The street vehicles on Leone were human driven, which felt a little strange after so much impersonal transport back on Earth. The government here had tried, three years ago, to install the subsurface grid system, but widespread rioting by the various transportation unions—fearful of unemployment—had put the idea on the shelf. The government was proceeding at a slower pace, phasing out cabs by not issuing new licenses and permits, thus creating, eventually, a demand for better service. At that point, they would step in and modernize the system—but at present, the cabs still ruled the street.

Alain took the taxi to L'Bruko Park, the vast expanse of wilderness area near the center of the city. There he wandered with apparent aimlessness through the twisting paths designed for children, lovers, and naturalists. He came to one spot, north of the central lake, unmarked but committed to memory, where he left the path and disappeared from view behind a thick clump of bushes. The ground here looked undisturbed, which was a hope-

137

ful sign. He dug at the base of one bush with his fingers until he was able to pry up the small metal box he had buried there two years earlier.

The box contained a thick wad of hundred-cedi notes and a z-beamer, which he quickly pocketed. He looked longingly at the rest of the contents: another complete set of false ID documents. He dared not use them, though, because they'd been supplied to him by the Agency itself and would be watched for. The point of this cache had been to escape from the Leoneans in case of emergency; he'd never thought he might need it to flee from his own side.

He closed the box with a sigh and reburied it. He would have to obtain a new identity without any help from the Agency this time. The procedure he had described to daPaz, that of becoming a farmer, a miner, or a logger, was the poor man's desperation method—simple, but not the most desirable solution. There were a few other possibilities he wanted to try out first.

With his pockets full of money and a z-beamer tucked safely away, he felt more confident of his abilities to weather the coming storm. Leaving the park, he checked into a nearby hotel and began making some calls.

Upon her arrival two days earlier, Joby Karns had set up a command post of her own in a rented apartment. She stayed far away from Alain's old store; if he should defect to the Leoneans—a possibility she had to consider —he would not then be able to tell them where she was. She did set up a watch on Alain's former quarters, on the off chance that he would be stupid enough to return there.

Her next step was to contact all of Alain's immediate subordinates, to let them know that she would be directing their efforts personally for the time being. She asked for reports on the missions against Project Cepheus and was dismayed to find that nothing new had been learned during the time she was en route from Earth. That situation would have to change, drastically.

She also informed people that Alain had gone over to the other side and was now to be considered a traitor and a threat to their personal welfare. Some of the agents expressed shock at that, but they were hardly in any position to question the word of the Agency's chief of Operations. Joby received assurances that any attempt Alain made to contact them would be reported to her immediately.

She put out feelers through standard channels, offering a reward for Alain's hide. After consulting with some of the local agents, she hired some independent "bodyguards" to form her own small army. Her ostensible reason for this was that she did not want to take any of her regulars away from their primary task of penetrating Cepheus, but there was another motive as well: the agents on Leone were all, to some extent, personally loyal to Alain—and despite what she'd told them, she didn't want to take a chance on any of them freezing up when the time came to kill their former associate.

She expended no effort at all on monitoring the spaceport. Alain would come, she had no doubts about that, and the spaceport was too obvious and too public a place for her to do anything. This was not Earth, and she had less than no authority—the local government would be delighted to pick her up on the slightest pretext if they knew what her mission was. She had to act with discretion.

Most of her energies were concentrated on breaking the barrier around Cepheus. Cracking that case would, she was sure, salvage her position even if her quarry got away completely. There was time enough to deal with Alain when he showed up.

The call came in on the third night of her stay. The caller was Patrick Kossa, and he was not a regular agent of the TIA at all. He was one of the comparative handful of people in this business who could make a living at it on a free-lance basis, selling his information and services to whichever side he thought would pay him the most. According to what Joby had heard, he was 85 percent reliable—which was considered quite good in the field.

"I received a call from a mutual friend," Kossa told Joby. "It seems he wants a complete new persona—new

139

face, voice, identity package. I thought you might be interested."

"I am. How much?"

"He's offering me 10,000. I figure it would be worth at least twenty to you."

The man was lying, Joby was sure. A complete facial transformation, a vocal cord change, and identity papers could not possibly cost more than 5,000 cedis here on Leone; even assuming Alain was offering Kossa a generous tip to maintain his silence, the figure should not have been that high. Joby knew she could bargain Kossa down a bit, but that would take time she didn't particularly want to spend. The money was the least important factor at the moment; she wanted to get this business wrapped as quickly as possible.

"You've got a deal," she said. "Payment upon final delivery. Where and when?"

"There's a fountain near the northeast corner of L'Bruko Park. Tonight at midnight. I'm supposed to be alone and unarmed."

Joby considered the plan. The area would be wide open. Even though it would be dark, Alain would have his telepathic sense to warn him of the approach of any strangers. She'd brought only one telepathy interference cap with her, and she intended to use it herself; the rest of her men would have to go mentally naked.

She realized that she couldn't let Kossa attend that rendezvous—Alain would see instantly from the man's thoughts that he was being double-crossed, and might be able to escape. It would be better if *no one* showed up within range; Alain, at least, would be there, and she could close her net on him without the bait.

"I want you to stay away from there," she told Kossa. "I want to avoid anything spooking him. Besides, you wouldn't want to be hurt when we close in our circle. I'll get back to you when the job's done." She hung up before Kossa could say another word, then summoned her men. They would have some plans to go over, and there were only a couple of hours left before midnight.

Laya Mendes cowered in the corner of the cellar as the older woman stood over her with a broom. "How did you get in here, you little tramp?" the woman's voice boomed.

Laya cringed. It was not the woman's menacing posture that affected her; Laya, though small, was young and agile—almost birdlike—and she could easily have evaded any physical menace from her attacker. Nor was it the shouting, exactly, that disturbed her. Rather, it was the *force* the woman was projecting without realizing it. There was a power in her hatred and anger that Laya could feel almost like a physical blow.

"Through . . . through the window," she replied in a tiny voice. She pointed up at a panel where the late-afternoon sunlight streamed into the basement of this apartment complex. Beside the wall was the furnace and a pile of empty boxes she had used as a makeshift ladder for climbing up and down to the window.

"Get out," the woman insisted. "Get out before I beat you." She waved her broom menacingly over her head.

As far as Laya was concerned, the beating had already begun. The woman's hostility crashed against the inside of Laya's skull like pounding waves against a rocky shore. "I didn't hurt anything, honest. I just needed someplace to sleep."

"Well, you won't do it here. I won't stand for any freeloading human rats stinking up my basement. Get out!"

The woman, tired of idle threats, started advancing on the cowering girl. Laya shrank back still further at first; then, as the broom descended, she made a sudden dash for the far wall. The blow missed its mark, and the older woman turned slowly to try again. By the time she could raise her weapon for another strike, Laya had scampered nimbly up the row of boxes and was squeezing through the narrow opening to the outside world. In addition to fear, hostility ruled her mind, hostility toward the old woman who was chasing her from her refuge. The boxes she had climbed teetered of their own accord, then toppled down on the woman who'd chased Laya out.

The woman cursed as the boxes hit her, then shouted after Laya, "Good riddance! Don't you ever let me catch sight of you again!"

Laya was in a dingy alleyway, running barefoot through the slimy layer of water and filth. Even though there was no danger of the woman's pursuing her out here, she continued her rapid flight to put as much distance between herself and the source of her pain as possible. Her head was pounding, and she could not stop the tears from clouding her vision. She ran out to the street and down a couple of blocks before another alley presented itself. Only then did she stop to regain her breath.

Being chased out of her "home" was nothing new to Laya. It happened on the average of once every couple of weeks and had been going on for years. She had to stop and think hard to recall living any other way.

Her ancestry had been a mixture of black and Hispanic, leaving her with brown eyes, long black hair, and a skin like rich cocoa. Both her parents were killed in an accident when she was ten years old, and she had been sent to an orphanage school to continue her education and upbringing. While the orphanage was not like home, she had adapted quickly. All went smoothly for the next two years.

The onset of puberty came as a special blow to her, for along with the normal confusion every young girl faces at that stage of life came the strange sensations inside her head. It seemed as though everyone around her was shouting, and she could not tune them out. When she tried to tell people about it she was taken to a series of doctors, who gave her medication they said would help. The medicines did a variety of things—some made her sleepy, some made her wide awake, some made her itchy, some made her see strange things—but not a one of them made the uncomfortable sensations go away. Her supervisors grew more and more impatient with her, and when she kept insisting that she didn't feel well, they took to beating her. She ran away, was caught and returned to the orphanage, where she was severely punished for her transgression. She was finding, though, that she could use the strange feeling inside her head as an asset as well as a handicap; it gave her the ability to outguess her opponents. The first chance she had she ran away again and had been running ever since.

She tried escaping to the farm country at first, but a little girl alone stood out too badly and made people ask too many questions. Getting food on her own was more of a problem; she'd been a city dweller all her short life and was unsure how to survive in the wild. Reluctantly, she returned to the city; there were more minds impinging on hers here, but there were also garbage cans, junk piles, and deserted buildings to help her live. The whole city of Port Mombarra became her smorgasbord, and she had been living off its riches for five years now.

During that time she matured into an attractive young woman—but the special pain within her mind also grew and would not give her peace. She never starved, but she was never fully safe, either. She avoided contacts with other people as much as possible, because adults frightened her and hurt her. They repeatedly chased her from whatever home she found, hounding her mercilessly.

Laya would not have called herself unhappy—she'd had very little experience of happiness in her life to compare her present situation with. She just existed and accepted.

After her eviction from the basement she wandered for several hours looking for a new home. Her wanderings took her to the neighborhood bordering L'Bruko Park; she liked the park because of its restful atmosphere but would not go there during the day because there were too many people. She kept, for the most part, to the narrower streets and alleys, where there was less opportunity for a chance encounter with anyone who might chase her away.

After a while, she found a promising spot: a row of old houses standing empty, condemned, and awaiting demolition in a couple of weeks to make way for some newer project. She explored until she found an open door, and let herself in. The house was dusty and deserted, with just an old bucket and some dust cloths left behind—ideal accommodations for her needs.

Laya settled in one dark corner and curled up to get

some sleep. She disliked the day; there were too many people up and about. Nighttime belonged to her. As soon as it was truly dark, she would go out hunting for food.

In the meantime, she rested.

chapter 15

The night was dark and still as Alain entered L'Bruko Park from the eastern side. Leone had two major moons, the larger being more than half as bright as Earth's moon. Both satellites were above the horizon now, but their glow was hidden by a thick overcast that threatened rain momentarily. A cool, damp wind blew into Alain's face as he walked, and he tightened his cloak around him. It was not the sort of night when he enjoyed being outdoors, but he was pressed for time and could not be choosy.

As he walked, he slipped one hand into the inside pocket of his cloak, closing his fingers around the smooth plastic of his z-beamer. The weapon was a comforting weight in his grip. He had little fear of muggers—Port Mombarra's population was not yet so densely packed that its crime rate would rise to extreme proportions . . . and anyway, Alain would be able to mentally detect any such criminals long before he encountered them, and change his path to avoid them altogether. There were other dangers, though, that the night held in store for him.

He did not completely trust Patrick Kossa. The man was a weasel, and Alain knew from previous dealings that Kossa's mind was a black pit of twists and convolutions. But Alain had gone through his list of contacts one by one and had been turned down repeatedly. "You're hot," they all told him. "I'm sorry, I'd like to help you. You've been straight with me in the past. But the pressure's on, now, and there's nothing I can do. Good luck." Seven times he'd been rejected, with the story being almost identical each time.

Kossa was the only one who hadn't turned him down. But then, Kossa would turn down almost nothing that paid good money. *I notice he didn't warn me that I was being hunted,* Alain thought. *Is he assuming I'm well aware of it, or is he trying to lull me off guard?*

Alain wished he'd been able to read Kossa's mind to see whether the free-lancer was planning a double cross. Telepathy was impossible over the phone, though; it required physical proximity. But there was little alternative to the gamble tonight; he would just have to take precautions and hope for the best.

The promised rain was materializing as a light mist by the time Alain neared the fountain where the rendezvous was to occur. He checked his thumbwatch. Five minutes till midnight. No need to panic just yet. He remembered from previous experience that Kossa was hardly the most punctual man to deal with, although he had stressed to the free-lancer that if there was any delay, the deal was off. With his life on the line, he could take no chances with any foul-ups; a delay might indicate a trap.

Alain did not approach the fountain itself, which was in the center of an open area; he stayed well within the thicket of bushes around the clearing, where he could keep the fountain in view. He opened his mind up to its most receptive state, hoping to pick up some clue to what was happening. He detected fragments of thoughts from at least three different minds right at the very limit of his perception. It was conceivable that three other people might be strolling near this section of the park at this hour, but . . .

His hand tightened around his gun, and he took it out of his pocket, just in case.

Midnight came, and still no sign of Kossa. Alain frowned. *I'll give him one more minute, in case his watch is slow. If he's not here by then, he's lost his chance.*

He started to detect something, an itch at the back of his mind. Just a few weeks ago he never would have noticed it, but his powers had sharpened so immensely in that time that it registered feebly on his consciousness. It was not the normal pattern associated with human thought, but it was not something totally unfamiliar, either. It took him a couple of seconds to recognize it for what it was, simply because it was something that by all rights should not have been within forty-five light-years of Leone.

A telepathy interference cap!

Neither Leone nor any of the other inhabited planets knew about Earth's success in developing telepathic agents. Telepathy was the major secret weapon in the TIA's arsenal. It had been discovered as the almost accidental offshoot of a series of parapsychological experiments fifty years ago. A clever administrator had recognized its potential immediately and spared no expense to develop it into a working tool for the Agency. All of Earth's schoolchildren were now routinely tested, unknown to them, for signs of the still-rare talent, and those showing potential were marked for future observation. Later, if the talent persisted, the person would be recruited into the Agency in some capacity.

Other psychic abilities, such as telekinesis and teleportation, had also been tested, but the prognosis for them was not nearly as favorable. After a short while, those experiments were abandoned to concentrate more fully on telepathy.

When the breakthroughs had come, the decision was also made to keep telepathy a secret from the rest of the universe. The "purloined letter" gambit had been used, and Alain had always admired its cleverness. Instead of drawing tight security rings around the project—which in itself would have invited an all-out attempt by the enemy to find out what was happening—the Agency allowed rumors to leak out that it had agents with incredible powers. It was reported that all of Earth's agents could read everyone's innermost thoughts, plant ideas in other people's minds, teleport from one place to another on a planet, kill by means of mental concentration, move heavy objects through the air via telekinesis . . . the list of impossibilities went on. The rumors were so incredible that no one could possibly believe them, yet every so often the Agency let them slip out again. In addition, the impressive ParaPsych Foundation was established to study the psychic sciences. The result of this overkill was that no one believed anything of the sort—a perfect smokescreen for the real telepaths working in the field.

For this reason, Earth was the only planet that had any reason to develop the telepathy interference cap in the first place. The fact that one was on Leone could only mean that someone had brought it here from Earth, someone who wanted to keep his thoughts secret from a telepath.

The significance hit him the instant he recognized the cap for what it was. As he'd feared, Kossa had set him up for a trap. He could only detect the one interference cap, but he detected those other unshielded thoughts, meaning there were at least four people pursuing him. At the moment they were all, except for the person wearing the cap, at the extreme limits of his range—and Alain hoped to keep them at least that far away.

He had no way of knowing yet whether he had been spotted. He made no sudden movements, but slowly started to back away from the fountain through the park's dense undergrowth. The rain was coming harder now, a sudden downpour that soaked right through his supposedly waterproof cloak to his skin. The water made the ground muddy and treacherous, but the driving sound of it would cover any slight noises he made as he moved.

The cordon around him was starting to tighten. He could feel the approach of other minds around the perimeter of an imaginary circle as it closed in toward the fountain at the center. There were at least half a dozen minds radiating their thoughts, their various streams of consciousness jumbling into a vast blur so that he could not count the exact number. They were moving cautiously inward, keeping alert for any movement that would give away their quarry's presence. That meant they hadn't spotted him yet. Alain thanked God for small favors.

Suddenly the minds stopped advancing. Alain stopped

too and waited. He could still hear no sounds over the driving of the rain, but he could tell from his pursuers' minds that *they* could—they were all radio linked with one another to coordinate their efforts. They were receiving a message now from the woman *(Joby?)* who was directing the attack. She had spotted someone with her night goggles, a form moving stealthily through the bushes. It would undoubtedly be their target. The location she gave pinpointed Alain exactly, and she ordered all her forces to converge on that point at once, firing at will.

Alain could no longer hesitate, or he'd be at the center of more firepower than he could possibly handle. Abandoning caution, he started running in a southwesterly direction—deeper into the park. The foliage would at least offer him some protection; if he let his pursuers catch him out on the street unprotected, he would make a much easier target.

Several of the hunters spotted him now and raised the cry against him. A z-beamer sizzled, scorching its ray into a tree a meter to Alain's left. Alain fired back in the direction of the shot. He doubted that would stop his pursuers, but it might slow them down a bit and make them more cautious before darting into the open. He wished, not for the first time, that his telepathic abilities were directional, so he could tell exactly where his adversaries were. He could tell by the strength of the signals approximately how far from him they were, but not in which direction.

A couple of them were getting very close indeed. Alain thought he spotted a movement to his right through the curtain of rain. He fired in that direction and was rewarded by a mental cry of alarm; his shot had come close, at least, and the man had slipped and fallen trying to avoid it. Alain raced on through the torrent and the darkness.

There was some confusion in the enemy's minds now, as their quarry put up more resistance than they'd expected. That confusion was contagious; because he'd opened his mind wide, he was extra susceptible to their emotional chaos. He had to fight at the panic building in his own mind as it caused him to stumble momentarily; if there was ever a time to remain clearheaded, it was now. But he dared not shut down the mental input from his adversaries; he needed too badly to keep tabs on them.

He burst suddenly out of the bushes onto a clear path of gravel. For just a moment he was in the open, and he gave an extra spurt of speed trying to cross the path to the trees beyond before he could be spotted. But his effort was too late. The deceptively gentle hum of a z-beamer filled the air, and he felt a flash of pain as the ray narrowly grazed his left arm. He stumbled forward once again, but managed to keep his balance and continued running. He made it across the path without further incident and plunged into the foliage on the other side, grateful for its concealment.

The pattern of thoughts around him was constantly changing—some faded out with increasing distance, others seemed almost to melt together. The small part of Alain's mind that could afford to interpret such things reasoned that he had broken out of the circle in which he'd been trapped, and was outdistancing at least those pursuers furthest away. He stopped worrying about running into anyone directly ahead of him and just ran forward.

He topped a small hill and found himself confronting the pond—though some generously called it a lake—that occupied the center of the park. He tried to change direction, but his feet slipped out from under him on the muddy ground and he went sliding downhill to the very shore of the pond. He landed on his left side, sending another stab of pain through his wounded arm. The splashing sounds he made as he rolled to his feet could not help but have alerted his pursuers to exactly where he was. As he stood up again, he momentarily lost his sense of direction, taking a step deeper into the pond before realizing his mistake and turning around.

The rain was a solid pounding sensation on his head and body as he ran, skirting along the edge of the pond to the west side of the park. There was another small hill to be scaled ahead of him before he could once again reach the safety of the trees. He got halfway up, slipped on the wet turf, and slid all the way back to the bottom. A z-beam sizzling into the mud just a dozen centimeters to his right gave him new incentive, and he raced up the hill once more. This time he made it all the way, clearing the top and running into the comparative safety of the grove beyond.

His wet cape, drenched by the rain and by his fall into the pond, felt like a sheet of lead dragging down on his shoulders. It slowed him down but, at the same time, he dared not stop to take it off; that would cost him the few precious seconds that were the only gap between himself and death. Gasping deeply now for breath, he pushed on.

The course he steered among the widely spaced trees was a zigzag pattern, random enough—he hoped—to keep any of his followers from drawing a steady bead on him. The density of the bushes on the other side of the pond had helped hide him from his pursuers but had also served to slow him down. With the trees more spread out over here, he could make much better time.

Time must have telescoped for him during the run, for he suddenly found himself running beyond the confines of the park, out on the empty street. This late at night, and in this kind of weather, there was no traffic abroad, no hope of any witnesses saving him. He could not go back into the park now; that would be flying directly into the teeth of the pursuit. With a prayer that was as short as it was fervent, Alain raced across the street to the other side.

The street facing the park had once been a very fashionable shopping district, though its respectability had slipped in the past decade. Shops with large display windows confronted him, all securely locked for the night. Alain looked left and right, but the nearest cross streets were too far away; his pursuers would have a clear shot at him before he could hope to round a corner.

When there's no way around an obstacle, you go through it, he told himself grimly. Putting up his arms in front of his face to shield his eyes, he ran full tilt at a store's display window. The glass shattered into a million shards, and each one seemed to leave a cut on his body. At the same time, the act of smashing the window started up a loud howling and hooting as the store's burglar alarm began sounding. That was an unexpected, but not unwelcomed, dividend; it meant the local police would soon be on their way to investigate, and his TIA pursuers would vanish into the night rather than be caught with z-beamers and no decent explanation. At the very worst, Alain might be picked up and charged with breaking and entering—but his treatment in a Leonean jail was apt to be kinder than what he could expect from Joby and her army of killers.

He had no intention of getting caught by anyone, though, if he could avoid it. Picking himself up off the display area littered with broken glass—and cutting himself even more in the process—he ran through the darkened store, occasionally bumping into counters that he didn't see until too late. He raced to the back, hoping to find an exit onto an alley.

Behind him, his pursuers slowed as they approached the broken window. The thought was occurring to them that their quarry might have picked out a hiding place within the darkened store, prepared to pick them off one by one as they came through the window after him. But the orders coming over their radios from the woman who had organized them *(yes, it was Joby; Alain got a sudden clear image of her in the mind of one of the men)* urged them to press on before the police arrived, so reluctantly they came through the window after him.

Alain found the back door, but it was locked. Looking around frantically, he spotted a window that would serve his purpose. Undoing the catch, he pried it up and slipped quietly into the alley, closing the window again behind him. He hoped he could confuse his followers temporarily into thinking that he was hiding somewhere inside the store before they came out back looking for him.

Along the other side of the alley were the backs of old houses—it was hard for him to make out much more than that. He started up the alleyway, hoping to make it out onto one of the streets, but then stopped. He could hear Joby's directions to her troops as they filtered through the men's minds. She was sending half her force to search the store and go through to the back, while splitting the rest up to go around the flanks on either side. There would be no escape that way. He would have to go through one of these houses to the street on the other side.

He had been concentrating for so long on the mental howling of his pursuers that the presence of another mind took him by surprise. This was a much gentler, more subdued mind at the moment, but it was very close by. It was aware of him, watching him, and a strong sense of apprehension was forming. He looked up and scanned the windows of the houses that looked down on the alley, but could see nothing.

The beeping of approaching police cars could be heard in the distance, and Alain sighed with relief. If he could hold on just a few minutes longer he would be safe. He allowed himself to relax just a little bit.

"Behind you! Look out!"

The words came from the emptiness above him, coming clearly over the beating of the rain. Alain swiveled, gun ready—but a fraction of a second too late.

The gunman at the far end of the alley had a clear shot at his target—but *something* slightly deflected his aim just as he fired. The z-beam hit Alain squarely on the right side of his ribcage, sending a searing wave of heat through that entire side of his body. Even as he was turning, his hand was readying a return shot, and his own beam lashed out down the alleyway, striking his antagonist. The man who'd shot him fell to the ground, dead.

The slashing mental death trauma only added to the pain of his z-burn. Alain dropped his own gun and fell first to his knees, then on his face, splashing down on the wet ground and getting a few drops of water in his nose. His mind was spinning, too dazed for him to even curse his own carelessness. The pain on his right side robbed him of all thought; he was left with only the instinctual need to get away, to crawl to a place of safety. He struggled to pry himself up on his left knee and pull himself along the ground with his hand, but he only traveled two meters before he collapsed once more onto the ground.

The rain pelted down on him, and he could move no further. A dark shape loomed over him, but he was not afraid. The thoughts reaching him from this newcomer were confused, frightened, tentative, but not at all hostile. It was not one of the human predators Joby had sicced on him. Turning his head a little, he looked up, but could see only a vague silhouette against the falling rain.

Help me, he tried to say, but didn't even have the strength to make his mouth form the words. Unconsciousness overtook him, mercifully blanketing out the pain in both his mind and his body.

chapter 16

Laya was never sure what instinct compelled her to cry out her warning to the hunted man in the alley below her window. Perhaps it was because, even from her safe vantage point, she could feel the desperation that flowed through his mind like a mighty river. She herself had been living as a fugitive for the past five years; she knew his plight only too well and could empathize with it. She had not felt close to any other human being since her parents had died, but the stranger below somehow evoked strong feelings of kinship, touching emotions she didn't even know existed.

Even so, she had never intended to do anything more than warn him of the danger she sensed from the end of the alley. The words escaped her mouth involuntarily, and almost too late. But it was unthinkable that she should get further involved with the dangerous situation below. She had enough troubles of her own without taking on any more.

And yet, there was that poor man lying helpless on the ground, in serious pain. There were more people chasing him, she could tell, and she could also hear the beeping of approaching police cars. Trouble was piling up thick and fast, and without knowing any of the particulars of the case she automatically sided with the fugitive. Her own problems seemed tiny at this moment compared to his.

Before she knew what she was doing, she was rushing out of the safety of her hiding place to stand beside him in the alley. The rain plastered her hair down on her forehead and neck and dripped off her nose as she looked at the figure lying at her feet. The man struggled for a moment to rise, then turned his head upward toward her. His eyes were glazed, and the pain he was suffering hit her like a z-beam in her own side. His mouth moved to form words, but nothing came out. His meaning, though, was conveyed to her as clearly as though he had shouted: *Help me.* Then he passed out, and his mind was muted to her senses.

She couldn't just leave him here to be discovered or killed. Bending down, she grabbed him under his armpits and began dragging him back into the house she was temporarily calling her home. Ordinarily he might have been too heavy for someone of her tiny size to carry by herself, but Laya's hard life had toughened her far beyond normal expectations. She hauled him through the open back door, put him down for a moment to close it behind them, and then continued dragging him over to one corner of the room.

She started peeling his wet clothes off him, then suddenly became very embarrassed at doing such a thing to a man. Her parents had raised her with strict standards of propriety, and that training held even to this day. She ended up compromising with her sense of modesty, removing his shirt, boots, and socks but leaving his trousers intact. The burn area on the right side of his ribcage was bright red and already starting to blister badly; she could feel heat radiating from it just by putting her hand near the wound. She went into another room and carried back a large canvas dust cloth that had been left there, draping it over the man's body to keep him warm.

The police cars were very close now, and the fugitive's original pursuers were starting to flee themselves. But the police, too, could mean trouble, as Laya knew all too well from previous experience. They would know from the burglar alarm that someone had broken into the store across the alley. After searching it and finding no one there, they would begin searching the immediate neighborhood—including these deserted buildings. Laya could not possibly drag her unconscious man away from here without being spotted; yet somehow she knew she dared not let him be found, either.

She would have to provide a decoy—herself. If they saw her running away from the area they would assume that she was the one who had broken into the store. They would chase her and forget all about searching the area. Laya was confident enough of her abilities to think she could get away with it. She had run from the police on many previous occasions and had an arsenal of tricks at her disposal. She was fast, she was agile, she was young, and she knew this part of the city intimately; there were dozens of cracks to squeeze through, cellars to hide in, drainage pipes to offer refuge. She would not be caught.

She paused just long enough to cover the man's body completely with the cloth, so that any policeman glancing inside casually would see only a heap in one corner. Then she went upstairs and went out the window onto the rooftop of the adjacent house. She had to wait a minute in the pouring rain until a policeman came out into the alley to investigate; then she knocked a roofing tile loose so the man was certain to notice her and started running. The chase was on.

For two hours she led the police on a convoluted circuit of downtown Port Mombarra, going over rooftops, through alleys, around and around the bushes of L'Bruko Park. When she was convinced she had led them far enough away from her home in the deserted house, she hid for an hour and a half in the cellar of an apartment complex. Then, when she thought it was safe, she spent another forty-five minutes returning to her home, making sure that no one spotted her or followed her along the way.

The man was lying just where she'd left him, still unconscious. He had thrashed around a little in his discomfort and had knocked the cloth partway off. She removed it the rest of the way and examined the injuries.

The man's face and hands were bleeding from a multitude of small cuts, but Laya could tell that they were minor. More serious were the burns. The right side of his body had swollen up into a series of ugly blisters, and around them was a band of fiery red. Laya noted, too, a smaller band of blisters on the man's left arm, probably from another, less serious wound.

Laya stood a small distance away, observing with confusion and uncertainty. The man was in shock; his entire system was screaming its pain into her mind. But she had no medical training, knew of no treatments to alleviate her patient's suffering. He could easily die there on the floor while she stood by, helpless.

There were exercises she had done in the past when she herself was sick or injured, but whether they would work on someone else was another matter. Still, anything was better than her idle staring, so she prepared to try.

Kneeling beside the unconscious body, she shut her eyes and slowed her breathing down to a bare minimum. Closing her ears to the sound of the rain outside, she turned off all her external senses and surrounded herself with a cloud of nullity.

Normally when she was sick, she would now be able to isolate the illness, concentrate her mind on it, and force it away. But her body was whole and well, and she blended perfectly with the induced mental grayness. She would have to reach outside herself this time to deal with the injury.

Slowly she lifted her mind upward and peered over the boundaries of her psyche. The other's injury was instantly apparent, a bright glowing redness in the fog like a bed of molten lava. Laya approached it gingerly, feeling the heat before she was even very close. She reached

156

out a mental finger to touch it and burned herself in the process; she retreated quickly with a whimper and leaped back within her own safe walls.

This, she realized, was more serious than anything she'd ever dealt with before. The healing would hurt her as well, and still she would have no guarantee of success. Would she have the inner resources necessary to cope? Was it worth the risk to herself merely for the life of a stranger?

She lay curled up within herself for a long time, afraid to make a decision. Occasionally she would peek over the walls, only to see the glowing red still confronting her. The burning area seemed a little larger each time she glanced at it, as though it were a slow fire consuming the man's soul.

At last she could stand it no longer. Crossing over her boundaries again, she neared the redness once more. The fire seemed to beckon her down to destruction. She reached out for it. The pain was worse than she remembered, but she did not back away this time. Instead, she slowly spread her mind out like a blanket over the lava pits. She had to scream as the heat seared her own psyche, but she forced herself to endure it. As an afterthought, she conjured up all the images of coolness she could think of—snow, frost on window panes, ice cream, swimming pools in summer—anything to counteract the effects of the heat.

She found herself permeating the psyche of the man and, in some senses, his body as well. Her mind was touching all the spots of pain within him, soaking the pain out, taking it upon herself.

When at last she could suffer no more, she pulled back to regroup her forces. As she looked at the redness, it did appear to have halted its expansion, perhaps even shrunk a bit. The area was not as hot as it had been, either. She had done some good—but there was still a long way to go, and she had no more strength now.

She pulled back into herself and opened her eyes. She found herself gasping for breath and drenched in sweat. Lying down on the floor beside the unconscious man, she fell into a deep sleep that lasted longer than she intended.

Morning had already broken when she finally woke, though the sky was still dark and raining heavily. A quick glance at her patient showed his condition to be unchanged from last night. The blisters still looked bad, and the only external thing Laya could think to do was sponge them with water. It would at least cool some of the burning she could sense with her mind. Picking up the old bucket in one corner, she went outside and gathered some of the rainwater that was falling so copiously.

Ripping up the dust cloth that had covered the man, she wet some of the strips and used them to daub at his sensitive skin. She was careful to make her motions gentle so as not to pop the blisters, and was relieved to find her ministrations having some effect. Even though the man was unconscious, she could detect a slight lessening of pain in his mind when she applied the cold compress.

The blisters extended down below the man's belt level, and she could tell that his trousers were rubbing against the burned area and causing pain. As embarrassed as she was at the idea, she would have to take his pants off as well.

Gingerly she peeled off his trousers and underwear. She had seen little boys naked before, but never a full-grown man; the sight so disturbed her that after staring at him for a few minutes, she raced out of the room and huddled by herself in a corner, trembling.

The rain had stopped for a while outside before she got herself under control once more. Slowly she walked back into the room and looked at the man's naked body again. She forced herself to stare, despite the fact that it caused her to perspire and made her breathe slightly faster. Her body, just emerging from adolescence to womanhood, felt a tension and excitement she could not have begun to explain.

When the worst of the effects began to subside, she resumed her task of sponge-bathing the injured man.

Again she could sense the relief as her damp cloth cooled the inflamed skin. As she brought the cloth down near the man's groin, however, she was startled by the sudden erection of his organ. She backed away immediately, fearing she might have accidentally hurt him by doing something wrong. She got conflicting impressions radiating from his mind, however, and the phenomenon subsided after a couple of minutes, so she figured no permanent damage had been done.

She ate some of the food she'd scavenged last night before the stranger had come, and then tried some more of her psychic healing. The red area was not quite as large this morning, the pain not quite as severe. Again, when she finished, she felt she'd done some good—but there was still so far to go. She returned to consciousness and sponged him off some more, surprised to discover how good it made her feel just to touch his body. As she worked, subconscious memories were stirred up—memories of dolls she'd played with as a little girl. She continued alternating her treatments of psychic healing and sponge baths until midafternoon when, utterly exhausted, she fell asleep once more.

She awoke just after sundown with a monstrous appetite. Her patient still had not recovered consciousness. She sponged him down again, then ate the few remaining scraps she had cadged. She would have to go out on a hunting expedition again at once, and this time find enough food for the two of them, in case the man woke up and needed something.

She was gone for ninety minutes and came back with an armload of tasty garbage to find the man writhing around on the bare floor. He was still not completely conscious, but the deep state of shock had worn off and now some of the pain was seeping into his mind more strongly. Laya could feel it in her own mind almost as badly, as though her own ribs had taken the z-beam. She went immediately into a short session of the psychic healing, which eased some of his pain. The sponging also helped reduce his thrashing but could not stop it altogether. Again as she moved her hands near his groin,

159

there was the same sexual reaction as before. Laya was getting used to it by now.

She ate her meal slowly, watching him in the darkness. Her night vision had so sharpened over the years that she could almost make out every tiny detail of his body, even in the unlit house. The strange feelings she had experienced this morning were returning, and she was upset; she'd hoped they would just go away of their own accord, but they returned like a tide that kept pulling her toward her patient.

She fought as long as she could, but her impulses won out. As she gave the man his next sponging and the erection response occurred again, she reached out with one tentative hand to touch the rigid organ. The reaction was almost instantaneous—a series of seminal spurts that made her back away once more in alarm. She had to wipe the sticky white fluid off her with disgust, and it was more than an hour before she could steel herself to come near him again.

Near daybreak his thrashing increased once more, this time accompanied by loud moaning, some incoherent babbling, and increased thought activity. Laya could only make out a word here and there, but the thought patterns revealed a great amount of fear, anxiety, pain, and . . . something else. It felt like desire. She herself was familiar with the desire for food—and there were definite traces of hunger in the man's mind—but the desire was even stronger for other things, things she could not quite understand.

His presence was confusing and disturbing to her. She spent some of her time roaming through the rest of the house, trying not to think of him. The mental pull was quite strong, and the feelings he aroused in her were so mysterious that she was unsure what to do. At times she regretted ever having rescued him—and yet at other times, just running her hands lightly over his body brought on a warmth and a tingle that were almost painfully intense.

The man spent slightly over two more days in this state of almost constant delirium, while she treated him with sponge baths and mind touches. Then one evening near sunset, as Laya walked past him to go into the next room, she could see that his eyes were open and he was staring at her.

chapter 17

To Alain, those first few days of recuperation were a time of blissful relief from his various afflictions, mixed occasionally with horrid nightmares of pursuit through mazes and down long, dark tunnels. Sometimes his pursuers were faceless zombies; sometimes they were lupine animals with the face of the young man he'd killed weeks ago and with long, sharp fangs; and sometimes they were incredibly sexy incarnations of Joby Karns. In those last instances, she was always on the verge of catching him and performing sexual acts upon his body when the dream would dissolve into the gray velvet curtain of his deeper oblivion.

He was aware, on some level of his mind, that he was not dead, that someone was taking care of him. But beyond those primal facts, nothing penetrated the shock and the damage to his bodily systems. He existed purely on an ethereal carpet to which mundane concerns could not adhere.

Eventually, reality began to intrude on his private universe. The pain was the first to reach him, robbing him of the peacefulness that should have been there. Hunger and thirst crept in subtly, a gnawing ache in the very center of his being. There was the alternating of light and darkness, day and night. The cool feeling of water against the blazing heat of his wound washed relief through his body, and the touch of light, caring hands brought stimulation of a deeper kind.

There was also the touch of another mind upon his own; but this was not painful as such contacts had increasingly become since the onset of his telepause. There was a light, airy feeling, like that of a feather caressing the inside of his head, its touch so soft that it was not even a tickle. Had he been capable of thought then, he would have wondered at its gentleness.

The awareness that his eyes were open filtered in slowly to him, with the knowledge that he was seeing the real world once more. There was a large dark shape moving back and forth in front of his field of vision, but for a long time that was all he could tell. As he continued to observe placidly, the shape stopped moving and he heard a tiny gasp. It was accompanied by a burst of mental confusion. Belatedly he made an effort to focus his attention more directly to find out what was happening.

As his eyes adjusted for distance and room light, the shape resolved itself into a dark-skinned young girl, staring at him almost as though he were a mummy risen from his coffin. She seemed at first to tower over him, but then his mind allowed for the difference in position—he was lying at her feet, looking upward. Actually, she was not so tall at all; if he were standing, she'd come only to his shoulder level.

The girl was barefoot and dressed in rags that seemed pinned together rather than sewn. She was filthy, her long black hair a mass of mats and snarls. She was thin and bony, the hollows of her cheeks and the slight discoloration of her eyes giving evidence of an inadequate diet. Toughened muscles stood out along her arms and legs, though; she obviously led an active life. There was a quality of tension about her, like the constant activity of a sparrow; but when she was actually moving, it was with the grace and agility of a jungle predator.

He supposed she looked quite pretty underneath all the dirt and unkempt apparel . . . and that thought almost brought stronger desires to the fore. He quashed it ruthlessly and made his mind stick to facts only.

He tried to sit up, and the slight motion brought with it a sharp stab of pain along his right side. The pain triggered memories of his last conscious activities—the chase in the park, the escape through the store, the shooting in the alley. Suddenly all the desperation of his predicament returned, forcing him over the threshold to complete awareness. His eyes narrowed as he reexamined the girl standing before him.

"Who are you?" he asked suspiciously. His voice was weak and cracking because his throat was so dry.

Although he was hardly a threat to anyone in his present condition, the girl backed off a couple of steps as he spoke. She kept staring at his face, almost afraid to answer. Finally she summoned up her courage. "Laya," she said. "Laya Mendes."

He let his mind open to the thoughts she was radiating, hoping to learn more of the situation. Although she looked nearly full grown, he could tell by the shape of her thoughts that her mind was still far from completely formed. There was a childlike simplicity to the patterns of her ideas, and her concepts were not overlaid with the heavy emotional connotations that he normally associated with adult minds.

He'd had contact, once or twice, with the minds of mentally retarded people, but Laya's mind was not like that. Her ideas were quick, darting things, and he'd always associated that with intelligence. The intellect was here, but raw and untrained; a mind somehow far less developed than the body it served. It was a butterfly of the soul, flapping beautifully about but leaving no real impression on the world behind it.

There was some other fuzzy quality he tried to see in her thoughts, a buzzing like the psychic equivalent of feedback. It disturbed him greatly, for it was a sensation he'd experienced before and he knew he should recognize it; but his brain was still shaking off the effects of shock, and he was not thinking at his brightest just yet.

"Where am I?" he next asked the frightened girl. "What happened to me?"

The girl was obviously afraid of him, though she was making a masterful effort to control it. In a series of simple sentences, she stammered out the story of how she rescued him, took him into this old house, led the police away from the scene, and tended his wounds. As Alain listened, he was also following the story as she visualized it in her mind. It confirmed his earlier opinion of her; she might be unpracticed in verbal skills, but there was intelligence within her skull.

Laya's story ended with surprising suddenness, leaving a conversational gap in the air between them. The two people stared across space at one another for a minute before Alain could think of anything else to ask. That feedback quality in her mind was so tantalizingly familiar it was driving him to distraction. "Why did you save me?" he asked.

Laya looked even more confused than she had before. "I don't know," she confessed. "You were so scared. You were running away from them, like I'm always running away. You're . . . I don't know, you're like me."

As she said that, Alain was struck by the missing factor he'd been trying to place. Of course she would think he was like her. Laya was a telepath! A latent one, to be sure; because the Leoneans didn't know the truth about telepathy, they had no way of developing it in their people. Laya would be able to pick up emotions, strong mental images, anything that was deeply affecting the minds around her, but she wouldn't be able to explain it. The strength of her latent abilities was impressive; now that he knew what he was looking at, Alain could evaluate it more fully. On Earth, Laya would have been tested and considered an incredible find; the Agency would have given her extensive training and made her one of their top agents for certain. But here on Leone, that talent was doomed to be thrown away.

He was still puzzled, though, by the girl's situation. She was obviously a fugitive herself, which was why she felt sympathy for him. Who was *she* running from? He couldn't pull that information directly from her mind, because she considered it such a basic fact of her life that she seldom thought about it. *Never mind that for now*, he told himself. *There'll be time to explore it later. What matters right now is that you're in a safe place and being taken care of.*

He tried to smile through his pain, to reassure her of his friendship, and he also tried to project his feelings of gratitude as much as possible. "Thank you for saving me," he said. "Do you have anything to eat and drink? I'm feeling very weak."

He could almost feel her relaxing. "Sure," she said. She still had some of the rainwater saved in the bucket. It was dirty from having rags dunked in it repeatedly, but at least it was wet. She cupped her hands in it and brought it up to Alain's mouth. He drank greedily, and she had to recup her hands at least a dozen times before his throat felt comfortable again.

With his thirst eased, he became more aware of the growling in his stomach. He started to ask her for food, but her own telepathic abilities anticipated his request. "I'll get some food now," she said, going into the next room.

She was back a few seconds later with a box of garbage. Alain looked inside at what she was offering him and wanted to retch, but he didn't have the strength. "What's that?"

"Food," she replied—and then, seeing the disgust in his mind, she added defensively, "It's what I eat."

"I don't think I'm that desperate yet."

"You must eat," Laya insisted. "I can tell you're hungry. You need strength."

"Maybe, but not from that. Look, there's some money in my pants pockets. Why don't you buy some real food?" Laya gave him a blank look, and for a second Alain had a fear that he'd gone beyond her comprehension. "You do know what money is, don't you?" he asked quickly.

"Of course," she said. "I'm not stupid."

Alain cursed himself for letting his doubts about her become so obvious that she could read them. The shoe was on the other foot now, and he himself would have to be careful what he thought, lest it be picked up and misinterpreted. He could see from her mind, now that she was thinking about it, that she knew perfectly well what money was; on those rare occasions when she found any she had used it, childishly, to buy herself some sweets. Money entered her life so seldom, though, that she normally gave

165

it little thought. She hadn't even considered that the stranger might be carrying some money with him.

She went to his pants now, lying in the corner, and took out his wallet. She told him there was a market open at night a few blocks away, and he recited a short shopping list for her, loading it in favor of protein and fruits. She was gone for an hour, then came back with most of what he'd requested, along with a big bag of candy. *Well, she deserves it*, Alain thought, smiling at her.

She had to help him eat, breaking the food into bite-size pieces without benefit of utensils and handfeeding them to him. He chewed slowly and swallowed carefully, but even those simple actions made him wince. After only a few bites he had to stop, and after a moment, he threw up what he'd just eaten.

They kept trying, and eventually Alain managed to keep some food inside his stomach—surprisingly little, considering how hungry he felt. But it was a start, and he knew he'd do a little better the next time.

It was quite dark by now, the only light being what drifted in through the windows from the street. Alain lay back to relax for just a moment, then realized he'd drifted off into a fitful sleep. He awoke from an ambiguously sexy dream and thought for a moment he was alone. Then he sensed her across the room, her mind wrapped up inside itself with the intensive meditative control that many mystics worked years to perfect. As he stirred, she came out of her trance and looked at him. "Do you want to eat some more?" she asked.

Alain's stomach was still a bit queasy. "Not right now."

There was silence for a moment before Laya spoke again. "What . . . what's your name?"

Alain hesitated. What name should he give her? He knew that Laya by herself was no threat, but if she would fall into the wrong hands she might be used against him. Better to lie for now and correct the situation later, if need be. "Call me Richard," he said.

"Richard." She said it as though the name left a metallic taste in her mouth. She probably knew he was lying, but she did not call him on it. "How old are you, Richard?"

The question startled him. He knew she was curious about him—that much was only natural; but he'd expected her to ask why he was running from those people. Perhaps running was so natural to her that she took it for granted. "Thirty-eight."

In the darkness across the room, Alain could see Laya's silhouette nod. "I'm seventeen," she replied. "Almost eighteen. I'll be eighteen in three months. That's when my mother said I'd be grown up, when I was eighteen. Is that true?"

Alain smiled. "It takes some people longer than others. There really isn't a magic day." But he could not completely shut the thought from his mind that physically Laya looked quite full grown—and that thought, in turn, spurred his sexual feelings even further. He could feel the warmth of her femininity even in the darkness. It penetrated the entire room, oozed into his mind alongside the constant pain from his z-beam wound. Laya was so naive, so virginal—and so close. He could . . .

He broke off that line of thought abruptly—so abruptly, in fact, that he could sense the girl was startled by it herself. *Even if she were a raging nymphomaniac,* he told himself sternly, *you're too feeble and in too much pain to do anything about it.*

To force himself to think along other lines, he said aloud, "Tell me about yourself, Laya. Why are you living in an abandoned house? Why do you have to eat garbage? What happened to your mother and father?"

Laya had repressed the memories for a long time, living only from moment to moment, and Alain's questions were not ones she faced willingly. She sat silently in the darkness, and Alain had to prod her some more before she would start talking. The story emerged reluctantly, piece by piece, and more than once Alain had to calm the girl to prevent her from running into the next room to escape his inquisition.

He hadn't realized that life could be so hard for a telepath on a world where that talent wasn't accepted—but then, as he thought back into history, he realized that insane asylums had been filled with people who "heard

167

voices" or claimed to know what others were thinking or just went around screaming because they couldn't stand to be in proximity to others. *She has no trimethaline to shut out the background,* he thought. *Just like the situation I'm now in. That must be hell on an untrained adolescent. No wonder she's so gun-shy of everyone.*

As Laya imparted her story, she gradually became more at ease with her patient. Alain did everything he could to encourage that feeling. He sensed in her a loneliness that mirrored his own, and he began caring for her in a way he had never allowed himself to care for a woman before. She was so helpless yet tough, naive yet wise that she touched nerves within him he would never have suspected.

They spent another three days together in the deserted house. Alain spent a lot of that time sleeping while his burns were healing with agonizing slowness. Every time he woke, though, there was Laya ready to tend his wounds and talk with him. Once she got used to the idea of speaking there was almost no stopping her, and she gushed forth on an amazing variety of subjects, whether she knew anything about them or not. She asked him many questions about himself—questions which he, for the most part, brushed aside with quick, shallow answers or outright lies.

Their minds were growing closer during this period also. Laya had never met anyone else who shared her telepathic abilities, and most of Alain's contact with telepaths had been early on during his training—and never in quite such an extended session as this. There were times during a pause in the conversation when he would test her, throwing her small balls of thought in one form or another to see how she would react. She was startled at first, but soon caught on to his trick and began to smile knowingly at him when he did it. In time, she even began throwing them back at him, and the two of them started a game of telepathic "catch" without a word ever being spoken on the subject.

Although he was impatient with the slow rate at which his wounds were healing—he hated having to be fed and washed like a baby—Alain was in no particular hurry to return to the outside world. The longer he remained in this abandoned house—out of sight, out of contact, out of circulation—the colder his trail would become. It would seem to Joby that he had vanished from the universe without a trace; she might become convinced that he had departed the planet for other pastures and leave to explore that possibility—or just abandon the chase altogether. Unlike the situation on Earth, where every second had counted against him in his efforts to escape, he felt that here time was quite definitely on his side. Joby was the one with the deadline; he could wait.

The hardest part of his ordeal was when Laya was treating his wound. He wasn't really sure what her psychic healing abilities might be, but they did seem to work; he knew he should never have survived such a wound without medical attention, and he'd heard enough about faith-healing not to question the process. He also had her continue the treatment of washing the wound frequently with a wet cloth. He was too weak to do it for himself, and she was only too eager to oblige him. The longer they were together, the more eager she seemed to become to run her fingers gently over his bare skin—and that was causing problems for him.

The sensuous caress of her fingertips was arousing him almost past the point of endurance. After trying unsuccessfully to hide his erections the first few times, he gave up disguising his reactions and just suffered through them with embarrassment. He could tell that Laya was intensely curious about it, but she sensed his embarrassment and, for once, showed enough tact—or was it shyness?—not to broach the subject.

On the last night they spent at the house, Laya was sponging his body as usual and Alain was lying on his left side with his eyes closed. The scent of her unwashed body was filling his nostrils. At first it had offended him, but now it was a smell he associated strictly with her. It was the odor of Laya, and if not completely pleasant, it was at least irresistibly warm, loving, and feminine. Without thinking, he reached up with his right hand and gently stroked the side of her arm as she knelt over him.

The result was like an electrical shock. Laya was an adolescent girl whose strongly repressed sexuality was only now beginning to emerge. She'd been reading the sexual desire in Alain's mind for days, and it had been feeding her own. His sudden tender touch produced a current of wonder and delight that she could not try to hide. The emotion flowed from her mind into his, feeding the fire there still further.

Laya bent lower and, instinctively reading the need in his thoughts, began stroking his body more passionately. His automatic response was an increasingly passionate series of caresses that raised goose bumps along her skin. Twisting over onto his back, he brought his left hand up as well, reaching behind her neck to pull her head down toward his. Their lips met, and as she telepathically read the mental cues he was sending, her mouth opened tentatively to allow his tongue to enter.

Gently, so as not to aggravate his wounds, she lowered herself down on top of him, their bodies pressing tightly together as the mental energy flowed back and forth between them. His hands ran over her ragged clothes, searching instinctively for ways to remove them.

No! he thought suddenly. *She's just a girl, too inexperienced to know what's happening. I mustn't be such a bastard that I let my gross appetites take advantage of her naiveté. I care for her too much.*

Weak but determined, he pushed her away from him. She felt the sudden coldness in his mind and responded with confusion and disappointment. She had received an emotional bucket of cold water squarely in the face, and while she was not sure what was supposed to have happened next, her bodily reactions were telling her that something was being denied.

The two of them peered at one another through the darkness for a moment. Then Laya stood up and ran from the room, only to collapse in the adjoining chamber, crying. Alain lay back and closed his eyes, feeling her unhappiness radiating even from the next room. "I'm sorry, Laya," he whispered to empty air. "I'm sorry."

chapter 18

The next morning, Alain insisted that they move into a hotel. He was becoming worried that their presence here might be discovered, and he was in no shape to run from any police called in to deal with intruders. Although he was still very weak, he could at least stand and move around slowly, and he was certain that lying on a hotel bed would be infinitely better for his recuperation than lying on the bare floor here.

Laya was disheartened at first because she thought—especially after the events of the night before—that he meant to leave her. But Alain wouldn't think of it. She would be coming with him, he insisted. He still needed someone to look after him, and he certainly couldn't risk going to a doctor or hospital; they would ask all sorts of embarrassing questions. Besides, he owed her a great debt for saving his life, and one way to repay her was to give her a better way to live than just scavenging through the city like an animal. Laya was nervous, at first, about making her reentrance into human society, but Alain was firm and persuasive.

Alain had checked out of his previous hotel before going to the supposed rendezvous in the park, because he had expected his future to be settled in some manner. He'd brought a great deal of money with him to pay Kossa, and he had even more stashed in a bank. His and Laya's first stop of the day was a clothing store, from which they both emerged looking far more presentable for human company. Laya, though still unwashed and with her long hair snarled and matted, looked especially beautiful to him now that she was in proper clothing rather than her old rags. From the clothing store, they went to a moderately priced residence hotel, where they rented a large suite with two bedrooms.

That, although he didn't mention it to Laya, was another reason Alain had wanted her to come with him. She provided a very convenient form of camouflage. If there still was a search going on for him, the searchers would be looking for a man alone; a couple might escape their notice altogether.

Alain's strength lasted barely long enough to get them up to their room, and then it deserted him. He collapsed on the floor, and Laya had to drag him into his bed and undress him once again. She was on the verge of ripping up a sheet and wetting it to cleanse his burns when he regained consciousness enough to advise her that they might have less trouble from the hotel if she used a towel for that purpose.

Despite the fact that their surroundings were more luxurious, both Alain and Laya were less comfortable here. In the old house they had been the only two human beings in the immediate area, and their minds were free from the constant intrusion of other people's thoughts. Here, however, they were constantly under a mental barrage of emotion. Alain's telepausal headaches, which had almost vanished in the old house, returned afresh. Laya's sensitivity increased as well, reminding her why she had run from human society in the first place. Picking up each other's disquiet only amplified the feelings for both of them.

They kept to their room almost exclusively, ordering all their meals from room service. The pattern of their lives remained largely what it had been before in the old house, except that now a tension existed between them that hadn't been there earlier. Each was very careful about accidentally touching the other, lest emotions be raised to the same uncomfortable level as that one night. Laya came near Alain only to wash or feed him; the rest of the time she remained at a discreet distance, averting her eyes

172

whenever she found him watching her. Their mental games of "catch" were dropped by implicit mutual consent; they were afraid of being too close again.

Alain grew progressively stronger. The burn in his side was still a constant fire, giving him little peace, but the massive shock it had brought to his system in general was wearing off. His appetite returned in full, and he ate ravenously to replenish the energy stores he had so depleted during his period of recuperation. Four days after checking into the hotel, he was able to walk around for long periods at a time without having to lean on Laya for support. He could put his clothes back on and suffer only minimum discomfort from their rubbing against his burn.

And as his strength increased, he found himself thinking more and more about the future. The thoughts were not happy ones. He had escaped Joby's clutches on three separate occasions; she was not the sort of person to take a defeat like that lightly. The high command at the Agency was going through a period of paranoia—the rapid replacement of Joby's predecessor had told him that. She might, by this time, have been "terminated" herself for her failure to reel him in; if not, she would certainly be desperate to do so. In any event, whoever was now in charge of the department would be after his head, with no holds barred.

Alain simply did not have the resources on his own to hide from that thorough a search. He knew full well what powers the Agency had at its disposal when it wanted to go all out against someone it considered a threat. He himself had been in on several manhunts. The Agency had a long and vindictive memory.

He would need professional help if he was to survive. But there weren't that many professionals to choose from. His own side was ruled out, and after his experience with Kossa, even the free-lancers could not be trusted. That left only the enemy—a choice Alain would have preferred not to make.

The Leonean counterintelligence corps was quite capable of providing the new identity he would need to live out the remainder of his life in peace. But everything in the espionage business had a price, and the price for these particular services would be high indeed. He would have to agree to sell out Earth and the TIA completely before the Leonean government would agree to such a deal.

He had no qualms left about betraying the Agency *per se*. They had been the ones to abandon him first, driving him straight into the arms of the enemy. They deserved no sympathy. What he would regret was the necessity to betray all his colleagues as well. There were many good people he had worked with on Leone over these past six years, and the Leoneans would insist on knowing the identities of all of them. They would want a detailed list of names, dates, places, and activities—and Alain would provide them for the favor of remaining alive.

He consoled himself with the fact that few of his former friends would die because of his actions. A spy whose identity is known to counterintelligence is little threat—and, in fact, can be a great asset. If his superiors don't know he's been compromised, he can be fed false information to mislead his own side unwittingly and kept under observation to reveal the rest of his contacts. Only those informants on the highest levels, who knew too much about too many things, might meet with fatal accidents.

It was a sad ethical choice to be forced into, but Alain didn't hesitate to make it. He wanted to live, and the cost of living was going up every day.

Laya could sense the turmoil swirling in his mind, and it made her very uneasy. She didn't know what he was going to do, but she could tell it would entail his leaving her—and that was something she didn't want. In just the short time she'd known him, her life had done a drastic turnabout—enough that she didn't want to go back to her old ways of scavenging garbage from the bins behind restaurants and stores. Alain had to spend a great deal of time convincing her—on both a verbal

174

and telepathic level—that he would not be deserting her completely, that he would come back for her and try to help her find a better life. He owed her that much and more. But she needed a lot of convincing.

The act of defection was not a straightforward process. Simply walking into the offices of the Leonean counterintelligence forces would be viewed as the mark of an amateur, and while they would listen politely to what he had to say, they would discount it as being too obvious a trap. Even if such a defector were genuine, his own side would know about the defection the instant it happened and would take preventative countermeasures.

On the other hand, every government's counterintelligence corps encouraged defections from the other side. There were established channels to contact and procedures to follow, and the counterintelligence officers made sure that these procedures were well known to all the professionals working against them—just as every agent, no matter how loyal to his home planet, kept abreast of what those channels were. Situations in the espionage game could change more rapidly than the weather, and one always had to know which way to jump.

Leaving Laya back in the room, Alain went out one morning to a public phone several blocks from the hotel. He called a particular number, and when a woman answered, he outlined his dilemma in the vaguest possible terms. He was given another number and told to call it later that afternoon. He did so at the appointed time—from a different phone—and dropped a few pertinent names and facts to let the man on the other end of the line know that he was neither an amateur nor a crank. The other man, suitably impressed, suggested a meeting for that evening, to take place at a public event. Alain suggested one particular men's room at the jetball stadium during tonight's game, and the other agreed.

The rendezvous went smoothly. As the two men met, Alain insisted that they move to a different men's room, to avoid the possibility that the Leoneans had bugged the first one since the time the rendezvous was established. Alain told a little more about himself and specified his requirements. They spent a while dickering over sums of money before reaching a mutually satisfactory figure. The Leonean said that he could get approval from his superiors but in return would need Alain's full cooperation. Alain could see from the man's mind that the other was wary of a trick—only natural, under the circumstances—but was speaking honestly when he promised to give the money and the new identity as the price for information. The Leonean offered to take Alain to a place of safety right now. Alain was tempted, but decided against it, saying aloud that he had a few loose ends to wrap up first. They arranged a meeting for the next morning and separated once more. There was a simplistic attempt to follow him, but Alain eluded it and returned to his hotel unobserved.

Alain did not tell the Leonean that he was a telepath. That was the one secret he intended to keep forever, if possible. He had to hold something in reserve, after all, in case the Leoneans, too, double-crossed him.

Laya knew the instant he walked through the door that something had changed, that he would be leaving her. The disappointment and fear radiated from her mind at a babbling rate. He tried to project calm assurance that everything would be all right.

"I have to go away tomorrow morning," he said, "and it may be for a little while. If it's at all humanly possible—and if I'm not double-crossed—I'll return for you and take you somewhere better than this. But for both our sakes, this is something I have to do.

"In the meantime, I've made arrangements for you to be taken care of. I've paid the hotel bill for two weeks in advance, plus enough extra to provide all the food you could want during that time. I know you're not completely at ease here, but at the very least you'll have two weeks without fear, without running, with all your material needs taken care of. If I'm not back within two weeks—well, I probably won't be able to come back at all. Here's the rest of my money; it's not as much as I'd like to leave you, but it'll buy you some food and some new clothes. You might try going out to the country, getting a job on a farm or something; you may have less trouble picking up stray thoughts and emotions if you're away from the crowds of the city."

He held out to her the packet containing his money. She stared back at him, unmoving. He could read the chaos boiling inside her mind: indignation that he could treat her so coldly, anger that he was deserting her, sorrow that he would be gone, desire to be with him again, hope that he might return, self-pity that she was losing the only person since her parents who'd cared about her—all those and more swirled in a bright confusion through her brain.

Without taking the packet, without speaking, Laya ran into her bedroom and slammed the door shut behind her. Alain stood for a moment looking at the blank door, knowing he had hurt her and wishing there had been some other way to go about this. But there was none. Where he was going, she would not be able to come. The Leonean counterintelligence officers had made a deal for one, not for two. Even if Alain told them she was innocent of any involvement, they would still tear her apart to prove that, and she was emotionally incapable of standing up to that stress. Under pressure, she might even reveal the nature of their telepathic abilities—and then she and Alain both would be in serious trouble.

He laid the packet down on top of a bureau; in the morning, when she was less distraught, she would see that he was right. He went into his own room, got undressed, and stretched out gingerly on the bed, staring up at the darkened ceiling and mulling over the unhappy twists of his life that had led to this night.

Sleep was slow in coming. His own nervousness about the events of tomorrow compounded the eternal oppression of his telepause to give him a raging headache. In addition, his own feelings of unhappiness seemed dwarfed by those emanating through the walls from the adjoining room. Laya was going quietly crazy, certain that her entire life had been shattered and she didn't even know why. Alain knew he could never explain it to her.

He did manage to sleep, fitfully, for a short while, but it was still dark when he woke up sweating. He'd been dreaming that Laya was in trouble, that he'd been unable to rescue her. His breathing was labored, his muscles tensed. He lay there in the dark, letting consciousness come to him completely once more.

As his mind cleared of the final vestiges of sleep, he heard a sound from the next room. Laya was crying. Throwing back the covers, Alain got out of bed and padded across the carpeted floor to her doorway. The door was still closed against him. He knocked gently but received no acknowledgment. Opening the door, he walked in.

Laya was sprawled prone on the bed, her face buried in her pillow. Her entire body shuddered as she cried, but the sobs were muffled slightly by the pillow. "Laya?" he said softly. There was no physical response, though he could tell from her mind that she had heard him. She was just ignoring him, for reasons that were not clear even to her.

He crossed the room quietly and sat down on the edge of the bed beside her. Putting his hands on her bare shoulders, he began massaging them softly. "Please don't cry, Laya," he said. "It'll turn out all right. You'll see."

"You won't come back," she sobbed. "Something bad's going to happen, I know it." Her tears slowed but did not stop altogether.

"That's nonsense," he replied, not sure whether it was or not. "I'll be back."

"You're lying to make me feel better." Laya sniffed back the remainder of her tears.

That's the problem dealing with another telepath, Alain thought. *You can't reassure her when you're not*

178

at all confident yourself. "I'll move the sun and the moons to get back to you. I promise you that. You know I'm not lying there."

He turned her over on her back so that she was looking straight up into his face. Their minds met and their glances locked; in that instant, a bond was cemented that only death itself would be able to break.

"Yes, Richard," she whispered.

He bent his head down toward hers. His only intention was to kiss her lightly on the forehead, but as his lips descended Laya leaned her head back so that her lips met his. Her arms reached up and encircled his body, pulling him gently down on top of her as she drew his mind into hers.

The momentary flash of guilt hit his mind again, but this time Laya was ready for it. With a strong mental push she banished it from his thoughts almost as though it had never existed. Their minds flowed together, becoming one interlocking unit—as, eventually, did their bodies.

The flame of his telepausal sexual desires jumped the gap and lit the adolescent fires within her own soul. Their love blazed out of control, bouncing back and forth from one mind to another, feeding off their mutual need and growing only stronger as it progressed. Each experienced completely the other's joy, which doubled the sensation for both. The outside world ceased to exist as they locked themselves up in the universe of their own minds.

As the light of morning crept slowly in through the window, Laya smiled at Alain. "I love you," she said aloud, while the full flavor of that love filled his mind.

"I love you too," he added—and for perhaps the first time in his adult life, he really meant it. "I really do have to leave this morning, but you can bet I'll be back. After this last night, no force in the universe will keep me away."

Laya's smile broadened as she snuggled closer against Alain's body—and for the first time since his telepause had started, Alain felt truly happy.

chapter 19

Colonel Kesse Rombolo leafed carefully through the thin but growing file on the new defector. *Earth's chief-of-station for the entire planet. How fortunate for me, if my luck is to be believed.*

The colonel was a very precise man. He was neither tall nor bulky, but he gave the impression of being both because his always immaculate uniform fit precisely every curve of his rotund body. His curly black hair was cut so close to his scalp that it was almost a knitted cap. The edges of his mustache were as precise as his barber's razor could make them. He did not believe in waste or ornamentation.

On the surface, this Cheney fellow's story looked legitimate enough. The TIA was indeed known for its internal politicking, and being on the wrong side of a dispute, as he claimed to be, might indeed make him a hunted man. The z-beam burn on his side was certainly real enough, and the incident in the park that he described was verified with police reports of that night. The man was intelligent, knowing procedures backward and forward, so there was little doubt that he *was* a top TIA agent. Already he had confirmed some facts that Rombolo's organization previously knew about the TIA operations here on Leone. The price Cheney was asking for his cooperation was quite reasonable by most standards within the business; he could have insisted on a larger fee without difficulty.

Col. Rombolo should have been very happy with Cheney . . . but he wasn't.

It was the timing, mostly, that worried him. If this

had happened three months ago or three months from now, he would have had few doubts at all. But coming as it did right at the crucial moments of Project Cepheus made it a mystery, and the colonel did not like mysteries. To him, all things should be neat and easily understood.

The TIA—along with a good many other intelligence agencies—was naturally curious about Project Cepheus. They were so curious that they were sending in wave upon wave of assault troops to try to discover what was going on within the closely guarded wing just down the hall from where Rombolo now sat. His guards had captured an infiltrator from the TIA just last night trying to break into the Cepheus wing.

So—with all their forces directed against a target on Leone, why would they suddenly turn on their presumably best agent and try to kill him? It was an act of pure irrationality—and the TIA, for all its silly internal squabbling, could scarcely be termed an irrational organization. It was still the best-run, most efficient intelligence-gathering network in the galaxy, the one from which all others were more or less derived. Was he truly to believe that they would cast out one of their best men at a time when they would need him the most?

There was another answer that appealed more to the precision-loving colonel: Cheney was a plant. As a defector, he was prime bait to snare any counterintelligence officer. No one could afford to turn him down; what better way to get him inside a line of otherwise sturdy defenses? Once inside, he would talk to his hosts' content; the TIA was so desperate by this time that they'd willingly trade half their organization for a crack at Cepheus. All the information Cheney gave would be true, making him ever the more trustworthy. Then, when the defenses had relaxed just enough, he would slip through, find what he wanted, and slip out again. Cheney was, after all, a prime agent.

So far, Rombolo had nothing to go on but guesswork. Cheney had shown no interest whatsoever in any of the Ministry's secrets. The code name Cepheus had been deliberately dropped once in his hearing, and he had not reacted at all. But then, Cheney would be playing it cool, ever the tough professional. When he did decide to make his move, it would probably be too late to stop him.

Rombolo dared not let it get that far. Cepheus was the most important project the Defense Ministry had handled in the past century, and it was his responsibility to see that it remained uncompromised until the Ministry chose to release the information publicly. To fail in that duty meant the end of his career, possibly of his life. From the little he'd been told about the project's progress, negotiations were now at the critical stage; nothing must go wrong.

He could not afford to pass up any information this Cheney gave him—but on the other hand, he could give Cheney no chance at wrecking Cepheus. *For the moment, he decided, I can let him dangle by the thinnest of threads. But one false step, one mistake and he's a dead man. I'd rather lose a defector than lose Cepheus.*

The first order of business Alain insisted on when the Leoneans picked him up was to have one of their doctors examine his z-beam burn. The doctor frowned when she saw what had been done, but she had been connected with the espionage services long enough not to ask why Alain hadn't gotten medical help sooner. Alain could see from her mind that she was frankly amazed he was still alive. She gave him injections and rubbed his side with ointment, but said that the delayed treatment would not be completely effective and that he would probably be badly scarred for the rest of his life. The z-beam had also nicked the edge of his liver, causing a small touch of jaundice. She told him he was under no circumstances to take alcohol, and she insisted that he be put on a special diet.

The next step before he talked was to arrange for his payment. Major Ofarda, who was to be in charge of his debriefing, showed him the papers and new identity they would create for him, and introduced him to the doctors who would give him a new appearance and voice. They finalized the details of Alain's stipend, and Alain agreed to the arrangement. With that much settled, they began their debriefing sessions in earnest.

Alain spent three days in Major Ofarda's office, sitting

in a comfortable chair and answering questions that the major read to him from a prepared list. Most of the questions dealt with the organization of TIA's forces on Leone, along with names of informants and contacts within the Leonean government. Alain answered every question as fully as he could, but volunteered nothing. It was bad enough he had to betray the people he'd worked with; he intended to do as little of it as he could get away with. If the Leoneans didn't know the proper questions to ask, that would be their loss.

Being back in crowded buildings increased the pain from his telepause. When he was alone, he spent his time stretched out with his eyes closed, letting the pain roll through his body in waves. When he was with other people he masked most of the symptoms, explaining any lapses as being caused by headaches.

Alain had few complaints of his treatment. He was fed well, within the limits of the diet the doctor had set for him, and he was given a room within the Ministry Building that, while small, was adequate for his comfort. Major Ofarda was a tough man, but honest; Alain could see from his mind that he intended to honor the agreement they'd made, which made the entire process worthwhile, if unpleasant.

There were subtle indications, though, that there were deeper mysteries occurring within the Ministry. Wherever Alain went, there were two guards assigned to him. They escorted him to the cafeteria or down the halls, and they stood outside the door to his room or to Major Ofarda's office while he was being questioned. Alain had hardly expected to be given the run of the premises, but there was a tension in the men guarding him that seemed out of proportion to the situation. His one mild attempt at a joke about running away brought them instantly alert, and Alain could see that they'd been given orders to kill him if he displayed the slightest suspicious behavior. He quickly became a model prisoner.

The rest of the Ministry, too, seemed to be walking on eggshells. One whole wing of the building was sealed off due to some special project, and even the most casual conversations in the cafeteria were strangely guarded.

Even Major Ofarda was under the strain. While reading Alain a list of project code names to see if the defector recognized any, the name Cepheus was mentioned. When Alain showed no response, Ofarda's mind was almost flooded with relief.

This Cepheus thing must be important, Alain surmised. *If I were still playing the game I'd probably make it my target. But I don't care anymore. I'm out of the business, and they can keep their secrets. I don't want them.*

The subject of telepathy also came up, in passing. As one of the routine questions on his list, Major Ofarda asked Alain whether there was any truth to the persistent rumor that the TIA had telepathic agents. Alain was ready for it.

"I've heard that rumor a few times myself," he said. "Frankly, I think it's silly. If Earth had people who could do even half of what those rumors say, they wouldn't be paying guys like me to go out and risk our necks on the trivial stuff. They could just have one of their mindreaders sit back and look into his crystal ball and give them all the answers."

"But is it possible, do you think?"

Alain shrugged. "Anything's possible, I suppose. I know they have a big research project studying it. But I never worked in the field with anyone who claimed to be a mindreader, or acted like he was."

That answer seemed to satisfy Ofarda, and they moved on to other subjects without the matter ever being raised again.

On the morning of the fourth day, instead of asking more questions, Ofarda said, "We captured one of your former associates trying to break in here the other night. We've tried to get him to talk, but he's far less cooperative than you are. We were wondering whether you might have better success with him."

"I'm not sure. If he's one of the people who used to work under me, he's bound to hate me for defecting, and he might tell me even less than he's told you."

Ofarda considered that. "You may be right. Nevertheless, my boss, Col. Rombolo, thinks it's worth a try."

Alain didn't have to be a telepath to know he was

being tested. Not that the Leoneans were faking the situation—there was no need for that. They probably did indeed have a TIA agent prisoner. But they wanted to see how far Alain's new loyalty to them would extend, and this gave them the ideal opportunity.

"Your wish is my command," he said aloud. "I'll try my best, but I can't guarantee results."

Major Ofarda and the two guards escorted him down to a small cell in the lower levels of the building. The atmosphere was decidedly warmer here, the accommodations less luxurious. Alain was shown into a cubicle with cinderblock walls where a man named Jeremy Riis was seated at a table.

Alain knew Riis as one of the covert operations specialists who drifted onto Leone from time to time for selected missions. He was not a regular here, but the two men had worked together in the past and knew each other casually. Alain asked that he be left alone with Riis, and to his surprise, his request was granted. The guards retreated only as far as the outside of the door, however.

Riis glared as Alain sat down across the small table from him. Riis's face was bruised and swollen, his eyes bleary; the Leoneans were far behind Earth in their development of truth drugs, and so normally resorted to the older methods of extracting information, such as beatings and sleep deprivation.

"I'd be lying if I said it was nice seeing you again, Jeremy," Alain began. "You look terrible."

Riis said nothing. He and Alain both knew that, though they were physically alone, this room was being monitored; nothing they said or did would be missed by the Leoneans.

"I do wish we could have met again under more pleasant circumstances," Alain continued. A line of small talk looked to be his best gambit for drawing Riis out of himself; the man's mind was on edge anyway from his ordeal, and a stream of meaningless cheerful trivia from someone he now hated was bound to jar something loose.

Sure enough, Riis exploded. "Jump off me, you traitor! I don't have to listen to you."

"I'm afraid you do. They sent me in here to question

185

you, and I don't want to disappoint them. You don't have to talk to me, of course, but if you don't they'll probably start doing some more nasty things to you. I always liked you, Jeremy—I don't want to see you hurt again."

"Don't you, really?" Riis's laugh was harsh and hysterical. "Look at my face, Cheney. Look close. See what these wonderful friends of yours have done to me?"

Alain looked back at him for a moment, then raised his shirt to show the large dressing covering his wound. "This is what my other friends did, my friends from Earth. They didn't mean to, of course—they were hoping to kill me outright."

"Serves you right for going over."

Alain shook his head. "They did it before I even considered changing sides. Their reasons were purely political; even now I don't know who I offended, but somebody wanted me dead. Wouldn't you change sides if your own people started gunning for you?"

Riis said nothing. He had vented his anger at Alain and was lapsing back into stubborn silence.

"Let me at least ask you some questions, then, so I can say I tried," Alain continued. "Who sent you here?"

A quick flash of Joby Karns fled through Riis's mind and vanished almost at once. "It wouldn't be Joby by any chance, would it?" Alain asked. Once again there was a mental confirmation, but the only outward thing Riis did was sneer.

"I know she's on Leone, directing the hunt for me," Alain went on. "You wouldn't happen to know where she is, would you?"

The image of an apartment building flitted through Riis's mind, but all he said was, "I don't know who you're talking about."

"You wouldn't know how to reach her either, I suppose."

Riis's mind rewarded Alain this time with a phone number. Out of habit, Alain memorized it for future reference.

"Well, then, let's move on to other things. Where were you trying to break in? What was your target?"

More images, these confused and much more esoteric.

Alain had a hard time following them—telepathy worked far better on visual impressions and emotions than on intellectual concepts.

An idea occurred to him. He began listing some of the code names Ofarda had recited to him, ending with Project Cepheus.

Jackpot! Although Riis gave no outward indication, his inward reactions were shooting off wildly. There was strong emotional connotation intermingled with Cepheus, and intermittent images of Joby and others. This was an important project to Earth as well as to Leone, and the TIA was pulling out all stops to crack it.

Maybe I've been flattering myself too much, Alain thought. *Maybe Joby's really here to find out about Cepheus, and I'm just a bonus thrown in.*

"Was there anyone else working with you?" Again, more visual images reached him from Riis's mind; some of the faces were familiar, some were not. But Riis refused to say anything.

This is slightly frustrating, Alain thought. *I've learned some information from him, and I could learn a lot more, if I chose. But I can't tell any of it without letting the Leoneans know I'm a telepath. They'll have to settle for what they can drag out of Riis themselves.*

He stood up. "I really do wish you'd been more cooperative, Jeremy," he said. "It would have been easier for everyone all around. From what I understand, the Leoneans are determined to get the information out of you, no matter how much it hurts. I only hope you survive it."

The string of obscenities Riis hurled at him as he left hurt him deeply, but he pretended to ignore them.

Colonel Rombolo joined Major Ofarda in watching the monitors as Cheney interrogated their prisoner. Although he had personally stayed away from the case so far, he took a great interest in this test that might show him whether Cheney was indeed a plant, as he suspected. Ofarda was a capable officer, but Rombolo had not shared his suspicions yet for fear his subordinate might make some slip to alert Cheney.

"Certainly isn't an aggressive interrogator, is he?" Rombolo commented as they watched.

"People's styles differ," Ofarda shrugged. "He might feel we've overplayed the hard line and is trying a new tack. He's been with the TIA all his adult life, he still may have some residual loyalties that prevent him from going all out against one of their men. He's been completely cooperative with me so far. A bit lackadaisical, perhaps, but I have no doubts about his sincerity."

At that moment, Cheney mentioned Project Cepheus. Rombolo stiffened and paid even closer attention to the scene before him. Nothing else Cheney did was at all suspicious, but that one question had been the tipoff.

"Send Cheney to my office as soon as he's done there," the colonel ordered, standing up and walking abruptly from the room. He didn't bother to wait for Ofarda's acknowledgment.

Cheney knows about Cepheus, Rombolo thought. *As soon as I find out how much he knows, he'll have to die.*

chapter 20

When he left the interrogation room, the guards escorted Alain to a new office and he was brought before an officer he hadn't met before. The nameplate on the desk identified him as Colonel Rombolo, although the man didn't bother introducing himself. Alain could read nothing but hostile, suspicious thoughts from this new questioner and was immediately on his guard. *I wonder what I've done to make him distrust me so much.*

Rombolo was blunt. "Where did you hear about Project Cepheus?"

"Two days ago, I think, from Major Ofarda. He mentioned a list of code names and asked which ones I'd heard of before. Cepheus was on that list, but it was one I was unfamiliar with at the time. Is it important?"

"Don't you know?" Rombolo sneered.

"How could I? I only heard that one mention of it a couple of days ago. For all I know, the major could have invented it just to test me."

"If you didn't know whether it was important, why was it the last code name you mentioned to Riis during the questioning?"

Alain saw his mistake and cursed himself for his stupidity. He'd learned telepathically how important Cepheus was, and had used that information in questioning Riis. But there was no way he *should* have known it if his story were correct. Rombolo was quite right in being suspicious of him.

"I used a number of the names Ofarda mentioned to me, just to see whether Riis would react," Alain replied. "It was just coincidence that Cepheus came last." The explanation sounded lame even to him—CI officers did not believe in coincidence. But it was better than nothing—and at least possible if not plausible.

Rombolo frowned. Alain could read the doubts in his mind, and the obsession he had with Project Cepheus. Apparently that project was more important than Alain had realized; Rombolo obviously felt that it superseded everything else, and that any sacrifice—even a prime defector—was to be made to keep it secure.

Alain's heart sank. He had honestly hoped that here, at last, he would find the refuge he so desperately sought. And now, because of some supersensitive project he'd been totally unaware of, even this haven was no longer safe. Rombolo's mind was clouded with doubts about letting Alain live. Alain's answer had eased the fears only a little, enough to make the colonel waver— but some other incident could revive those fears at any moment. Alain would have no future with the Leoneans, either.

But what kind of a life was there left for him? Hopping from world to world, stealing to stay alive; trying to keep one step ahead of both the TIA and, now, the

Leonean intelligence forces as well? He was planning not just for himself, at this point, but for Laya as well; their lives had been inextricably joined, and he knew he could never leave her behind. But surely she deserved a better fate than to be an interstellar fugitive.

He brought his mind back to the present with a sharp snap. Rombolo was talking, probing further into Alain's supposed knowledge of Cepheus, and it would not do to be caught thinking of something else. The more doubt he could plant in Rombolo's mind, the longer he would live to plan his future.

By concentrating his mental efforts, he was able to anticipate everything the colonel asked and come up with answers that sidestepped the issue as much as possible. Finally, annoyed with himself for being unable to expose Alain completely, Rombolo dismissed him back to his room for the rest of the day. He was still uncertain whether to have Alain killed or not, and Alain dared not wait around much longer to let him decide positively.

On the way back to Alain's quarters, he and his escorts passed the heavily guarded wing that he assumed was the location of Project Cepheus. That project had assumed more importance to his life in the past few minutes than it previously had held, and so he gave the corridor a much more thorough glance. Three guards stood in a rigid posture beside a checkpoint desk that was outfitted with a computer terminal. Access past the door behind the checkpoint could only be gained, he was sure, by presentation of proper computer-coded ID—maybe even voiceprint and fingerprint checks as well. His professional's mind rated it beyond the abilities of a mere telepath like himself to weasel through that entrance.

His two guards ushered him into his room and locked the door behind him. He could tell from their thoughts that they were taking up their customary posts on either side of the doorway and would remain there either until the next mealtime or until Alain was once again summoned for questioning. They weren't due to be relieved for another five hours.

Alain lay down on his bed for a few minutes, contemplating his strategy for escape. When he had that set, he got up, went very deliberately into the tiny bathroom, and stuffed one of the flimsy towels into the trashcan. Bringing the can out into the middle of the main room, he lit the towel with his pocket lighter. The material smoldered for a moment before igniting, then burst forth with a creditable flame.

Alain raced to the door and began pounding on it desperately. "Help me, quick, my room's on fire!" he yelled. He could tell he'd been heard by the sudden confusion that flashed through the minds of the two guards outside. Seeing their uncertainty, Alain pounded and yelled some more, until finally one of them unlocked the door and looked inside.

The acrid smell and the sight of flames leaping upward convinced the man that this was not a trick. He raced inside the room to help, his companion at his heels. Alain waited until both were inside, then closed the door behind them. A quick, unexpected kidney chop made the second guard double over with a low groan. His compatriot, hearing the sound, turned his attention from the fire and started reaching for his gun.

His action came far too late, however. Alain moved toward him, delivering a solid jab to the solar plexus. As the man doubled over, Alain finished with an uppercut to the jaw that sent the man reeling against the wall. The guard slumped unconscious to the floor, and Alain turned his attention once more to the second man, gasping on the ground. A blow on the back of the man's neck with a heavy ashtray put him out cold too.

Alain quickly turned the trashcan upside down, burning his fingertips slightly in the process but smothering the flames. There was no point, after all, in letting the building's fire detectors become aware of the blaze and set up alarms all over. Although that would have provided an interesting diversion, he wanted to escape with a minimum of attention.

After stripping his two captives down to their underwear, Alain ripped the sheeting off his bed into strips and bound the men hand and foot. The leftover pieces of cloth served very nicely to stuff in their mouths as gags.

Alain dressed himself in the uniform of the taller guard. It fit a trifle snugly, but he was hoping not to be seen closely enough for that detail to matter. Slipping out of the room, he locked the door behind him and walked purposefully down the corridor.

The Leonean Defense Ministry was a labyrinth of halls, stairs, ramps, and levels, many of them crowded with other uniformed people. Alain had been afraid his white skin might give him away, but there were enough other whites in uniform that he was not a standout. He kept his eyes straight ahead and walked at a brisk pace, as though he knew precisely where he was going and had just enough time to get there. No one stopped him.

He'd been walking in large circles for five minutes, trying to find an exit, when he passed the Cepheus wing. As he walked by, his curiosity was piqued. His chances of getting any help from the Leoneans were now completely smashed. But if he learned something about Cepheus, he might be in a position to bargain with someone else. If Joby had come all the way here from Earth to supervise personally the operation against Cepheus, then the TIA obviously considered it very important. Perhaps he could make a deal. At any rate, it would be better than the chance he'd have without the knowledge.

He would have no chance of breaking through the security system on this main floor where the project headquarters was located. The checkpoint security he had seen would easily spot his masquerade. But the floor below this might not be so well guarded—and all he needed for picking up information was proximity to the right people. It didn't matter whether he was alongside them or underneath.

He roamed through the Ministry for another fifteen minutes before he found the right level and the right location. He was starting to worry. His absence from his room could not remain unnoticed forever. He'd initially hoped for an hour or two, but he could count on nothing. He had to hurry.

There were guards along this corridor too—the Leoneans were taking no chances that enemy agents might break in here and tunnel upward into the more secure area above. But they had no idea that they might have to protect against mental tunneling. Alain walked briskly past the guards, ignoring them, and went into a stall in this floor's lavatory.

Thus assured of some privacy, Alain sat down, leaned back and allowed his mind to go as blank as he could make it. Three months ago he would never even have attempted something like this—the range of normal telepathy was extremely limited. But the telepause had increased his sensitivity to an enormous extent, and it was certainly worth a try now. He had little left to lose.

Impressions crowded his mind. The floor he was on was not a busy one, but one level up was a beehive of activity. There were dozens, maybe hundreds, of people up there involved in Project Cepheus, with thoughts passing through their minds in a babble that was worse than trying to listen to random conversations at a crowded party. Some of them had their minds on their jobs, others on personal matters. All of them were thinking at high speeds, engaged in various activities that might or might not have been related to Cepheus. To Alain, it was a pain so intense it was like a spear being driven full force into his skull.

It's no use, he thought. *I'll never make sense out of that*.

He had started to pull his mind back in, to close it within the boundaries of his cranium once more, when he felt the strangeness. It just brushed at the edges of his consciousness, a tiny quality of difference overshadowed by the sheer volume of everything else—but he knew it was nothing he had ever experienced before in his life.

It slipped past him before he could grab at it and hold on, but even when it was gone, it left an odd after-impression—much like putting a copper coin in the mouth leaves a metallic aftertaste on the tongue.

He shook his head, as though to clear it. Even with the after-impression still strong on his mind, it was hard to believe he had not imagined what he'd felt. He could not define it—and that in itself made him suspicious. Whatever it was, it might very well be the central concept behind Cepheus—and even if it wasn't, he had to know more about this strangeness, if only in self-defense.

Bracing himself for more pain, he opened out his mind once again. This time, knowing better what he was looking for, he was able to filter out much of the background garbage and concentrate instead on finding the strangeness. Time and again he forced himself to reject impinging impressions that might have been of some interest, while he searched for what he knew had to be there. The thought occurred to him that whatever it was might have vanished forever, a transient phenomenon, but he put that out of his head and went on with his search.

There! He struck it again, and this time grabbed on tightly. It was something near the limits of his perception, almost drowned out in the general babble—but definitely not a figment of his imagination. Once he had it located, he pulled himself in toward it, concentrating all his powers in that direction and totally ignoring everything else.

It was a mind, but it felt different from any other mind Alain had ever experienced. It was not an animal; he had, on occasion, looked out through the brains of lesser creatures, and this was not at all the same. This was an intelligent mind, a mind capable of reasoning and self-perception. But it was definitely *not* a human mind.

The implications of that were so stunning that he almost broke his concentration and lost his hold on the subject. He forced himself to press deeper. This new mind thought in different patterns, along different logical circuits. It perceived the universe in subtly different ways. Visual images that reached Alain were almost impossible for him to decipher, until he realized that they were not stereoscopic—they were looking out in different directions from the being's head, scanning both sides at once like the eyes of a fish. It was that thought, more than anything else, that made him realize what he was sensing.

A Dur-ill!

Alain pulled his mind away almost instinctively, his imagination reeling. He had, of course, never met a Dur-ill, nor read one's mind before. Like most other people, all he had seen were pictures in the history tapes—pictures of tall, skinny bipeds with gray, scaly skin, enormous gaping mouths, and eyes on either side of their heads. The treaty of over a century ago had guaranteed that neither race would violate the territory of the other, ensuring no contact between the only two known intelligent species in the galaxy.

As far as public knowledge went, there had been no contact since the end of the war. But now there was at least one Dur-ill here on Leone, kept under constant guard. That was what Cepheus was all about, and Alain could now see the reason for the incredible secrecy. The tight security around this section of the Ministry effectively kept the rest of the galaxy out—but was it also serving to keep the Dur-ill in? What was a Dur-ill—or possibly more than one, he reminded himself—doing on Leone in the first place?

He pulled his mind in tightly now, trying hard to reason the problem out. The Dur-ill was kept buried deep within the Defense Ministry, and that fact conjured up several possible conjectures. For one thing, security would be tightest here. If he was a guest, he could be better protected—and if he had come here as a spy or an attacker, he could be better guarded.

But was the Dur-ill here on a hostile mission? Leone was one of the human systems closest to the boundaries of the Dur-ill Empire; it would be the logical place to attack if the Dur-ill, for some reason, wanted to renew hostilities between the two races. But if the Dur-ill had attacked Leone, why this intense secrecy about it? It would make more sense, Alain reasoned, to start screaming the alarm to anyone who'd listen. Leone might not want to trust Earth with the information, after the way Earth had treated its colonies during the first war, but the shadows of the former colonial alliance were still in existence; the Leoneans would certainly want to resurrect the old mutual defense pacts. Yet the impression Alain had gotten from Col. Rombolo's mind was that Project Cepheus was to be kept secret from *everyone*.

Then, too, there was the code name itself. A "project," almost by definition, was a plan conceived and carried out in a deliberate manner. If the Dur-ill were here as a captive, then the effort to interrogate him might be termed a "study" or perhaps an "operation." "Project Cepheus" had the ring of long-term endeavor to it.

Suppose, then, that the Leoneans either invited or brought the Dur-ill here. The implications of that made Alain's head swim. An alliance between Dur-ill and Leone—any sort of alliance, be it for trade or, God forbid, military assistance—would shake up the power structure within human-occupied space beyond recognition. Earth would suddenly find itself a has-been world, the mother planet whose children were now looking elsewhere for affection. Up to this point, no matter how much the former colonies hated Earth for abandoning them during the war, they still looked to Earth as the center and originator of all human culture. But if Leone accomplished this alliance . . .

All his old instincts returned to him in a flash. Oblivious to the mental pain now, he set to work at a feverish pace to ferret out more of the riddle as it was known to the minds above him. His mind jumped from target to target, from secretary to project officer, examining, sifting, discarding or preserving any little snippets of information that passed his way. Time lost all meaning to him as he pieced together the puzzle the Leoneans above were unwittingly handing him.

What human beings had never known until just recently was that the war a century ago had been as harsh to the Dur-ill Empire as it had been to Earth's—perhaps even more so. While most of the battles had been fought in human space, the cost to the Dur-ill in terms of lives and materiel had been staggering. By the end of the war, they had completely overextended themselves. They were just barely able to put on a good show of solidarity to sign the final treaty, and then their empire shattered into a thousand pieces. Old interplanetary hatreds flared. Civil wars ensued. Some worlds were totally annihilated; many others were decimated so badly that they reverted to more primitive levels of culture. Some even lost the technology of space travel. The Dur-ill–inhabited planets now had even less in common than did the human ones. The empire was extinct.

The Leoneans had discovered this mostly by accident, when one of their military training flights had inadvertently strayed into Dur-ill space and undergone a forced landing on one planet there, a world called Wandatta. Upon its return with this startling revelation, the Leonean government had begun a series of flights to the Dur-ill world, increasing the contact and trying to formalize an exclusive trading and military agreement. The Dur-ill ambassador was here now, hammering out the final details. Negotiations were at such a delicate stage that there was daily contact between the two worlds. Rather than risk subradio communications, which might be intercepted, a small scout ship was launched each day from the Ukonë military spacefield outside Port Mombarra with secret dispatches, and returned the next day with answers from Wandatta. When it was finally accomplished, the treaty would be announced to the rest of the human galaxy as a *fait accompli*—the most incredible diplomatic achievement in man's history.

As the final pieces sorted themselves out in his mind, Alain leaned back against the wall, utterly exhausted. His body was soaked in sweat, his hands were shaking, and his eyes were having trouble focusing. His mind had been exploring others for so long that his own body felt unreal to him. But he felt more triumphant than ever before in his life. The biggest puzzle humanity had ever seen had fallen into his lap, and he had solved it by himself. He, Alain Cheney, alone!

He looked at his thumbwatch and discovered, to his horror, that two hours had elapsed since he'd first discovered the Dur-ill mind. While he could detect no general outcry for him yet, he had certainly used up any safety margin he might have. Any second now, the two missing guards would be discovered. He had planned to be away from the Ministry long ago, and now his escape was imperative. He could not allow this information to die with him, not after all he'd been through to get it.

He wiped off the perspiration and left the lavatory trying hard to look cool and businesslike. But it was hard to keep his excitement bottled up. *With this information, he thought, I'm a free man. Not even Joby will touch me when she learns what I can tell her.*

chapter 21

He had almost made it out of the building when the alarms went off. Loudspeakers blared, people started running, confusion was all around him. Alain pretended to become a part of the confusion, letting his telepathic abilities carry him along with the rest as he made his way slowly toward the outside.

Most people did not know what the fugitive looked like, and the few patrols that did were easy for him to avoid because he could sense them coming. He reached the outside without serious incident, stole a limousine waiting for some important officer, and drove into the center of town, where he abandoned the vehicle and walked the rest of the way to the hotel where he and Laya had been staying.

He slipped in through the service entrance when no one was looking and took the elevator up to the floor of their suite. Suddenly he found himself feeling very frightened— not of being captured again, but rather that he would find Laya gone with his money, that she had given up hoping for his return (even though it was far less than the two weeks he had promised her) and left the hotel, to disappear forever into her former anonymity.

He did not have a key to the room with him—he had not wanted to bring into the Leonean Defense Ministry any clues to Laya's existence—and was afraid he'd have to knock on the door and wait outside. But even as he approached the room he could feel the power and flavor of her mind. She seemed to have grown only stronger since he'd left her, and he marveled at the potential she must possess.

Even though she had not been warned he was coming, she sensed his mind before he reached the door. She ran to it, threw it open, and raced out into the hallway to meet him. She was in his arms, kissing him, and their minds were welding once again into the same solid unit they'd known on their last night together. They stood there embracing for several minutes before Alain gently separated. "We'd better go inside," he told her. "We've got work to do, and we have to move fast."

"Oh, Richard, I was so worried for you," Laya said as she walked with him back into the suite and closed the door. "I was afraid you'd never be coming back."

"I told you I would, didn't I? And there's no harm now in letting you know that my name's really Alain, not Richard." Laya accepted that fact without comment as she watched her former patient cross the room to the phone set.

Alain pushed out of his mind the pleasure of being with Laya again. The next few hours would be crucial, and he would need all his wits about him. Recalling the phone number he'd learned from Riis's mind, he called Joby, hoping she'd be in.

His former secretary answered and gasped when she saw his face appear on her screen. "Hello, Kalere," he said as though he'd never been away. "Patch me through to Joby at once."

"Who?"

"Don't try to fool me. You know perfectly well who I mean. If I'm not talking to her in thirty seconds, I'll hang up and never call back."

"Just a second." Kalere's face disappeared from the screen, to be replaced for a moment by the restful flow of colors that was the holding pattern. In very short order, though, those colors were replaced by the image of Joby Karns, looking startled and bemused at the same time.

"This is certainly a pleasant surprise," she said.

"I'll bet it is. I've got a deal for you."

Joby's beautiful face tightened in a frown. "This is past the dealing stage, Alain. I'm sorry, but that's the way it is. You'd know I was lying if I said anything different, so why pretend?"

"I know what Cepheus is," he said quietly.

Alain wished it were possible to read minds over the phone, for his simple sentence froze Joby for nearly fifteen seconds. She kept good control of her facial muscles, but he could see in her eyes a confusing parade of thoughts passing through her mind. "What makes you think I'm interested?" she asked at last.

"You weren't going to lie to me before, please don't start now. I've got it, you want it. Let's start from there."

Joby sighed and nodded slightly. "All right. I want it. What do you want for it?"

"I want you to call off the hunt. I want to be left alone. I want to be free."

"I was afraid you'd say that. It's beyond my power, Alain. I didn't start the hunt in the first place, and I don't have the authority to stop it."

"Good-bye, Joby." He started to reach for the switch, making sure she could see his gesture.

"Wait a minute," she cried, letting some of her real desperation show through. Alain did not hang up, but continued watching her with cold eyes. *Let her sweat for a while, like I did*, he thought nastily.

"Let's at least talk about it," she went on. "Maybe . . . maybe I can think of some way around it."

"That sounds a little more like the Joby I knew. We'll talk face to face, my field, my conditions."

"Name them."

"There's a location known in the local references as Rendezvous Spot Three. Ask any of your people where it is, they'll know. We'll meet there in three hours. You're to fly in with a personal copter, unarmed and alone. No interference caps, either—I know how to sense them. Remember, now that I'm telepausal I'm extra sensitive—I'll know the instant anyone approaches. If you're not going to deal fairly, don't bother coming; I'll see any double cross in your mind."

Joby's eyes narrowed. "How do I know this isn't just a trap to kill me?"

"If I'd wanted you dead, I could have done it weeks

ago aboard the *Bakalta*. All I want is out, Joby, and you're the only one who can give it to me."

Joby thought that over for a moment, then agreed. "All right—alone, unarmed, in three hours, Rendezvous Spot Three. You've got a date, sailor."

She winked at him and signed off. Alain smiled in spite of himself. She hadn't called him "sailor" since they were both in the Academy together and he was taking the classes in spaceship control. *Somewhere along the way it fell apart,* he thought, *but we sure did have fun for the brief while it lasted.*

Laya was watching the now-empty screen coldly. "Who was she?" she asked.

"A fossil," Alain said. "A piece of the past that can never be recaptured. But at the moment, a very useful one."

"I don't like her."

Alain could feel the incipient jealousy roiling up from the depths of Laya's mind, and he laid his own calm like a blanket over her fears. "Nobody said you had to, darling. And please—you have no need to be jealous of her. Anything that happened before I met you is ancient history, of purely intellectual concern. But we need Joby at this moment if we're going to weather the storm that's about to hit. Trust me. If all goes well, she'll soon be long gone."

Laya came up from behind him and put her arms around his shoulders, her nimble fingers deftly massaging his chest. Alain knew he should be making preparations for the meeting with Joby, that there were precautions he should be taking in case she double-crossed him, and that he had to devise long-range plans for escaping from Leone with Laya. But as her mind opened up to his once more, beckoning him inside, all of that was pushed to the back of his thoughts. It had been several days since he'd left her, several days of missing her and wanting to be once more in her arms. The rendezvous with Joby was three hours away.

It could wait for a little while, at least.

Rendezvous Spot Three was a grain storage depot, a large wooden building just on the outskirts to the north of

Port Mombarra. It was owned by a holding company of the Terran government and had seldom had any grain stored in it during its existence. Sometimes it was used as a staging area for covert paramilitary missions; a large percentage of the time it merely stood empty, far enough away from everything that no one ever bothered to examine it closely.

From his position near the door, Alain could see the copter coming closer through the clear sky. One thing he had to say for Joby, she was always prompt. He turned away from the door, walked to the middle of the large room and sat down on the seat of a lift truck. Now if only Joby would stick to her side of the agreement, they could transact their business and be away from here in half an hour. There were still so many things to take care of. . . .

As the copter touched down just outside, Alain scanned it with his mind. Joby was in it, definitely alone, and there was no trace of telepathy interference caps. He could not tell for sure whether she was indeed unarmed; she wasn't thinking about that particular subject at this moment, but knowing she was approaching a telepath, she was making sure her mind projected all kinds of peaceful, nonviolent thoughts. Alain was not worried. He would have enough warning if her mood changed to be able to defend himself.

Joby paused at the threshold, then stepped resolutely forward into the dim interior of the building. Alain could tell she felt dwarfed by the enormity of the warehouse, but she was resolved not to show it. As her eyes became accustomed to the dimmer light, she spotted Alain sitting on the lift truck and walked toward him.

They stood for a moment facing one another awkwardly. Joby broke the silence. "Here I am," she said. Lifting her arms out to her sides, she added, "Care to search me?"

In that instant, the thought flashed through her head that she didn't really mind because she knew Alain would not find anything. She was definitely unarmed, so Alain knew he needn't bother. "In my youth," he said, "that might have been a very tempting proposition. But I'm old and bitter now, and I'm frankly tired of all these stupid games we play with ourselves. Put your arms down and let's get this business over with."

Joby obligingly put her arms down and gestured with her head toward a level area on the back of his lift truck. "Mind if I sit down and make myself comfortable, then?"

"Be my guest."

She sat down beside him then—close enough for him to know that she was still, after all these years, a highly desirable woman, but not close enough to let him think she was vamping him. Her perfume tickled his nostrils and triggered a rush of pleasant memories. Had she worn that scent because it was what she'd worn when they'd been lovers back at the Academy, or was it her usual perfume? He couldn't tell—her mind was not on her perfume at the moment. It was filled with nothing but Cepheus.

"Why, Joby?" he asked suddenly.

"Why what?"

"Why everything? Why did the Agency try to kill me? I was perfectly loyal, I did a good job, I didn't get mixed up in any office politics. Why the sudden obsession to have me eliminated?"

Joby's shoulders sagged slightly. It was as though she realized that Alain was a man she didn't have to pretend with, and the relief that brought was almost physical. "It's been standard Agency policy for the past ten years, ever since we first discovered what telepause was and what it was doing to our people. A telepausal agent is a threat to the network and must be eliminated."

"Again, why? Sure, it's a disease, maybe like leprosy. But why the death penalty?"

"We learned that a telepausal agent is unreliable. The mental anguish he suffers from his inability to block out background thoughts becomes worse with each passing day. He goes mad, he begins babbling. His sexual drives increase to the point where he can't control them. Even in an ordinary citizen these would be dangerous symptoms; they're intolerable in a spy. As the telepath becomes increasingly irrational, the odds of his being captured by the enemy increase enormously. He could be induced to reveal everything he knows in a matter of days, or even hours. The very nature of his illness would alert them that we have a working telepathic system. For the Agency's own sake, he has to be removed from the scene."

Alain was lost in thought as her words hammered home. He knew she was telling the truth, he could see it in her mind. What was worse, he could see it in his own mind. All the symptoms she was describing, and that Dr. daPaz had described to him earlier, were indeed coming true. Soon he would be a raving madman with enormous sexual appetites, both a burden and a threat to society. It was a bleak picture. But it did not really answer his question.

"But why do you have to kill?" he persisted. "The 'official lie' that Dr. daPaz first told me was that there was some sort of retreat where telepausal agents were taken. Couldn't we just have been retired gracefully and . . ."

He stopped suddenly. The mention of daPaz had triggered a flash of memory in Joby's mind. The doctor was dead. Although he had feared the worst, Alain's anger was still kindled by the murder of the man who had saved his life.

"DaPaz is dead, isn't he? That's one more stupid, senseless murder you can be proud of."

"It's not my fault. I had nothing to do with that. Dekker was the one who killed him. If it had been up to me, I'd have put him in prison for a while, that's all."

She was telling the truth, at least as far as she knew it, but that didn't make Alain feel any better. He said a quick, silent prayer for daPaz's soul and did not look at Joby.

"And as for putting telepausal agents in some sort of clinic," the woman went on, "it was deemed both more efficient and more humane to put them out of their misery all at once. When a racehorse breaks its leg it'll never recover; you have to shoot it to relieve the suffering."

"You'll have to excuse me if I find that simile less than enthralling."

"It's not a decision I had anything to do with. It's been policy for ten years. You were one of the best agents I had—I didn't want to lose you, particularly not with this Cepheus mess coming on us so suddenly. But you wouldn't believe how neurotic everything is in the higher echelons these days. If I had even hesitated about killing you, they'd merely have gotten rid of me and replaced me with someone who had even fewer scruples."

She put a hand on his arm. "Believe me, Alain, the thought of killing you was not one I enjoyed."

Alain pulled his arm away, stood up, and walked a few paces from the lift truck, his back to her. "We agree on something, at least." He spun around to face her. "But you now have a second chance. Call off the dogs."

"I told you, I can't. It's policy." There was a ragged edge to her voice. "Alain, my career, my entire life is hanging by a thread. You're that thread. If I fail now, I'm finished."

"Excuse me while I shed a tear."

Alain forced himself to think of other things than the emotions that were flowing through Joby Karns at this moment. He sensed the desperation she could not conceal from him. She was showing him more of her basic human frailty in this moment than she'd shown to anyone in over a decade—and because of his position, he could not afford to sympathize.

She started pulling herself together after his rebuff. "I won't beg, Alain. I still have some pride. I came here to make a deal. Name your terms."

"I'll give you Cepheus if, in return, you get the Agency off my trail. Lie to them, you're good at that. Tell them you killed me. I'll do my damnedest to disappear, so no one will ever know you didn't."

"But if you slip, if they should somehow find out . . ."

"You'll have Cepheus. It's big, believe me. When you know what it is, I think you'll agree that getting raped by the entire Leonean army would be a small price to pay."

Joby stood up and walked around to the other side of the lift truck. She appeared to be deep in thought, but it was all for dramatic effect; Alain knew that her mind was already made up. "You win," she said at last, turning to face him. "As of now, I have just killed you, after I tortured you into revealing what you knew about Cepheus. You won't have any more trouble from my people, I promise. But now you have to live up to your end of the bargain."

Alain was about to speak when he was interrupted by

205

a voice coming from the doorway. "That's enough, you two. You're both traitors."

Standing in the doorway were Morgan Dekker and two other men. All three had interference caps on their heads and z-beamers in their hands.

chapter 22

So intent had Alain been in his conversation with Joby, and so concentrated had he been on reading her mind to make sure she wouldn't double-cross him, that he had failed to notice the slight nullity that signaled the approach of telepathy interference caps. They masked their wearers' thoughts so well that his mind had to be open and receptive to pick them up.

He turned first to glare accusingly at Joby, angry that she had somehow set him up. But he could see from her mind that she was every bit as startled and frightened as he was. This was a surprise to her too.

She recovered her bearings quickly, though. "Morgan, you're just in time. Take him and . . ."

Dekker shook his head. "I no longer take orders from you. Glazer was right, you are a threat to the Agency. You'll betray it to enhance your own glory—I heard everything you said in here. The game's over. First, I'll finally kill Cheney, then I'm taking you back for your own trial. Or perhaps," his eyes narrowed, "perhaps I should kill you here too and save everyone a lot of trouble."

Joby's own temper flared. "Don't be a fool, Morgan. This may be our best and only chance to learn about Cepheus."

"The Agency's security comes first, Joby. And the

Agency can't be secure as long as the two of you are alive." He raised his gun to fire at the two figures standing before him.

Even as he did so, however, a small bottle was arcing through the air from the loft above them. It shattered at Dekker's feet, bursting instantly into flames. The three men in the doorway backed off instinctively; one of them, however, was not fast enough—the fire caught some of his clothing and he began to burn.

Even before the bottle hit the ground, Alain was in motion. He had prepared a series of fire bombs in case of a double cross and showed Laya how to ignite them. She was hidden upstairs in the loft, and during the interview with Joby, she had been scanning the surrounding area for traces of interlopers—but without experience of the interference caps, she also did not detect them until it was too late. But at Alain's mentally shouted order, she had now thrown the first of the bombs.

Alain dived to one side, behind the lift truck and out of the men's line of fire. Joby, unprepared for the sudden rescue, stood out in the open for a moment, then quickly dived alongside Alain, out of range. As Laya hurled more fire bombs at the front doorway, the walls of the building themselves caught fire and started to burn. Thick black smoke began to sting everyone's eyes, and the smell of blazing wood made them choke. Alain gave a quick mental shout to Laya that she had done enough damage for now and should come down out of her hiding place and escape with him.

He found Joby looking up at him. "This was none of my doing, Alain. I swear I didn't know. . . ."

"Relax, I know that. Let's worry about getting out of here." He looked quickly over to the hiding place of the rented car that had brought Laya and him here, but it was on the other side of the building, cut off from them by the flames. He turned back to Joby. "Where exactly is your copter sitting?"

"Over on that side of the building, maybe twenty-five meters away."

Laya leaped down out of the loft, landing neatly beside them. Her sudden arrival startled Joby a bit, but the

Terran woman was always quick on the uptake. Laya had been the one who threw the fire bombs, and thus a friend. Alain took Laya's hand in his and started running in the direction Joby had indicated. Joby, after a second's hesitation, followed them.

Alain tried to sense the presence of the interference caps as he ran, but there was too much confusion around him. He took out his own z-beamer and fired randomly ahead of him into the smoke; if any of Dekker's men were in his way, that would at least keep them honest.

Even Alain was startled by the speed at which the warehouse caught fire. It seemed as though one second he had been facing Dekker and his men, the next he was running for his life through walls of flame. A burning beam crackled, then crashed to earth just a few meters away. Laya was clearly frightened by the hell she had unleashed, and Alain had to devote at least part of his energies to soothing her panic.

They reached the side door, and Alain opened it cautiously, peering out to see whether any of Dekker's men might be waiting for them here. There was no one in sight, so he quickly ushered the two women out of the burning building. Joby's copter was positioned as she had promised, sitting tantalizingly two dozen meters away.

The three started sprinting for the copter to make their getaway complete, but they'd covered less than half the distance when Dekker's car rounded the corner of the building, catching them in the open. Seeing the fugitives, the car's driver accelerated straight toward them. They froze for an instant, but this time it was Laya who recovered her senses first. Taking one of her remaining fire bombs, she hurled it straight into the path of the oncoming vehicle.

The bottle broke and the flames shot upward just as the car passed over it. The explosion of the fire bomb ignited the vehicle's own fuel tank, and the entire car blew apart in a burst of flames. The death traumas of the occupants were screams of agony in Alain's and Laya's minds. They stumbled but were so intent on their own survival that they continued on. The fugitives reached the waiting copter without further incident.

Alain helped Laya climb into the two-seater vehicle, then climbed in himself. As Joby, too, started to get in, he pointed his gun at her. "Sorry," he said. "This is where we part company for good."

Joby seemed confused, unwilling to understand. "We can all squeeze in there together. It'll be a little crowded, but . . ."

Alain shook his head. "This is the end of the line, Joby. You'll have to find your own way back."

"We had a deal."

"You're in no position to make deals," Alain said coldly. He kept his gun pointed at her while he started the copter's engines with his other hand. "The way I read things, you were just fired as Operations chief. You have no more authority with the Agency than I do now."

The copter's motor hummed to life, and the blades began rotating. "Alain, they'll kill me," Joby pleaded.

He looked her straight in the eyes. "No they won't. You're an even better survivor than I am. You'll get through this somehow." The copter rose into the air as he spoke, leaving Joby standing alone on the ground looking up.

The wave of hatred that came from Joby's mind rolled over the both of them like molten lead. "You bastard, Cheney!" she shouted. "Come back here."

With great deliberation, Laya threw a fire bomb directly down at Joby. The agent saw it coming and ducked instinctively away, but she could not dodge fast enough. The bottle burst to one side of her and the blaze flew up into her face. Her beautiful long red hair caught fire and soon was flaming for real. She fell to the ground shrieking, rolling onto her side in an attempt to smother the flames. Then the copter passed through a cloud of the black smoke from the burning building, and Alain could see no more.

He said nothing aloud to Laya about the incident as they flew, and he tried to keep his thoughts under control as well. He felt very little sympathy for Joby; anything that had once been between them was long dead. He had plenty of other thoughts to clutter up his mind.

The momentary exhilaration of escape was giving way

to the deepest despair he'd known since that night on Earth when daPaz had told him the truth about telepause. He had escaped the Agency's clutches once again, but what good was it all? Where was there left to run? The TIA was determined to kill him. The Leoneans were determined to kill him. And if they didn't, the telepause would finish him off soon enough anyway. What was the point in living?

Suddenly he felt the cool, gentle touch of Laya's mind on his. *This* was what there was to live for. As long as he and Laya were together, they were a complete universe unto themselves, and nothing could touch them. She had so much to learn that he wanted to teach her. She would be the mark he would leave on the universe to note his passage. Somewhere, somehow, he had to find the freedom to do it.

He tried to clear his mind of the chaos and depression that were choking it, and Laya helped him sweep away the debris. Where could they go and not be found? Within a few more hours the Leoneans would be thoroughly organized, and they'd tear this planet apart to recapture him. Even if he went to some other world, either the Leoneans or the TIA would catch up with him. There was no planet in the galaxy where he could be safe.

Or was there? The thought had been buried so deep within his brain that it took a while to emerge into the light. Perhaps there was no world in *human* space where he could hide—but he had just learned that the Dur-ill planets were no longer the closed door everyone had believed they were. What if he and Laya could reach one of those? Not Wandatta, certainly, but there were theoretically hundreds of others to choose from. Some of them, according to what he'd learned, had even lost the art of space flight. He and Laya could go there, hope to be taken in. They would be different, they would be aliens on a strange world—but it was a chance. They had *no* chance if they stayed in human space. There would be communications difficulties with their new neighbors—but he and Laya were both telepaths and could work out some means of conveying ideas. It *could* be done.

Laya could not read his specific thoughts, but she did

sense the growing optimism in his mind, and she fed it with her own youthful enthusiasm. He turned to her, his own ardor building along with hers. He had to explain the situation to her; he had to make sure she knew what they were getting into before making the decision that would commit them irrevocably to that course.

He told her everything—about his job, about the tele-pause, about the chances of their finding a Dur-ill world. She listened avidly, then nodded when he was through. "Yes, of course I'll go."

"But you'll be constantly surrounded by aliens, beings who are totally different," he argued.

"I am now. You and I are different from everyone around us. As long as you'll be with me, that's all that matters."

"But I'll die in a few years—the telepause will see to that. And you'll be alone again."

"No." She shook her head emphatically. "After knowing you like this, I can never be alone again. Whatever happens, I'll be far better off than I was before you came. I love you, Alain." And the feeling she imparted in his mind left no doubts at all about the solidarity of their mutual emotions.

The decision was made, their course committed. There was yet to be found only the means of their departure.

The Ukonë military spacefield from which the scout ships of Project Cepheus took off was naturally guarded; but the security, though tight, was not the stranglehold that existed back at the Defense Ministry. It was thought to be a peripheral target at best and was guarded accordingly. And the Leoneans had no idea the missing Terran agent would be showing up here.

The air lane for civilian copter traffic passed within thirty kilometers of that base. As long as he stayed within the established pattern, Alain knew he was safe. When he reached the closest point to the field, he darted out of the traffic flow and headed full speed for the installation. In less than a minute, his radio came to life, warning him that he was trespassing on government property. He ignored the warning. Shortly thereafter, a second warning reached him, this time ordering him to turn around or face dire consequences. He ignored that too.

The third warning was an order to land his vehicle immediately or be shot out of the sky. The spacefield was now within easy view. Alain pretended to comply with the order, slowing his speed and dropping his altitude until he was hovering just slightly above the ground—but he was still moving forward toward the base. A group of patrol copters were flying out to meet him.

Suddenly he shot up to full speed, zipping along barely a meter above the ground. He and Laya were buffeted about inside the cabin as he guided the vessel on a crazy, zigzag course. The patrol copters swooped down and commenced firing; their shots were tearing up dirt all around Alain's craft. The invading copter shook at one point as a shot from the defenders ripped off one landing runner; the craft listed to one side, but it still flew on.

No pilot with any regard for life or limb could have accomplished what Alain did that evening. A sane man would never have played such dangerous games with the ground, which is every pilot's enemy. Alain's copter swooped up and down erratically, sometimes almost bumping the ground, skimming dangerously past trees and bushes and power lines. The defenders must have thought a madman was at the controls—and they wouldn't have been far wrong. Alain had absolutely nothing to lose and was aiming to win.

His sheer daring enabled him to fly past the defending group of copters without sustaining serious damage to his own vehicle—but there were other hazards ahead. The alarm had been sounded all over the base, and personnel were scrambling to their defense positions. A front line was already forming as Alain buzzed in low over the open spacefield. The defenders could have shot at point-blank range, but they were too busy scattering and running for cover as the copter swooped recklessly right through their midst. Now that the copter was inside the outer perimeter, Alain was not too worried about the Leoneans using their big guns; they'd be concerned about hitting some of their own men or equipment. This battle now would be fought on a more personal scale.

As he buzzed the field, he scanned it for what he'd been hoping to find—a small, already fueled scout ship. He knew from his "research" at the Defense Ministry that such ships were making regular runs between Leone and Wandatta. If such a ship were ready now, he and Laya still had a chance; if not, their luck had finally run out.

There did seem to be a ship down at the far end of the field, near a small blockhouse. Alain gunned the copter for it, unmindful of the artillery going off around him. Another line of defenders formed between them and the scout ship. This batch, braver than the last, gave no indication of scattering as he flew straight at them, but held their ground and fired directly at the copter. At a mental signal from Alain, Laya tossed her last fire bomb into their midst. The results were more than satisfactory; the few soldiers who were not caught by the blast and the flames ran for cover against any further bombardment.

A stray shot from somewhere hit the tail of the copter. The steering rod seemed to go crazy in Alain's hands as his machine slued wildly around and off course. He tried righting it, but half the controls were dead and the copter insisted on going at a diagonal to the direction he wanted. Instead of heading for the scout ship, the copter was now flying directly at the blockhouse.

It was too late to do anything about the direction—they were almost on top of the blockhouse. In one last desperation move, Alain slowed the craft's speed and ordered Laya to jump out to the ground. Without bothering to see whether she did so—there wasn't time—he jumped out himself.

The field on which he landed was hard and rough. He bounced along it as he landed, ripping his clothing and jarring his teeth. He came to rest on his left side with his arm bent under him at an awkward angle. There was pain there, but he hadn't heard any snap; he hoped it was merely a sprained wrist as he struggled, dazedly, to his feet.

The copter continued along its erratic path, smashing broadside into the concrete blockhouse. There was the sound of wrenching metal, followed almost instantly by an explosion. The ground shook, and Alain reached up with his right arm to shield his eyes from possible flying debris. There were screams of anguish as people ran from the blockhouse, their clothes and bodies aflame.

Alain picked himself up and ran. He could sense Laya also running toward the ship; she was aching and bleeding from a number of cuts she'd received in her fall, but she was young and in exceptionally good condition. She'd fared even better than he had and was streaking toward the scout ship. Her mind reached toward his, and together they formed a tight mental lock to coordinate their efforts.

A soldier appeared suddenly in the ship's hatchway, gun in hand. Perhaps he was a pilot who'd been checking out the ship when the invasion occurred, it was hard to say. But as he saw Alain running toward him, he instantly aimed his weapon to fire. Alain had his own gun in hand, but there was simply no time to stop, raise it, and shoot at the man threatening him. He would be picked off without a chance to fight back.

Then a curious thing happened. The gun flew out of the soldier's hand, much to his own amazement. It landed on the ground a few meters away, but he never had time to retrieve it. Given the exra seconds, Alain had time to bring his own weapon into play and the soldier fell from the hatch.

Alain reached the ship first and climbed awkwardly up the ladder one-handed, favoring his left wrist. He had just climbed through the empty hatch when Laya reached the ship, scrambling up the ladder like a monkey. He pulled her roughly inside, then closed the hatch behind them. Gun in hand, he led the way as they explored the rest of the small vessel.

They were indeed alone in here, much to Alain's relief —although, if they didn't act quickly, that status was subject to change. He found his way to the control center and checked the instrument panel. The scout ship had been built to be flown by a crew of four, meaning he would have to do the work of several. But the radio officer's function was not critical to his needs, and he was counting on Laya to be able to read some of what was

214

necessary from his mind. Trained or not, she would have to be his copilot.

He strapped himself into the pilot's couch and turned on the instrument panel. With great trepidation he checked the fuel monitors, but the worst of his fears were for nought—the gauges read full all the way down the line. This ship would take him as far as he needed into Dur-ill space. After all, he didn't have to save any fuel for a return trip.

The ship was finely tuned and had been kept in peak condition, so it required little in the way of preflight checkout. Alain noticed the Leonean copters circling warily overhead, not doing anything, but waiting for him to make his move. There was probably a major crisis occurring in Cepheus command right now, with the officers in charge of Ukonë base having to decide whether to destroy the ship along with the unknown assailants or try to recapture it. If Alain knew military command as well as he thought he did, no one of lower rank would want the responsibility for making the final decision, and it would take some time for them to find and brief anyone of appropriately higher rank.

He forced himself to be slow and methodical, despite the need for speedy action. The instruments to run this ship were laid out in a different pattern than he was used to, and his skills in spaceship piloting were rusty themselves. He had not only the pilot's board to monitor, but the other two as well. He gave Laya some idea of what she was supposed to be checking, and she helped as much as she could.

After only a few minutes—which seemed like hours—Alain decided they were ready. He primed the ignition sequence and, with a deep sigh and a prayer, set the automatic takeoff timer. He lay back on his couch and tried to make himself comfortable, at the same time giving Laya, who'd never been in space before, a short warning of what to expect.

The ship gave a roar beneath them and rose majestically into the air, through the cloud of copters that had been circling it. Despite Alain's warning, Laya whimpered at the unaccustomed pressure of extra acceleration. Even as they accelerated quickly through the atmosphere, Alain's eyes were darting over the instrument panel. The Leoneans had other defenses, spaceborn, and they were not free by any means.

Sure enough, the small scout had barely cleared atmosphere when they found a trio of orbiters closing in on them. These were drone ships, automatically operated, but the Leoneans were hoping they would keep him busy long enough for their piloted ships to get into position to stop him. Indeed, Alain had to spend the next forty-five minutes at the unfamiliar controls dodging his way through and around the robot vessels. By the time he'd left them behind, he could see the wall of cruisers speeding toward him.

There must have been at least thirty of the big ships, each one armed with the latest devices of mass destruction. They were fanned out in a hemispherical pattern around him, blocking him off from escape in that direction. For him to attempt to charge through their ranks would be nothing short of suicide.

But the Leoneans had made one fatal blunder. They had assumed that these mysterious agents wanted to reach another human-occupied world so that they could tell their superiors what they had learned. Accordingly, they had blockaded the direction leading back into human space, leaving a clear opening for the scout to go the other way. Alain waited where he was, watching the enemy ships approach until they were almost within range, letting them grow cocky at having outmaneuvered their foe. Then, like a mouse scampering back through its hole, Alain turned the scout around and zipped into the opening they had left him, toward Dur-ill space.

The commanders of the other ships realized too late what he was doing. They tried to give chase, but Alain knew that given any kind of a head start, he had the speed to beat them. The cruisers were built for firepower, not speed, whereas just the reverse was true of his scout ship. Within half an hour it was clear he had outdistanced them, and in another fifteen minutes they gave up the chase and disappeared from his screens entirely.

Alain closed his eyes with relief. At long last and

forever, he was free. But he could not relax entirely; Laya was having a great deal of discomfort coping with freefall and needed his help. He spent some time just holding onto her and soothing her by stroking her mind with his own. As he did so, his memory replayed the scene at the spacefield, the last battle of his life.

Suddenly he stiffened, mind and body tensing at once. "What's the matter?" Laya asked suddenly, sensitive to the change in his mood.

"That guard in the hatch, the one who was about to shoot me. . . ."

Laya grimaced. "Yes, I remember. It's lucky for us he dropped his gun."

"But that's just it. He didn't drop it. We ripped it out of his hand with just the power of our minds. Laya, that's something called telekinesis. It's not supposed to be possible, at least not on any kind of practical level. But we did it. You and I, with our minds linked together to form a single unit—we did it!" He was ecstatic.

She rejoiced in his ecstasy, let it fill her own mind and then bounced it back at him to reinforce the feeling. "We can do a lot of things," she said with simple conviction, hugging him even more tightly against her in the weightlessness of the cabin.

The warmth of their unity spread throughout the ship, and the darkness that had weighted Alain's soul vanished before the bright promise of the future. *Maybe telepause is an evolutionary stage before we move onto something even better,* Alain thought. *That's a possibility we'll have to explore more fully in the years to come.*

He looked into Laya's lovely face and smiled. *We've both got a lot of exploring to do, physically and mentally, before we're ready to give up.*

The scout ship zoomed outward at supralight speed, carrying them to a destiny of hope.

epilog:

iwagen

The narrow dirt track that served as a road wound between the hills underneath an orange sun and a green sky. The vegetation in the fields were hardy, weedy-looking plants called thistlefruits, just beginning to sprout their orange bulbs through the tops of their stems. The woman marveled at how alien and yet how natural they looked as she walked along. She was almost tempted to pick one and see how it tasted.

She had been walking since early morning and she was getting very tired. Walking, even nowadays, was an un-accustomed pastime for her—but this portion of the planet Iwagen was quite backward, and faster means of transportation just were not available. To make matters worse, her destination was well back in the hills—the strangers had settled as far from the town as they could and yet still be accessible. The woman sighed and continued walking.

A little boy stood at the top of one hill, looking down at the approaching woman. He had sensed her presence more than half an hour ago, long before she came into view. Years ago, he might have worried; today he was merely curious. She did not see him as she walked, and eventually he tired of watching her. He ran back, instead, to his house-tree to inform his mother of their approaching visitor.

Someone's coming, he thought, and his impressions, despite his young age, were sharp and clear within her mind.

His mother looked up from her washing and nodded. Though her powers were not nearly as developed as her son's, the newcomer's presence had gradually made itself known to her. "I know," she said aloud. "You'd better take your sister and hide out back, just in case. I'll talk to her."

The boy nodded and scampered off. The mother finished the piece of washing she'd been working on, then went out front to sit in the bower and await the arrival of their visitor.

Soon the strange woman made her physical appearance, walking at a casual pace down the dirt road. She was hot and tired, and even a little unsure whether she should be here at all. She caught sight of the mother sitting in the bower, and she waved but received no response. Even more uncertain, she shuffled forward until she stood at the opening of the arched bower leading to the house-tree.

"Hello," said the traveler. When the woman in the bower failed to respond, the traveler moved a little closer. "We were never properly introduced the one time we met," she went on. "There was hardly the time. But I'm sure you remember me. My name's Joby Karns."

The woman in the bower looked her visitor over. The last ten years had not been kind to Joby Karns. Her hair, once a long, lustrous red, was now dyed mouse brown and cut short. Her figure, once athletic and trim, had tended to flab. Joby was not fat by any stretch of the imagination—she had too much pride for that—but the pure animal tension that had once charged her body so sensuously was now sagging, and she had a double chin.

The worst change, though, was in her face. The right side of the countenance that had once been alabaster perfection was darkened and scarred. The scar tissue tightened up the face, bringing the corners of her mouth and eye much closer together than they should have been. That side of her seemed dead and mealy to the touch.

"Yes," the woman in the bower nodded. "I thought there was something familiar about your thought patterns. Everything else looks different, though."

There was a twinge within Joby Karns as she heard those words. "Yes. I have you to thank for part of that, at least. Looking back on it, I suppose I should even be grateful. I was on the run then, the same as you. If I'd gone to a plastic surgeon, he'd have charged me a small fortune to make my face unrecognizable. You did it free of charge." She started to give a little laugh, then realized how unfunny the joke really was. "They tell me in the village that your name is Laya."

"They told you correctly."

Joby shuffled back and forth slowly. "I, uh, I've had a long walk out here. Could I trouble you, please, for a cup of water?"

Laya stood up and, without a word, went into the house. She returned a few moments later with a handmade metal cup full of water. Joby took it gratefully from her hands and drank, then handed it back. Laya set the cup down beside her chair, then sat down once more. She continued gazing at Joby.

Joby stared down at her own feet for a moment, then looked up defiantly at Laya. "Oh hell, I might as well get it all out into the open. You hate me, and you have every reason to. There's nothing I can say or do that will make up for one instant of the suffering I caused. I know all of that, but I came anyway. I tracked through half the galaxy just to find you and Alain."

"You've found me," Laya said. "Alain's over there." She pointed at a small cairn of stones ten meters from the house-tree.

Joby lowered her gaze. "How long ago?"

"Six years. The telepause killed him, just as you said it would. It was much milder than you described, though, at least in his case. It was only the last year that things were really bad." She closed her eyes, remembering the pain Alain had gone through, and all her efforts to ease his troubled mind those last few months before he died.

"It's little consolation that I was right," Joby said. "I would have given anything to be able to change it. I did love him, you know, in my own way."

Laya could see from the other woman's mind that she actually believed that. *I guess a person can talk herself into almost anything in ten years,* she thought, but said nothing aloud.

"He was right too," Joby continued. "I did manage to survive. It wasn't easy, at first—I had Romney Glazer's agents tracking me all over the galaxy for the first three years, before he finally gave up. The TIA had too many other problems by then to worry about me.

"Not that it matters much what happens to the Agency anymore. Earth has been a second-rate power ever since Leone announced its liaison with Wandatta and formed the first link with Dur-ill worlds. We were present at Earth's last grasp for glory, and we were all the victims of its death throes. It's somehow comforting to know that I was the last Operations chief while the organization really meant something. In some ways, it's probably a good thing I never went back—it would have been hell watching something I loved deteriorate in front of my eyes and not being able to do anything about it."

"Yes," Laya said, "it is."

Joby looked startled, then embarrassed. "Oh. Alain. I'm sorry, I didn't mean . . ."

"I know what you meant," Laya said. "No need to apologize."

The other woman paced around in a small circle, avoiding eye contact with Laya. She pounded fist against palm, and Laya could feel anger rising to the surface.

"It all seems so terribly pointless when we look back from a vantage point of ten years, doesn't it? Me and Dekker running around trying to kill someone who's only going to live another four years anyway. Trying desperately to find out a secret that looks so obvious now, so simple. It changed the entire nature of the galaxy, and there probably wasn't much we could have done to stop it even if we had learned in time. We ran around in circles, biting our own asses, playing games with life and death as though we were about the most important, most serious task in the universe. And what does it all come to? This!" She waved her hands around to indicate the house-tree and the fields surrounding it. "I think we were all fools, so caught up in our own self-importance that we couldn't see the sense to anything."

Speak for yourself, Laya thought. *Alain was not a fool.*

Joby suddenly stopped her outburst, aware of Laya's critical gaze. "Sorry to be so hostile. I've got ten years of frustration and anger built up, with nowhere to vent it. I shouldn't burden you with it." She paused. "Although, come to think of it, I don't know what other reason I might have had for tracking you down after all this time. Guilty conscience, I suppose, or maybe I was hoping to find kindred spirits with whom I could commiserate. You're nothing of the sort though, are you? You've managed to make a new life for yourself, comfortable and content, while I . . ."

Laya watched Joby's mind back off from the admission of failure, the dissatisfaction, the constant efforts to rebuild her life the way it had been, only to meet with one disappointment after another. Instead, Joby changed the subject.

"Maybe, too, I came hoping to find that I was wrong, hoping that Alain would still be alive and had been able to achieve something worthwhile with his life, after all."

He has, Laya thought. *More than you could possibly guess.*

Joby sighed. "They told me, back in the village, that you had two children."

"Yes, Richard and Mara."

"It must be some comfort, then, knowing that Alain will at least live on through them. May . . . may I see them?"

Laya did not have to call. Suddenly both children were just there, standing in the archway of the bower looking out at the woman who'd traveled all this way to see them. The boy, eight, the girl, almost seven—both with dark hair and dusky skins, and a look of intelligence about

222

their eyes that seemed to reach far beyond their chronological ages.

Joby smiled at them. The children returned the gesture only halfheartedly. "The boy in particular—he has Alain's eyes," Joby said. "He's going to grow into an impressive man one of these days, I can tell. Maybe even better than his father, though that would be hard to do."

She turned to look back at the mother. "You're to be congratulated, Laya. You won, you and Alain both. I only survived. Hardly an achievement to engrave on a tombstone."

She straightened up and glanced over her shoulder at the road that led back over the hills. "I think I've over-stayed my welcome," she said. "If there ever was a welcome to begin with, that is. I make a pilgrimage across half a galaxy for a few minutes of superfluous soul-baring and then I leave again, no wiser than when I arrived. I'm still a fool, I think. Forgive me, Laya, I won't bother you again. Good-bye, and good luck."

Joby turned and walked dejectedly back along the road she'd come. Laya and the children stood silently, watching her go. Finally, when Joby had disappeared from view, Richard spoke—a combination of words and thoughts.

"I think, for the first time, I can feel sorry for her," he said.

"She startled me for a moment," Laya said, "with her comment about Alain living on through you."

Richard shook his head. "She was merely speaking figuratively. There was nothing deeper than that."

There was, his thoughts went on, no way she could have known just how significant an evolutionary step telepause was in human development. There was no way she could have guessed that the increased sexual desire was a need for progeny in which to pass along the soul and the talent; no way she could have learned that the pain and increased sensitivity bespoke the awakening of psychic powers beyond the puny levels of telepathy; no way she could have understood that all the anguish suffered in telepause was just the labor pain for a higher order of mentality seeking to be born.

Richard was, in part, Alain. Not a reincarnation, but a thought infusion, a merger of Alain's mind with that of his son to produce a union that was stronger than either of its components separately. In a similar manner, Mara knew that she was to be the receptacle for her mother's mind when Laya died after passing through the transitory stage of telepause. Knowing her brother/father, she knew it was something to be hoped for rather than feared.

Richard was telepathic to an extent even his father could never have dreamed of. His powers of telekinesis were growing stronger with each passing month. He had little doubt that, as his body and brain matured and his strength increased, he would also list teleportation among his talents.

When Laya died, their exile here on Iwagen would be complete. There were other telepaths in the galaxy—both of human and of Dur-ill stock—going through their lives in darkness, suffering the telepause and dying alone for lack of a midwife to see them clear to the higher existence. Richard and Mara would go to them, explain and help them, usher in a new era of intelligence and a new race of beings. In a way, Richard was impatient that his mother was still years away from telepause.

Laya sensed his impatience and stroked his hair lightly. Richard smiled. In the meantime, there was work to be done here. There were other fields to reap. The galaxy could wait a few years more.